**Kim Longinotto** is a documentary filmmaker whose latest film, *Divorce Iranian Style*, is set in the family law courts in central Tehran. She lives in London.

**Joanna Rosenthall** is a psychotherapist working at the Tavistock Marital Studies Institute in London. She also writes short stories and is now at work on a novel.

# cheatin' heart

women's secret stories

edited by
Kim Longinotto
and Joanna Rosenthall

Library of Congress Catalog Card Number: 98-86407

A complete catalogue record for this book can
be obtained from the British Library on request

The right of the individual contributors to be
acknowledged as authors of their work has
been asserted by them in accordance with the
Copyright, Patents and Designs Act 1988

Copyright © 1998 of the individual contributions
remains with the authors

Compilation Copyright © 1998 Kim Longinotto &
Joanna Rosenthall

First published in 1998 by
Serpent's Tail, 4 Blackstock Mews, London N4

website: www.serpentstail.com

Set in Plantin by Intype London Ltd
Printed in Great Britain by Mackays of Chatham plc

10 9 8 7 6 5 4 3 2 1

# contents

Acknowledgements  vi

Foreword  vii

Joanna Torrey  *Cheatin' Heart*  1

Rose Tremain  *Dinner for One*  14

Pat Cadigan  *Two*  32

Betsy Tobin  *The Clockmaster*  63

Amy Bloom  *Sleepwalking*  82

Claire Calman  *The Secret Voyager*  104

Claire Calman  *A Restricted View*  106

Gill Horitz  *About Time*  110

Janette Turner Hospital  *Flight*  121

Alyson Hallett  *Bone Song*  137

Erica Wagner  *Haircut*  146

Rosemary Friedman  *Southern Comfort*  156

Lorna Thorpe  *The Dead Lie Down*  166

Joan Diamond  *The Dowry*  178

Catherine Gammon  *Letter from an Upstate Prison*  185

Helen Lynch  *Half-mast*  201

Jude Weeks  *Old and Long Remorse*  208

Kathy Page  *The Question*  216

About the Authors  229

# acknowledgements

The editors and the publisher gratefully acknowledge permission to reprint the following stories:

'Sleepwalking' copyright © Amy Bloom 1991, 1993, reproduced by permission of Curtis Brown Group Ltd, London.

'Two' copyright © Pat Cadigan 1988. First published in *The Magazine of Science Fiction*, January 1988. Reproduced by kind permission of the author and Mic Cheetham Literary Agency.

'Bone Song' copyright © Alyson Hallett 1998. Reproduced by kind permission of the author and Greene & Heaton Limited.

'Dinner for One' from *The Colonel's Daughter* by Rose Tremain, published by Hamish Hamilton. Copyright © 1983, 1984 by Rose Tremain.

'Flight' copyright © Janette Turner Hospital 1995. First published in French in *L'Envolée*, Myriam Solal 1966. Reproduced by kind permission of the author and Mic Cheetham Literary Agency.

'Old and Long Remorse' copyright © Jude Weeks 1998. Reproduced by kind permission of the author and Greene & Heaton Limited.

# foreword

There's nothing quite so irresistible as a secret. The stories in *Cheatin' Heart* are all about secrets, dangerous yet desired. Some of them deal with the more expected meaning of secrets: keeping things hidden from the outside world, whereas others deal with darker, more solitary kinds of secrets.

Some of the stories have a lighter quality. In Rosemary Friedman's bittersweet story, a middle-aged woman indulges in forbidden love in tropical climes, in Jude Weeks' we are drawn into an intense childhood game which has tragic consequences. Others touch on more disturbing areas. Lorna Thorpe's story has a lilting style with a sinister undertone and a nasty twist at the end. Pat Cadigan's riveting tale explores the boundaries of mind, reality and sanity.

All the stories in this book have the qualities of secrets themselves. Their energy relies on the illicit thrill, the unexpected twist, or the unknown revealed. They are passionate, seductive and exciting and all touch on the forbidden, the feared and the destructive areas of life.

# joanna torrey

## *cheatin' heart*

After I made love for the first time, I went right home to tell my older sister. Diana was in bed with a book propped on her bent knees. We were in the same French class. She always did her *explication du texte* on time.

'You weren't at ballet,' she said, her eyes cool and narrowed. I sat down on the side of the bed. She picked up my hand by the wrist and brought it up to her face and sniffed. '*Mon dieu*,' she said.

All during supper she watched me with a small, disapproving frown, as though the sex smell on my hands had tainted her meatloaf. Dabbing at her mouth with her napkin following each bite, she talked politely to our father, something she usually only did when she wanted to borrow the car. 'Daddy, how was your day?' she said politely. The lead in the school play.

That night we were doing the dishes together. She said it was her turn to wash. This meant she got to choose the radio station.

'You're wrong,' I said, continuing to shape liquid bubbles into glistening, rainbow-filled penises at the top of the basin. 'It's my turn.'

I kept waiting for her to ask me what it had been like.

She pushed me from behind. I turned and pushed her

back hard so that she hit the counter. Plates fell from the dish rack and broke into clattering pieces. My father and mother appeared in the doorway each holding a different section of the newspaper down at their side and stood there frowning at us. His eyebrows were drawn together into one line. I swept the pieces into the dustpan, tiptoeing in my bare feet. Diana and I finished the dishes not saying a word and didn't speak for the rest of the evening.

Later in bed that night, I kept smelling my hand, between my fingers and along my wrists, trying to find the sex smell. I wanted desperately to find it under the soap smell, the dish detergent smell, the lost eight hours from the secret, scary, smeary tangle I'd been in. I lay there, thinking about going into Diana's room and covering her sleeping face with my open hand.

My sister and I once slept with the same man. I came back for Christmas break from college and found out that he was her new boyfriend. I'd introduced them, worrying that she would be lonely while I was away at school. I thought they could be friends. I was trying to expand my shoebox world by leaving town. She'd decided to go to the local college and was still living at home. We'd always shared friends when we were little, adopting them and then dropping them simultaneously without ever discussing it. When he called during my break, we said hello with exaggerated politeness and then I handed her the receiver and she got on and stayed hunched over for hours, the phone tucked into her neck, whispering to a man who used to kiss my breasts.

We were in the basement when she told me. She was jumpy and awkward and wouldn't quite meet my eyes. I got all hot and prickly at first, and then the blood receded in a wave and I stood there feeling very cool and tall and distant. Superior.

'That's okay,' I said.

When she looked up, she had hives all over her face and neck. She started to giggle. 'Remember, I'll always love you best,' she said. This was our little joke, the way we reassured each other. We'd stand in the kitchen in the wreckage of some evening. I'd blow cigarette smoke through the back screen door. She'd stand in front of the open freezer with her jacket still on, eating ice cream out of the carton with a teaspoon. I was the thin one, who turned away from food. She'd dip into all three flavors, the chocolate, then the strawberry, then the vanilla, channeling through until the spoon was mounded high with white, pink, and brown curls, over and over again, cold steam swirling around her head.

We were always forgiving each other.

Jim is leaning on the bar talking on the phone when I come into the Roost, the bar where Diana works. I'm waitressing at a hamburger/beer place a block away for the summer, just until I figure out what to do next. After all, we used to live like this, close together, our bedrooms side by side up in the attic. In a way it seems completely normal. All these years later, I still tuck her into bed at night, no matter what. Somehow, she manages to end up in her nightgown with her teeth brushed, lying in bed with the covers up to her chin, all settled and comfortable, while I'm sitting next to her, face unwashed, fully dressed, worrying about a man or a job or the end of the world.

Jim and I look at each other and roll our eyes up at the ceiling in mock exasperation. I'm sure he's talking to his wife. Jim is tall with sandy hair and wears jeans and a beat-up denim jacket with a tight T-shirt underneath. He's a regular who comes into the Roost at the same time every afternoon, opens his notebook and sets up a row of pens and sharpened pencils on the bar, and orders a bottle of beer. He's studying to be a veterinarian. He's the first older student I've ever met. His wife is a nurse who works the night shift at the local hospital and they have two small daughters. She calls him at the bar in the afternoon, reminding him to bring home milk or pick up one of the kids from her mother's. Sometimes I'll help Jim study for a test the next day by asking him how many bones there are in a horse's leg, or the scientific definition of mad cow disease. When he's thinking, he rubs his forefinger hard up and down between his eyebrows leaving a bright red mark like an exclamation point.

My sister hurries over to him the minute he walks in and puts a napkin under his beer, then hovers expectantly, caressing the air around him with her bar cloth. Diana and I have caught each other staring at him.

Diana is getting drunk. I can never understand why she does this where she works. She only drinks like this when I'm around and she feels safe. Her switching drinks is the warning sign, the signal that makes me slow down immediately, mid-sip. She orders her frothy, creamy, feminine drinks in this girlish voice. I feel my throat start to close when I hear her at the bar flirting with the night bartender who takes over her shift.

Breaking away from me, Diana runs over and leans against Jim, putting her hand right on the middle of his chest, her fingers spread open like a starfish. I walk up behind them and start playing with the pinball machine. She jumps up like an eager puppy, landing kisses all over his neck. Slinging her arm around his shoulder, she half hoists her hip up on to his. I continue to play, not knowing whether I'm winning or losing. When I turn around, she's over at the bar again, ordering another drink.

Lately I've been coming into the bar in the afternoon on

my days off to keep her company when it's slow, and sometimes we stay afterwards for the whole evening. I do this partly because I know that we'll probably never in our lives be together again like this. On these afternoons she's been teaching me how to carve whole lemons and limes into long delicate spirals, stripping them down to the white pith. She stands behind the bar in her red vest and black string tie, slowly polishing a beer glass with a white towel, instructing me. We both sip beer from long-necked bottles. Sometimes when the bar's completely empty she comes around to the customer side and we sit next to each other on bar stools, talking and drinking beer and eating peanuts from the wooden bowls set up along the bar.

Ever since I came to live with her at the beginning of the summer, we've been like a newly married couple. We talk about what I'm going to make for supper, and then I run out to shop and then home to cook. She shows up later with a bottle of chablis smuggled from the bar. We sit in the backyard at the picnic table until it gets dark and we light citronella candles. Lying back on the grass and looking up at the stars, we talk. It's easier in the dark, gazing up into infinity. Sometimes we leave the dishes on the picnic table all night.

'Did he keep the TV on with no sound and the stereo blasting when you did it?' Diana asks. 'And did he throw a white hand towel at you when he'd finished?'

We're sitting sideways in two old armchairs in the basement, our legs draped over one of the overstuffed arms, kicking the sides of the chairs. We do this automatically, the way your legs start pumping when you sit in a swing.

Diana has just finished cutting my hair, something that started way back when we were in junior high school. I think I keep letting her do this because it's one of the few times that she actually feels like an older sister. Years ago, she taught herself how to cut hair by studying a library book. She always made my hair shorter than I wanted it, no matter how much I warned her. Recently she bought this lethal plastic hair-cutting gadget that has a double-sided razor blade lurking beneath a two-inch-wide comb on either side. She starts swooping in at the sides and top of my hair until great sheaves of it fall away. There's no mirror down in the basement, but I can feel it. When I go to the upstairs bathroom mirror, I look as though I've just had brain surgery.

I remember how much I'd hated the thing with the towels, how it had made me feel dirty and damp as though he couldn't wait for the air to dry us off. I wasn't sure whether it had all been exactly the same for Diana, and whether that made it better or worse.

Her face is excited. 'Do you remember them? He had this whole stack of white towels in his closet. Did you see them?'

I'd wondered where he'd gotten so many small white towels, whether he'd robbed motel rooms for them. I remember the rough, bleached feeling of them between my legs and the way he hadn't watched me wipe myself, but had tossed the towel so that it landed across my thighs, then turned away to fiddle with the stereo. Later it was easier to imagine him with Diana than with me.


Walking a little unsteadily, she comes back from the bar holding a large, milky drink. I know it's no good taking the glass away from her. She gets this strange determination when she drinks and you can only follow her around and make sure she doesn't do anything too crazy. 'Hi,' she says brightly to both of us, moving in close to Jim and snaking her arm around his waist and locking her hand on to the one holding the drink so that he's belted in tightly next to her. He shrugs and smiles. It's Friday night and school is over for the week and his wife is away with the kids for the weekend. You can see the freedom in his eyes. Partly, he's enjoying this, and I want to leave, but I can't.

I go up to the bar and order another beer and get one for Jim. I don't really want one, but I want to hold something cold. Diana has a handful of marked quarters that she got from the night bartender and she's leaning all over the jukebox, practically climbing on top as she reads the songs, running one finger up and down the glass as if she's just learned to read. I know from experience that it feels warm as an incubator when you press against it, especially when you're drunk. A Hank Williams song starts up and she sways back toward us and stops right in front of Jim, so close that the top of her head touches his chin.

'Come on, let's dance,' says my sister. She starts singing 'Your Cheatin' Heart' really loud, tossing her hair back and forth in front of her face. She's pulling at Jim's hand, the one that isn't holding the beer. Reaching back, Jim hands me his beer to hold, then looks over at me and shrugs, lets her lead him toward the tiny dance floor in front of the jukebox.

I put my whole mouth over the opening of his beer, feeling the smooth glass ridge on the inside of my lips, tip the bottle back and take a large gulp, hold the beer in my mouth for a minute, thinking about our saliva mingling, then swallow.


They're the only ones dancing. Everyone at the bar turns on their stool to watch. Jim has both arms draped around her, looking embarrassed. He's acting as though he's dancing with her to hold her up; his arms go around her back and then droop down low so that they're resting below her waist, and the tips of his fingers are stuck in the back pockets of her jeans. Abruptly, she stops singing and snuggles into him, lacing her arms up around his neck and resting her head against his chest. He has to stoop down to support her. Patsy Cline comes wailing up out of the speakers. Diana screams and shoves Jim aside and comes running over and drags me on to the dance floor. 'Crazy' is our song. Draping her arms around my neck, she picks up my hands one by one, slapping one around her back near her waist and the other on her shoulder near her neck, trying to get me into the guy's position. 'Crazy for feeling so blue,' she sings, her breath hot in my ear. This time, I shrug at Jim. I remember when we used to practice dancing in the living room at home, taking turns being the boy. She always told me I was good at leading. I remember the waxy, scalp smell of her hair, and how I wondered, looking down at her, what a boy would feel.

Swaying side to side, she doesn't seem to notice that I'm not moving. After a second, I let my hands drop down by my sides and just stand there. She picks them up patiently again, one by one, and places them around her waist. Jim is leaning on the pinball machine, watching us. Suddenly Diana arches back dramatically in my arms toward him so that her hair cascades in a dark fan on the dance floor. Sensing the sudden downward movement before it happens, I catch her around the waist. We used to play Trust when we were little. It was one of Diana's favorite games. She would fall backwards with her eyes closed tightly and swing her head back and forth so that her long hair brushed the floor. She never seemed to be afraid. When it was my turn, I would never quite close my eyes all the way, but would peek out between a tiny slit in my eyelids. 'Cheater,' Diana would yell at me, just as the arms reached out for me, and everyone would pretend to let go.

I think Diana is confused about who she's dancing with.

I'm embarrassed with everyone watching. She keeps resting her head on my chest. Every time I get her to straighten up, her head lolls down and rolls back and forth over my breasts. I squeeze my arms around her tightly, trying to make her body less slumped and sleepy, but she's getting pretty comfortable dancing in my arms. I don't want to just leave her there. I gesture with my head to Jim to come and rescue me, but he pretends to not get what I mean. He heads over to the bar and I see him talking to the bartender and pulling out his wallet. They look over at us and laugh.

'I can't believe how Patsy died,' Diana suddenly says, lifting her head from my chest. She's crying and her mascara is smeared, but she still looks pretty. Ever since she saw the movie *Sweet Dreams*, and watched Jessica Lange crash into the side of a mountain in her plane and it explode into flames, she can't seem to get it out of her head. 'Crazy for thinking that my love could hold you,' she sings, gulping and sobbing at the same time.

'I think it's time to go,' I say.

'No,' she says, stopping short in the middle of the floor.

'You have to open the bar tomorrow. You should get some sleep.'

Right at that moment, Jim comes over to us and hands us each another drink. My sister must have asked him to buy drinks and then cut in on me, knowing that I would try to stop her if she went up to the bar. Her drink is tall and foamy with a big soda straw sticking out of the top with the paper still hanging off it.

A few minutes later, I'm standing behind her in the ladies room, bracing her forehead and watching the back of her neck strain, holding my breath to avoid the creamy smell of her vomit. She laughs drunkenly, turning her head up to mine, a big vein standing out in the middle of her forehead. I'm rolling the toilet paper in a thick white bandage around my hand, ready for the clean-up. I know it's time to take her home and that it will be a fight. She never knew how to throw up. I remember her at six, standing with her head straight up, her eyes terrified, vomit bubbling from her mouth. I would stand at the bathroom door in my nightgown, mesmerized by the purplish contorted face, the rolling eyes, the way my father held his hand on the back of her neck, showing her how to arch over the bowl.

'I love you,' she slurs, a cartoon drunk's voice, then her chest heaves again and the whitish speckled cream splashes over the side of the toilet.

The next thing I know, Diana is out the front door of the Roost, holding her drink in front of her as if she's delivering it to a customer. Jim and I look at each other and simultaneously turn to follow her. He stops by the bar long enough to shrug on his denim jacket and stuff his notebook into his bag. Obviously, he's not planning to come back tonight. I suddenly remember that he lives somewhere and has a family.

Jim has to unstrap one car seat and put it in the trunk before there's room for me in the back. There are books and bits of cookies and crackers all over the back of the car and a crusty bottle of milk propped up in the corner of the car seat.

I pick up one of the splayed, dog-eared books and hold it up to the window so I can read it by the streetlight. The car is an old battered Buick, and I feel a million miles away from Jim and Diana in the front seat. She's disappeared, and Jim is looking down. I assume she's now lying with her head in his lap. The book I'm holding is one where you do things: there's a Daddy with a scratchy patch of beard, and a lamb with a soft cotton-ball body. I go through the book stroking and pressing all the things you're supposed to. Most of the textures have worn away: the sandpaper beard is almost smooth and the lamb has only a few wispy strands of cotton wool still clinging to the dried glue. The honking horn, the finale of the book, is faint and nasal. I press it over and over, imagining Jim's kid picking it up and doing the same thing.

The sound finally attracts their attention, and both heads turn back to look at me over the front seat, my sister's eyes barely visible over the top.

'Let's go,' I say. I lean forward and start giving Jim directions to Diana's apartment. My chin is resting on the front seat so that my head is exactly between theirs. It used to be my favorite way to ride in a car. I would drape my arms over the seat so that my armpits rested on top and my arms hung straight, all the way down to where the back met the seat, smelling the damp, fresh sweat on the back of my father's neck.

My sister balances her White Russian on the dashboard and when Jim stops suddenly at a red light, it spills over in a dramatic splash of white, staining her black work pants and the dark upholstery. I'm thrown back against the seat. Jim slows down almost to a stop and starts to pull over, but then swerves to the center of the road and continues to creep along. I wonder if he's drunk. He reaches across Diana, whose head is burrowed in his armpit. Rummaging in the glove compartment, he comes out with a handful of paper towels. He dabs at the stains, looking at the road and then down, then back at the road. After a while, he gives up and stuffs the wad of paper towels under the seat. He adjusts the rear-view mirror. It's a weird feeling to be looking so intensely into his eyes, which are light and bright under the streetlight, while still looking at the back of his neck. My sister's head is turned sideways on his lap, her ear poking through her dark hair the way it did when she was a kid. The light turns green, and then red again, but no cars come along to make us move. Diana lifts her head and mutters, and Jim puts the car into gear and makes the final turn on to her street.

The second we pull into the driveway, she opens the car door and bolts up the front path without closing the car, pitching slightly forward like a wind-up toy. The screen door bangs behind her. Jim and I sit there, neither of us saying anything. I've been gathering all the cookie and cracker crumbs into a few neat piles on the seat. With a brush of my hand, I scatter them. Jim plays with the car keys in the ignition. The straw from Diana's drink is poking out of the ashtray, tied into the neat row of knots she always manages to make, drunk or sober. I touch the back of Jim's neck. He turns and looks at me, then leans across the front seat and opens the passenger door. I slide across the back seat and open the car door and get out, pause for a moment and slam it shut. The apartment windows stay dark. I slide into the front seat next to Jim and try to close the door quietly. The overhead light stays on. The faint stubble on Jim's face glints.

'I should go in and see if she's all right,' I say. We both sit there for a while without saying anything. Jim takes Diana's knotted straw from my hands. I've been playing with it, alternately sucking on the still-sweet, milky ends and trying to unpick the knots. He puts it back in the ashtray and keeps holding my hand. With my free hand, I pull the car door shut again, hard this time, so that the light goes out.


I'm sitting at the kitchen table, halfway through a huge meatloaf and ketchup sandwich. I made it for our supper, but we never got around to it. Diana stumbles out of the bedroom. Her eyes are bleary and her clothes twisted.

'Where's Jim? What time is it?' she asks, yawning and rubbing at the mascara circles under her eyes.

'He went home,' I say. I take a bite out of my sandwich and chew it slowly, sipping iced tea between bites. 'It's almost three.'

'He should have stayed,' she says, pouting, and sits down across from me. She tucks her knees up under her chin and wraps her arms around them. She's shivering. 'I was only taking a nap.'

'He said to say goodbye.' I push the plate with half of the sandwich still on it across the table. The ketchup is burning my raw lips. Diana finishes the sandwich in three large bites, cheeks bulging, eyes half closed.

She wanders over to the sink and finds a spoon in the drainer, then goes over to the freezer and opens the door and stands in front of it, swaying, looking inside.

'Still love me best?' she asks, not turning.

# rose tremain

## *dinner for one*

He said: 'I'll take you out. We'll go to Partridge's, have something special.' She took off her glasses and looked at him doubtfully.

'I don't know, Henry. I don't know that we want to make a fuss about it.'

'Well, it's up to you.'

'Why is it?'

'Why is it what?'

'Up to me?'

She bewildered him. For years she had bewildered him. 'It's your choice, Lal; that's all I meant. It's your choice – whether we go out or not.'

She sighed. 'I just thought . . .'

'What?'

'I just thought it might be better simply to treat it like any other day.'

'It's not "any other day".'

'No.'

'But it's your decision. You're the one who makes these decisions. So you let me know if you want to go and I'll ring up and book a table.'

He walked away from her, sat down in his worn red armchair, fumbled for his glasses, found them and took up the *Times* crossword. She watched him, still holding her glasses in her hand. It's funny, she thought, that whenever we talk to each other, we take our glasses off. We blur each other out. I suppose we're afraid that if we see each other clearly – too clearly – communication between us will cease.

'Six across . . .' he murmured from the faded comfort of his chair, 'two words, four and three: "Facts of severing the line".'

'Anagram,' she whispered, 'I should think.'

Henry and Lal weren't what anyone expected. Separate from her, he seemed to belong. He belongs; she doesn't, was what people thought. You could pull old Henry's leg and raise that boisterous laugh of his, but with her you didn't know where you were. Quite ordinary remarks – things that everyone laughed at – seemed to worry her. But she never told you why: she just closed her eyes.

There had been so many friends at the beginning. Henry and Lal had belonged then. 'Isn't my wife the belle of the ball?' he used to say. And there were so many balls, once, to be belle of. The changes had stolen gradually into her; the changes had begun after Henry came home from the War, so that people often said: 'It was the War that changed her,' and even to her face: 'It was the War that changed you, Lal, wasn't it?'

But she didn't agree with them. 'The War changed everyone' was all she'd say.

'It always seems . . .'

Henry looked up from the crossword. He was surprised Lal was still in the room. 'What, Lal?'

'Such a waste.'

'What does?'

'Going out. All that eating.'

'We can afford it, darling.'

'Oh, it isn't that.'

Henry took off his glasses. 'Well, I'm damned if . . .'

'Look at our stomachs! Look at yours. So crammed with food you couldn't push any more in. And mine, a dreadful bulge.'

'Oh, Lal, for heaven's sake.'

'It's horrible to eat and eat. What's it for? Just to make us heavier and heavier till we die with all this weight.'

'You're not fat, Lal. I'm fat! I'm not ashamed of it.'

'Why?'

'Why what?'

'Why aren't you ashamed?'

'Because it's *my* life. I can be any shape I choose.'

No, she thought, that's wrong. I am haunted by the wrongness of things.

'Henry,' she said, 'I hate it . . .'

'What?'

'I hate it when . . .'


Larry Partridge was a popular man. 'We're so lucky,' ran the county's favourite saying, 'to have you so near us!' They didn't mean Larry himself (though they liked his silver-haired politeness), they meant his restaurant which, every night of the week except Tuesdays when it was closed, was packed with them.

'This part of the world was a culinary desert before you came, Larry,' they told him, 'but now we really are lucky. Partridge's is as good as anything in London and so much more reasonable.'

Of course they had been cautious – caution before ecstasy – because, glancing through the windows of the old run-down pub he had bought, they had noted that the old run-down walls were becoming resplendent in indigos and fruit-fool pinks and this had made them nudge each other: 'Well, you can tell what *he* is, duckie!'

Now Larry's tightly clad buttocks circled their contented

after-dinner smiles. He extended to each table a limp-handed greeting and waited for the superlatives to flood his ears like warm water. 'You're so imaginative with food, Larry!'

'The sauce on the quenelles was out of this world, Larry.'

'We've had a superb meal, Larry, really superb.'


Larry's parents still lived in Romford. He had moved them from their council flat to a detached house. However, Larry's father still called him Lawrence. Lawrence: to say the name to himself was to remind Larry of his father, was to make him shudder as if the thin shadow of the man – neat in his dark-green suit and white shirt, ready for work, working all his life, never giving up his dull and hopeless work till one day he would die at it – passed between him and the sun.

For Larry, Lawrence was dead, buried hideously down in the greasy kitchens of the catering school. Lawrence, born in poverty, reared in repression, was the detritus from which Larry, in all his colourful glory, had sprung. He had sprung in 1964, the year he had met Edwin, and each year since then he had bloomed a little more.

'What can I say about Edwin?' Larry had asked his mother at the time. 'Except that I love him.'

Oh, but they were not prepared for this kind of love, she told him. They had never thought that their own Lawrence, so popular with all the local girls . . . No, it had not once entered their minds and she really did think he should have given them some warning, some indication that he wasn't what they thought . . .

Larry left his parents' flat in Romford and moved into Edwin's flat in Fulham. Edwin found him a job in a local restaurant. Lawrence in Edwin's careful drawing room became Larry, became lover and loved.

All the past, like a dirty old bandage no longer needed, began to unwind and fall off; Larry was healed.

Edwin's money purchased the pub in 1972. One end of the large building was converted into a flat and the move from Fulham was made. A year later, Partridge's opened, each of its walls a reflection of Edwin's taste, Edwin's imaginative eye.

Larry moved with perfect ease and happiness about his steel kitchen, liking his own little kingdom the better because just outside it was a rich land that he shared with Edwin.

'I do it with love,' Larry sometimes said of his cooking. But the great golden weight of his love for Edwin he seldom talked of. It hung inside him, a burdensome treasure that he knew would never leave him.

Visitors to Partridge's never saw Edwin. Larry's nightly ritual of passing from table to table to receive his cupful of praise did not include him. He was glimpsed occasionally; there was talk of him, even questions to Larry.

'But it's all yours,' Edwin had said to Larry when the restaurant opened. 'My bit's done. Don't involve me any more. Then the success and the glory will really belong to you.'

And even the invitations that came – to the lunches and the county cocktail parties – Edwin would never accept. 'You're their celebrity, Larry. Why muddle them?'

Edwin was never jealous. 'I am quite free of it,' he once said to Larry. 'I simply do not feel it. Jealousy is the vainest – in all senses – of the emotions. You must learn to rid yourself of that before it works its decay.'

But Larry had known no human relationship in which jealousy had not been present – sometimes screamed out, sometimes unspoken, but always there to stain and spoil.

And he knew that his love for Edwin was a jealous, greedy love. He thought to himself: 'Edwin is my life. How can I not be jealous of my own life?' Whenever Edwin went away, the weight inside him became a dead weight, immovable, full of pain.

When Edwin returned, he often wanted to run to him, discovering in his body a sudden miraculous lightness.

Daily, Larry watched Edwin for any sign of discontent. Three years younger than Larry, his hair was still fair and thick. With an impatient gesture of his hand, he would push back the flopping hair several times in an hour.

Whenever he was angry or agitated, he would push back the hair almost constantly.

Larry dreaded his anger. Its occasional appearance in a man as contained and rational as Edwin was unsightly. Larry couldn't look at him. He would turn away, trembling inside.

But in the hundreds of times he had turned away like this over the years, there was not one time that he had not dreaded to turn round again, afraid suddenly that all the hubbub of Edwin's anger was nothing but an echo and that, unnoticed, Edwin had quietly slipped away and left him.

Edwin did little with his time. He gave to unimportant things the careful attention of his hands. He grew roses. He did occasional pen-and-ink drawings of old houses, which Larry collected and had framed.

He made an elegant coffee table out of glass and wood. He wrote a little poetry, always laughing at what he had written and throwing it away.

Money had bought Edwin a studied indolence. 'I'm really a rocking-chair man,' he once said to Larry. 'The little motions I can make are enough.'

Certainly, they were enough for Larry. He was quite

content for Edwin to be just as he was – as long as he was always there.


Lal said: 'I've worked out that anagram.' Several moments had passed in silence. Henry had filled in two more clues in the *Times* crossword. Lal had walked to the study window and looked out at the bird table she festooned in winter with strings of nuts and pieces of coconut. The nuts were eaten, the coconut pecked dry: it was springtime.

Henry looked up. 'What was that you said, Lal?'

'Two words, four and three, "Facts of severing the line".'

'I've got that one, haven't I?'

'I don't know. It's "cast off" – anagram of "facts of".'

'Let me see, "cast off"? You're right, Lal. Good for you.'

Henry filled it in. Then he looked up at Lal standing by the window. 'Made up your mind yet, darling?'

Lal knew that he meant the dinner, knew that she had made up her mind. She didn't want to go out with Henry on that day.

A reward, she thought – a more fitting one for fifty years of marriage – should be to spend that evening alone, without him.

For the clear lines with which she encircled the petty wrongnesses of her life became each time like the lines drawn by aeroplanes in a blue sky: they fuzzed and were dissipated and the spaces where they had been were filled up, so that only a moment later you couldn't see that they had been there. Life went on in the old way.

In the mass of years she kept drawing and redrawing lines, kept believing that things might change one day and she would rediscover something lost.

'I have made up my mind,' Lal said. 'I think we should go out as you suggested. It would be nice to go to Partridge's, don't you think?'

'Well, I do.'

'Only . . .'

'What?'

'It's a Tuesday. Larry shuts on a Tuesday.'

'Damn me! Never mind, we'll make it the Monday. Why not? We can toast the midnight. As they used to say in the army, always better to have the feast before the battle; you might not live to enjoy it afterwards.'

Lal turned and stared at Henry. 'It has been a battle. The battle's going on . . .'

'Oh come on, Lal, not one of your frettings.'

'We never were really suited, Henry – only at first when we used to want each other all the time. We should have parted when that cooled off. We'd had the best of each other: we'd had all the wonderful things.'

'What rubbish you do talk, Lal. As couples go, we've been among the lucky ones. You name me the day when we've had arguments. I could count them on the fingers of one hand.'

'Not arguments, Henry, but a battle going on inside . . .'

'The trouble with you, Lal, is you think too much. We're old now, God bless us, so why not give your mind a bit of a rest?'

Lal turned back to the window. 'You'll book the table, then, Henry? I do think that if we are going to Partridge's, it would be safer to book.'


Spring arrived on the Saturday in the shape of a deep-blue sky and a softening of the breeze. Larry never opened the restaurant for lunch. 'It simply is not fair on Edwin,' he said. Instead, he usually prepared a light lunch for the two of them and they sat by themselves in the restaurant, enjoying its peace.

Edwin always washed up. He did the job so carefully that

their few plates and dishes sometimes took him half an hour, a half-hour usually spent by Larry, a cigarette in his curling mouth, in blissful contemplation of his friend. He took as much care over these lunches as he did over his evening menus.

After all, he said to himself, this is our home. Edwin has a right to my time. And to cook for Edwin was pure pleasure. Often, just before sleep, his mind would turn up some little dish that he would make for Edwin as a treat the following day.

Early on the Saturday morning, wandering out on to the patio (laid in intricate patterning of stone and brick by Edwin) Larry felt the warmth of the sun and decided he would lay a table for them outside, make them a cold lunch and serve it with a bottle of hock. He imagined this meal and others like it that they would share during the coming summer, and his imaginings laid on him a hand of such pleasurable gentleness that he didn't want to move.

Indeed was poor suffering Lawrence dead! He was dead without trace and only Larry, head crammed with joy, existed now.

'Larry!'

Edwin called him from an upstairs window. Larry looked up and saw that Edwin, whom he had left sleeping, was dressed.

'I'm going out,' Edwin called.

'Where?'

'Just out.'

'Oh.'

Larry knew that he shouldn't question him. This was what Edwin hated most.

'Will you be back for lunch?' he asked.

'Yes.'

He was relieved. They would still have their lunch on the patio and now, if Edwin was going out, he could spend the whole morning in the kitchen, do some preparation for the inevitably busy Saturday evening as well.

Larry waved to Edwin, saw him nod and then disappear from the window. He made himself stay where he was till he heard Edwin's Alfa Romeo roar out of the gate. Then he wandered into the kitchen and tied on his apron.

Larry made an iced tomato and mint soup, a cold curry sauce for a roasted chicken and a watercress salad. He spread a pink cloth with matching napkins on the wooden patio table and set two careful places, each headed by a tall-stemmed hock glass. He then went back into the kitchen, checked the contents of his huge fridge and larder against the evening menus for Saturday and Sunday, made a shopping list, took a basket and got into his car.

By the time I get back from shopping, he thought to himself, Edwin will be back; then I can open the hock.


When Lal woke on the Monday morning she experienced that bleakest of sorrows – the realization that a dream had tricked her with a few seconds' happiness and was now gone.

She had dreamed herself young. She had dreamed a bedroom in someone's country house and a corridor outside it which creaked under Henry's footstep as in the dark he fumbled his way towards her room.

She had laughed a secretive laugh full of joy as she lay under the clean linen sheet and waited for him. Their wedding was in a few weeks' time. Then there would be no more creeping down corridors: she would be Mrs Henry Barkworth and the strong white body under the silk dressing gown that now shuffled towards her, moving slowly, prudently, but running, running like a hare in its desire for her, would lie in a big bed beside her – hers. Yes, Lal remembered, there had been a great feasting of love between her and Henry. Sex had never frightened her as it seemed to frighten some women of her sheltered generation. To touch and be touched became, after Henry's rough taking of her, all. All life, save this, paled and receded into insignificance.

For days together she would not let Henry go to his office, but kept him with her in their wide, comfortable bed.

'We fit so well!' she laughed. 'How could anything be more perfect?'

Then came the War. Lal's children were both conceived during Henry's brief periods of leave and born when he was away. When the War was over and he came home, he made love to Lal like a weary stranger. She wept for what they had lost.

Lal sat up, rubbed her eyes with a white hand. It was strange that she could dream a desire she had long since ceased to feel. Life was so stale now.

We smell bad, Henry and I, she thought bitterly. We're blemished and fat and no good to anyone. Why do we go on and on?

The day was interminable. Lal felt bilious, as if the meal they would gobble up at Partridge's was already inside her. She felt like crying. But I've shed so many tears for myself, she thought wearily, why shed more? So the evening crept towards her.

She thought as she dressed for it of the wine Henry would order: a heavy claret that they would both enjoy but which, soon afterwards, would give her indigestion and a headache. Fifty years! We've had fifty years together, so now we celebrate, but the unremarkableness of all that time, the waste of it all . . .

'Cheer up, darling.'

Henry was breezy, tugging on his braces, smelling of aftershave, his bald head gleaming.

'Oh, was I . . .?'

'You've been miles away all day. Lal. Something wrong? Not feeling up to it?'

'What? The meal?'

'No! Not just the meal – the occasion!'

'In a way not. We don't need to make any fuss, do we?'

'No, no fuss. But a bottle of fizz at least, don't you think? I asked Larry to put one on ice for us.'

'Yes.'

Lal dabbed her face with powder. She had decided to wear a black dress – the one concession to her real feelings. Pinned to the dress would be the diamond and sapphire brooch Henry had given her on their wedding day.

There was a small bar just off the dining room in Partridge's; it was too small really for all the diners who congregated there, but was pretty and restful, done up by Edwin in two shades of green. A fine tapestry drape hung down one wall and now Lal leaned back against this, her head almost touching a huntsman's knee behind her.

One of Larry's lady helpers (he had two, both about forty-five and confusingly called Myra and Moira) had brought Henry the champagne he had ordered and he was pouring it excitedly like a thirsty schoolboy might a longed-for Coke.

'This is the stuff, darling!'

Lal smiled and nodded. She often thought that the reason for Henry's pinkness of face and head was that he did simple things with such relish.

'So,' he exclaimed, holding up his own glass, 'this is it then, Lal! Happy anniversary, darling.'

Lal only nodded at Henry, then took a tiny sip of her champagne. 'It's a long time,' she said, 'since we had this.'

The restaurant was seldom full on a Monday night. The little bar was completely empty except for Henry and Lal, so that to make some accompaniment to their sipping of the champagne Lal needed to talk.

'Larry's not around, is he? He usually pops into the bar, doesn't he, with his apron on?'

'I expect he's hard at work. We wouldn't want Larry doing anything but concentrating on our dinner, would we?' Henry said jovially.

'I like Larry,' she said.

'He's a clever cook.'

'I think he's quite shy underneath all that flippety talk and showing off his bottom.'

'Lal!'

'Well, he does, Henry. He shows it off all the time. Haven't you noticed the way he ties his apron so carefully, so that the bow just bounces up and down on his behind when he walks?'

'No, I haven't noticed.'

'I mean, a less shy person wouldn't need the bow, would he?'

'Haven't a clue, Lal.'

'Oh, they wouldn't definitely. You can tell that Larry's very dependent.'

'On what?'

'Not on what – on Edward or whatever his name is: his friend. He loves that friend and depends on him. Edward's more cultured than Larry is.'

Myra (Henry addressed her as Myra; but Lal nudged him, fearing it might be Moira) came to take their order. Lal ordered champignons à la viennoise, followed by stuffed pork tenderloin with cherry and Madeira sauce; Henry ordered a venison terrine, followed by veal cordon bleu.

Henry then chose a bottle of fine claret and sat back, one hand on his stomach, the other holding his champagne glass. It's not hard, he thought, to find one's little pleasures – just as long as one isn't poor. He smiled at Lal.

His work done for the evening, Larry took off his apron and hung it up. Only two tables had been occupied – not unusually for a Monday evening – and he hoped those few customers would leave early so that he could tidy up and go to bed. He sat down on one of his kitchen stools and took a gulp of the large whisky he had poured himself. But the whisky did nothing to lessen the pain Larry was feeling. The pain squatted there inside him, an undreamed-of but undeniable parasite.

Even his hands which usually moved so lightly and quickly were slowed by the pain, so that he had kept his few customers waiting for their meal, waiting and growing impatient. I must go out, he thought wearily, and apologize. Not do my little round to hear any praise tonight, but just go out and apologize for the delay, for the gluey quality of the Madeira sauce, for cooking the veal too long . . .

Larry sighed. He had said nothing to Myra or Moira. For three evenings he had kept going almost as if nothing had happened, so humbled and grieved by the turn his life had taken that he didn't wish to find a word, not one, to express it, but rather held it in – held it so tightly inside him that no one could suspect how changed he was, how absolutely changed.

If I can keep it in, he said to himself, then my body will assimilate it; it will become diluted and one day – perhaps? – it won't be there any more. It will have passed through me – only the vaguest memory – and gone.

'Bill for table four, Mr Partridge.' Myra, carrying four empty wine glasses, came into the kitchen.

Larry got off his stool and, taking his drink, shuffled over to the pine desk Edwin had provided for him at one end of the kitchen. He wrote out and added up the bill for a party of four – young people he had never seen before – and handed it to Myra.

If they're leaving now, Larry thought, then I don't have to go, not to the strangers. I'll wait till they've paid and gone and then I'll go and have a word with the Barkworths.

Larry liked Lal Barkworth. She looked at the world out of fierce brown eyes. Neither the eyes nor the body were still for long: only when something or someone managed to hold her elusive attention did she stop pacing and watching. Larry sensed that she tolerated him – as she seemed not to tolerate most people she met.

But remembering her staring eyes, now he felt afraid of facing her – knowing that she of all people would see at once that something had happened, that his gestures were awkward, his mind slow.

He refilled his whisky glass and sat motionless on the stool, waiting to hear the door close on the party of young people.

When he heard them leave and Myra came back into the kitchen with their money on a saucer, Larry got off the stool and, without looking in the mirror Edwin had hung above his desk to see if his hair was tidy, wandered out into the dining room.

Lal was sitting alone, smoking a cigarette. Forgetting for a moment that he had cooked two dinners, Larry wondered if she had come alone and had sat there all evening in silence. This sudden feeling of pity for her made him forget his pain just for an instant and smile at her. Lal smiled back.

Larry noticed that her brown eyes seemed bereft of some of their sharpness, almost filmed over. So it's all right then, he thought. She's drunk quite a lot: she's not seeing clearly, not into my mind – she won't guess.

'Hello, Larry dear.'

'Mrs Barkworth.' Larry held out a limp, hot hand and Lal touched it lightly.

'I expect we're keeping you up,' she said.

Larry looked round at the empty restaurant. 'Monday night – no one at the feast! Washday doesn't give one an appetite, I dare say.'

'We had a good meal.'

'Did you? Not one of my best, any of it. We all have our off nights, don't we?'

'Mine was very nice, Larry. I couldn't eat it all, I'm afraid. I never seem to be able to, not when it's something special. I used to eat well when I was young. Will you sit down, Larry? Henry's gone to the loo, he won't be long.'

'Oh, yes, I see. Well . . .' Larry felt confused.

He wanted to say: 'I thought you'd come alone', then realized that he'd cooked the veal for Henry Barkworth and here on the table of course were two wine glasses, two coffee cups.

He sat, gulping his whisky. Over the rim of his glass he was aware of Lal watching him.

'It isn't the same!' Larry blurted out.

There was a moment's silence; then Lal said: 'What isn't?'

'Oh . . . you know . . .' Larry couldn't finish the sentence.

To Lal's amazement, he had begun to weep, making no effort to disguise or cover his crying, his face awash with tears.

'Oh, Larry . . .'

Larry took another drink from the whisky glass, then stammered: 'I haven't told anyone. I thought I could keep it . . . inside . . . I thought no one would need to know.'

'Yes,' said Lal, quietly, 'yes.'

'But . . .' Larry put a fist up to his eyes now. 'I can't. It just isn't possible . . . when something like that . . .'

'Is it something to do with Edward?'

'Edwin. *Edwin*. That's his name. Not Edward. He was never like an Edward. Only like himself, like Edwin. And we were so happy. We were just as happy as – happier than – some married people. I thought we were. I thought I knew. And I never would have left him, never in my life, so how could he . . .?'

Larry's voice was choked with his sobbing. Facing him

across the table, Lal's body felt freezing cold. She reached out a hand and laid it on his arm. She was glad of the warmth of his arm under her cold hand. 'If...' she began.

Larry looked up. 'What?'

'If... he had just gone for a while perhaps, for a kind of holiday, a break from routine, well then—'

'No.'

'But why then, Larry? Why should he leave you?'

Larry pulled out a purple handkerchief and wiped his eyes. 'He...' Larry stopped, sucked at the whisky. 'It was on Saturday. I had thought... because of the sunny day, we would have lunch out on the patio. I made us the lunch. Edwin was out. I didn't know where because he didn't tell me. So I made this nice lunch for us and waited for him.

'But when he came back he said he didn't want any lunch and I said: "Edwin, I made this for you and I opened a bottle of hock and thought we could sit out in the sunshine..."

'He got into one of his rages. He wanted to get into a rage. He wanted me to do something silly like sulking over the meal so that he could rage at me and leave there and then. He tried to make me the excuse. He said he couldn't bear it the way I always spoiled him and did things for him and then sulked if he didn't like them, but I said: "Edwin, okay, I do that; I do that because I want you to like things and be happy with me, but that isn't enough! You couldn't leave, not for that."

'So then he had to admit – he had to admit that wasn't it. He was drunk – got himself drunk on vodkas so that he could tell me. It's someone called Dean, nineteen or something, no more than a kid. Edwin's been sleeping with him. Whenever he goes out, that's where he's gone, to sleep with him. He says he can't be... He says he's obsessed with him... He says he can't be without him.'

Larry stopped talking. His sobs were only shudders now. Lal kneaded his arm. 'Oh, Larry . . .'

'I'm sorry,' he blurted. 'I'm sorry to burden you.'

'No. Larry, I'm the one who's sorry, so sad, because I knew you had this – this precious kind of love. You see, I can't do any more for anyone now, but I was once very strong because I loved. I was so strong! I'm too old now. I just turn away. That's all I can do, isn't it, when everything's so ugly – just turn away. But you, Larry, you must fight to get him back, to get your love back. Life is so hideous without love, Larry; it makes you want to die.'

'Evening, Larry!'

Henry, jovially wined and full, staggered to the table. 'How's tricks, then?' he said.


Lal lay still. The meal lay in her stomach like a stone. Henry lay next to her, sweating a little as he snored.

As quietly as she could, not wanting to wake Henry, Lal got out of bed and crept to the bathroom. She made up one of her indigestion powders and sat on the edge of the bath, watching the powder dissolve.

When she had drunk it down, she belched and a little of the pain left her stomach, as if the stone had been blanketed by snow.

'There won't be another fifty, thank God,' she whispered, staring at her empty glass; but even though she smiled at this thought, she found that a tear had slid down her cheek on to her lip. Lal sighed. 'Oh, well,' she whispered, 'at least for once I'm not weeping for myself. I'm weeping for Larry.'

# pat cadigan

## two

He seldom touched her.

Lying on the bed on her left side, Sarah Jane thought about that. She heard the newspaper crackle as he turned the pages. If she rolled over, she would see him sitting at the small table under the hanging light, almost a solid shadow in front of the bright drapes screening out the early afternoon glare. It would be – was – a sight so familiar she called it a variation on the theme of their existence.

It might have been different if he touched her.

She had read in the magazines he was always buying her that people needed to be touched physically. Children needed hugs to thrive, married people who cuddled were happiest. Sometimes she wanted him to touch her so badly it was like pain.

'Michael?' Her voice was small and powerless in the room. He didn't answer but she knew he had looked up from the paper. 'Could we get married?'

He laughed briefly, without humor. 'No. No, we can't get married.'

She hadn't thought so. After a moment, she pushed up from the bed and wandered into the clean, clean bathroom to unwrap one of the water glasses. Her reflection in the mural-sized mirror looked peaked. The funny fluorescent lighting they used in hotel bathrooms sucked all the color out of her, leaving her like an old color photograph about to turn black-and-white. She patted her long, light brown hair and curled the ends around her fingers. Her face was bony, just like the rest of her, as though she were treading on the sunny side of starvation. It was her thinness, she decided, that made her look sometimes so much older and sometimes so much younger than twelve.

Behind the drapes was a sliding glass door that opened on to a balcony. Michael went on reading the newspaper as she stepped outside and stood in the sunlight with her hands clasped behind her back and her feet apart. A slight wind flapped her shirt-tails. Not exactly a portrait of a lady, she thought. But she had never figured on being a lady, not her. No chance. Ladies had graceful, refined forms, not bony bodies that were still growing, and they didn't wear thrift shop shirts and faded jeans, and they didn't stand like they had a plank between their legs. And they didn't live in and out of hotel rooms with men like Michael.

She leaned on the wrought-iron railing and looked down at the hotel parking lot, which was beginning to fill up with cars. The cars belonged mostly to middle-aged married couples, coming in for the hotel's Weekend Mini-Honeymoon Special. She had read all about it on a stand-up card by the telephone. Three days, two nights, complimentary champagne the first night and a special buffet brunch on Sunday morning, $90 a couple. She wondered how all those people would react to having her and Michael in their respectable midst. She imagined them walking through the crowded lounge together during the special buffet brunch on Sunday morning, while the husbands and wives stared. *It's okay*, she might say to them as they passed, *he never touches me. I'm twelve and he's almost thirty and we're just good friends*. Right. Michael would slap her silly if she told anyone he was closing in on thirty. He could pass for twenty-two or twenty-three. But a slap was a touch, anyway.

Inside the room, the phone rang. She closed her eyes. Michael picked it up on the third ring. She didn't listen in. That was one of the rules Michael had laid down in the beginning. He said when she could listen and when she couldn't and if she didn't abide by them, he would leave her. A strand of hair blew across her face. She dragged it away with two fingers and threw it over her shoulder. Even though she wasn't listening, she knew when he had put the phone down and she felt him coming to the open glass door.

'Sarah Jane?'

She turned around. He was smiling. For the millionth time, she thought how handsome he was.

'I got it set up for tonight. A game. It's safe and it's heavy sugar.'

She gave him a split-second, mirthless smile.

'It's not gonna be any different than the other times. Clean pickings.' He stared at her. When she didn't say anything, his smile broadened defiantly. 'I'm gonna catch a nap now. Wake me up at six-thirty. I'll take a shower and then we'll get some supper before the game, okay?'

'Okay, Michael.'

His mouth twitched with annoyance. 'Practice calling me Uncle Mike or they'll know something's up.'

'Okay. Uncle Mike.'

'Right.' He took a deep breath and let it out. His dark hair showed mahogany lights in the sun. 'No funny stuff while I'm asleep, got it?'

She blinked at him solemnly.

'I mean it.' He pointed his finger at her through the screen. 'I really mean it, Sarah Jane. I don't like any funny stuff, you know that.'

Her gaze roamed over his body. He wasn't a big man. She was nearly as tall as he was but he was solid, perfectly formed, without a bit of fat to him.

'Hey, why don't you put on your bathing suit and go down to the pool,' he said, his voice softening. 'Get a little sun. You could use some.'

She shrugged. 'Maybe. I don't know. I don't like being out in public in a bathing suit, you know that.'

'Jesus. You're the only female I know who thinks she's too skinny. I know broads that're living on celery sticks and water trying to get a shape like yours.'

'I don't have a shape.' She turned away and looked down at the parking lot. 'Even if I did, I still don't think I'd want to go out in a bathing suit.'

'You oughta get some sun, for chrissakes. You're a kid. You're supposed to go out and play sometimes.'

She looked over her shoulder at him sourly. Was he kidding?

His gaze dropped to his feet. 'Yeah. Well. Do whatever the hell you want, take some money and go have an ice cream sundae or something, I don't care. Just be sure you wake me up at six-thirty. And *no funny stuff*.'

Her face was expressionless now. 'Okay. Uncle Mike.'

She didn't go back into the room until she knew he was asleep. He had pulled the heavier drape behind the light one to dim the room and he was lying fully clothed on top of his bed with one arm thrown over his eyes.

Michael was the only person she had ever known who could sleep at his own command. If he decided he needed a nap so he could stay up all night, he would just lie down and be out in a few minutes. It was just another of his extraordinary features. Except he always needed her to wake him up.

She stood over him, wishing he'd move his arm so she could see his face. Michael's face did something to her; she never got tired of looking at him.

*You're a kid.* Twelve years old and hopelessly in love? Anyone else would laugh in her face if she said it out loud. Michael would laugh in her face but the laughter would be nervous because he'd know it was the truth. She couldn't help it. Michael was the only one, the only one she had ever found, maybe the only one in the world. All her life she had hoped to find someone like him. She had been afraid for a long time that perhaps no one like him existed, or even if one did, the person might not want her.

Michael rolled over, putting his back to her. She tensed but he was deeply asleep, unaware of her. She wanted to lie down next to him, just to be near him but if she did, she wouldn't be able to resist touching him and she knew what would happen then. He wouldn't have it; he was very firm. *No funny stuff.*

Would it have been any worse if he'd been, say, a married bank teller with three kids? She probably wouldn't have been able to get near him then. If he'd been a woman – well, that would have been completely different. Some nice woman, who would maybe have liked being kind of a mother or older sister to her. That would have been best of all. But Michael was what she had.

*Michael.* She mouthed his name. *Roll over facing me.* Without really meaning to, she pushed out a little and he obeyed in his sleep. His expression was peaceful, all his concerns set aside while he rejuvenated himself for the evening's game. She could see his eyeballs moving back and forth behind the lids. Dreaming. *Michael,* she implored silently, *share your dreams with me*. Because she had already pushed out once, she couldn't stop herself from doing it again. Her eyes closed and she had the sensation of drifting downward through still air, floating toward a region of fog and shadow. As she sank closer to it, it began to take on dark colors and there was a flickering of something like heat lightning playing in clouds.

Then she was with him. A jumble of images like animated balloons assailed her: Michael broke, Michael flush, Michael humiliated in school for some petty sin against classroom protocol. Michael meeting her for the first time in the laundromat. Michael and a woman – she turned away from that one. Michael when she had tried to touch him. When he hit her. Michael discovering she was telling him the truth –

*Okay, little sister, if you can really do that, tell me what that guy over there is thinking.* Standing on a sidewalk near a diner, Michael jerked his head at a man holding a flat paper bag under one arm while he waited for the light to change so he could cross the street.

*He's thinking when is the goddam light going to change.*

Michael laughed at her. *Brilliant, Sherlock. I'm no mind reader and I could have guessed that.*

She stared up at him evenly. *I wasn't finished.* And then she really gave it to him, not orally but direct, right between the eyes. He's-thinking-I-wonder-when-this-goddam-light-is-gonna-change-I-wanna-get-back-to-the-office-nobody-there-now-lunch-get-some-peace-piece-magazine-nice-one-all-women-crawling-all-over-each-other-oily-women-tongues-skin-oily-hard-oh . . .

Michael froze, unable to move while she gave it all to him, dictating the man's thoughts while he waited for the goddam light to change. Then the light did change and he was striding across the street quickly, swinging his arms, the small brown paper bag in his right hand moving like a pendulum.

*Where's he going?* Michael asked.
*Back to his office.*
*Where's that?*

*I don't know.*

*You don't know?!*

*I can only hear what people are actively thinking about. I can't get into their minds. They can't receive me. Nobody can. But you.*

He didn't give her time to tell him how lonely she had been, how she had run away from home six weeks before, how hollowly she had profited from the ability and how she had tried to give up using it and couldn't. But he took her back to his place, one room in a shabby building called the Hotel Cosmo (By the Day, Week, or Month, In Advance).

Something stirred in his mind. She'd been in almost too long; if she stayed much longer, he would become aware of her and wake up. But she needed the contact, God, how she needed it. Michael knew that. He kept her on short rations, letting her in only for a few minutes. He didn't like her crawling around in his head, it was a dirty thing to him. Except when it was useful.

Like for the games.

They might have done anything else. At twelve, she knew more about people than anyone should have known at any age and they might have done something grand, even if Michael insisted on keeping her out most of the time. Instead—

Her head filled with an unimaginably bright light and she was whirling in sudden disorientation. There was a feeling of falling and acceleration and it was as if she were plummeting past a thousand bulky objects, hitting every one of them . . .

When she opened her eyes, she was on the floor. Michael had hit her with the telephone book.

'What did I tell you, little sister?' He threw the slim volume at her. It bounced off her breastbone and one sharp corner dug into her stomach. 'Did I say no funny stuff or what.' He crouched over her, wrapping one hand in her hair. It was safe for him to touch her hair; hair was dead. 'Did I tell you no funny stuff? Answer me!' He jerked her head back.

'Michael, I couldn't help it.' Her voice came out in a high-pitched whisper. 'You know I've got to have—'

'You can *wait*, you understand that, you can *wait* until later when *I* say!' He forced her to her feet and shoved her at the bed. Her hair was still tangled around his hand and she cried out. He shoved her again, freeing himself from her roughly as she tumbled down onto the mattress. She got up, reaching for him but he had the phone book again and he batted her hand away.

'Michael—'

'Back! I mean it, girl, get back! I don't have to touch you to hit you!' He stepped forward and she threw one arm up defensively. For a moment, she thought he would strike her. Then he rolled the thin directory into a tight tube.

'Okay. Great. You just stay there on the bed and don't move.' He ambled around to the foot of the bed, watching her. She began to bring her arm down and he swatted it. 'I said, don't move!'

'No, Michael, Okay, I won't.' Her eyes burned, wanting to fill with tears but she wouldn't let them come. If she could just touch him, it would stop. The contact was instantaneous if they were physically touching but Michael was careful about that because she could paralyze him with it.

'Did I warn you about the funny stuff? Answer me!'

'Yes, Michael, you warned me.'

'But you did it anyway. Why.'

'I couldn't help it—'

'You *can* help it!' He slammed the phone book down on the bed inches from her other hand. 'You *can* help it, you've got the control and we both know it. You can keep from listening in on me or anyone else. *Why* did you do what I told you not to?'

Her throat seemed to be twisted as tightly as the phone directory in Michael's hands. 'I wanted to . . .' Tears filled her eyes after all and overflowed. 'I'm so lonely, you don't know—'

He slammed the directory down on the bed in front of her, nearly grazing her cheek. 'Don't you ever,' he said, low and gravelly and dangerous, 'don't you ever come inside me without I tell you to again. Don't you *ever. Don't you ever* – because I swear I'll really hurt you bad. And you'll never see me again. Now you think you can remember that?'

She nodded.

'You'll be goddam lucky if I let you in tonight after the game. That's when you get yours, girly, when *I* let you in. I can keep you out, you know I can. And I still might do that.'

'Please,' she whispered.

'Shut up. You better do right tonight, little sister. You better be on your best all night because if you're not, I might decide I like my old scams better. Are you taking this in?'

'Yes, Michael. Can I put my arm down?'

He stepped back. 'Get out.'

She scuttled across the bed, watching him warily, and backed toward the door. 'I – I need some money, Michael.'

He threw a crumpled ten-dollar bill at her. 'Get your skinny ass *out.*'

Moving quickly, she crouched to pick the money up off the carpet, still keeping her wide eyes on him.

'Little sister.'

She paused halfway out of the room, holding the door in front of her like a shield.

'Be back here to wake me at six-thirty or don't bother coming back.'

She dipped her head in a nod and slipped out into the hall.

She spent nearly an hour in the tacky gift shop off the lobby, drifting among the shelves while the clerk behind the counter tried to decide whether she was a shoplifter and wondered why, on his salary, he should have cared.

Out of boredom, she bought a *Vogue* magazine and a small bag of pistachio nuts with her crumpled ten-dollar bill and went out to the patio near the pool to sit at one of the umbrella tables. There weren't many people around and she was left to herself to methodically pry each nut open with her teeth and suck the meat out, staining her fingertips and mouth magenta while she stared at fierce-faced models cavorting in unlikely places in even unlikelier clothes. The pistachio shells made an untidy little pile on the metal table and the wind threatened to scatter them. Deliberately, she held herself tight and would not tune in on the few people who walked by and gave her curious glances. She didn't want to know what they were thinking, she didn't want to know what anyone was thinking ever again. She might be better off if she just walked away from the hotel, let Michael sleep until he woke up, whenever that would be, and tried to forget about him. Her own parents didn't want her back but maybe she could find a family to take her in. She could try to live like regular people, suppress the ability (she had never called it a gift) and maybe it would atrophy and disappear.

A woman advertising purple lipstick offered her a kiss from a glossy page. She turned it over, working a pistachio nut open on her bottom teeth. She might as well try to alter the basic rhythm of her heart or glue her eyes permanently shut as attempt to give up using the ability. It was still useful and having lived with it, she could not live without it.

Live without Michael? Go back to the way things had been before, having no one to get close to in the special way she needed? No one to provide the complement to the ability, to receive her, bind with her in a union that transcended the separateness of two minds in two bodies . . .

But Michael would never let things go quite that far with them. He opened up to her only so much but when he felt the start of the process that would have melded them together, he forced her out again.

In the beginning, she had tried to convince him it was the right thing to let the process continue to its conclusion. *Don't you see, Michael? It's supposed to be that way. Maybe we're not really two people . . . maybe we're one person who came apart somehow . . .*

But he didn't want to hear about that. If she didn't know who she was, *he* knew who *he* was and he wasn't half a man and half a twelve-year-old girl. If she didn't like the way things were, she could walk, he wouldn't stop her.

Whether he actually would let go of his meal-ticket she didn't know. He managed to keep a lot of his motivations hidden from her, even when she was inside him. Sometimes she thought if she ran away, he would come after her; other times, she was afraid he'd carry through on his threat to leave her.

And in the meantime, they were getting closer, whether Michael liked it or not. Every time he let her in, even just a little bit during the games or afterward, they drew that much closer. Someday he would have to let her all the way in. Either that or never let her in again.

She looked at her reddened fingers and tried to wipe them on her shirt-tail. The stain would have to wear off. She wished Michael would wear off, that he would somehow lose his capacity to receive her. There wouldn't be anything she could do if he just lost it. Then she wouldn't feel so desperately drawn to him, her compulsive, helpless love would fade and she could search for someone else. And if there wasn't anyone else, she wouldn't be any worse off than she'd been before she'd found him. Would she?

The last pistachio nut in the bag refused to open. She held it up to examine it. The shell was perfectly smooth all over, with no hint of an opening or even a seam where she could split it open. Licking her stained lips, she put the nut between her back molars and bit down, crushing both the shell and the meat inside to pulp.


She stayed by the pool, looking through the *Vogue* over and over again until it was time to go upstairs and wake Michael. He said little to her beyond telling her to change her clothes but his anger seemed to have passed. She kept thumbing through the magazine while he showered and when they went down to the dining room, she carried it with her without thinking about it.

'Why'd you bring that?' Michael said after they were seated in a corner booth.

She shrugged one shoulder. 'I don't know.'

'It's not exactly bright enough for reading in here. All this candlelight crap.' He looked around the dim, almost full dining room. 'Mr and Mrs America, getting away for a weekend from the kids they wish they'd never had. Isn't that right, little sister?'

'I don't know,' she said again.

'You don't know?' He had a sip of beer. 'Don't tell me you've been wandering around loose all afternoon and you didn't listen in on anybody?'

'I didn't feel like it.'

'You just read a magazine and ate those watchamacallit nuts.'

'Pistachio.' She looked down at her lap.

'You look like hell. You got red all over your mouth. What's the matter with you? Girls your age are supposed to be all uptight about how they look and you go around like that.' He blew out his breath disgustedly. '*Vogue* magazine, for crying out loud. I give you money for clothes and you go to the Salvation Army and come home with somebody's old rag they don't want anymore.'

She didn't look up. She couldn't tell him she went to the charity stores because the thoughts of the people who worked in those places were usually warm and comforting and permeated by something that lay in a grey area between kindness and love. Not like the thoughts of the people she met with Michael.

'All right, so what do you want to eat? You ain't even looked at the menu.'

'A cheeseburger.'

'A cheeseburger. Jesus. Come on, eat something real for a change. A cheeseburger. We're in a nice place here.'

'I want a cheeseburger,' she said firmly.

'A cheeseb—have a steak.'

She shook her head. This was Michael trying to be nice to her now, except he didn't really know how. She had to clench her teeth to keep from pushing out to him, to taste his mind and his self and show him how to love.

'You're having a steak. You gotta eat good stuff if you're going to keep your strength up. And coffee. I don't want you falling asleep on me tonight. I probably should have made you take a nap.'

'I can't sleep during the day.'

'Yeah, yeah, yeah.' He made a disgusted noise. 'You won't do this and you can't do that and you don't like to do the other thing. You're a major pain in the ass, Sarah Jane. You can't appreciate a goddam thing I do for you. If it weren't for me, you'd still be camping out in laundromats and parking garages, eating whatever you could steal. And you wouldn't have anybody for that funny stuff you're so hot to do. And what do *I* get for it? A big long face and crazy questions about can we get married. Cut me a break, little sister.'

'What do you want me to do?' she asked miserably, twisting the ends of her hair around her fingers.

Michael leaned forward with a nasty grin. 'Tell me what's going on with those two over there.' He jerked his head to her left. She turned to look and saw a middle-aged couple at another table. They were scowling down at their place settings, not looking or speaking to each other.

'What about them?'

'Tell me what's eating them.'

And this, she thought, was Michael offering to let her back into his good graces. She sighed. 'They're just a couple of married people here for the weekend.'

'Yeah, but look at them. I mean, take a good look at them. Listen in.'

She made a pained face.

'Listen in and maybe I'll let you stay in longer than usual after the game tonight.'

'You alway say that but you don't mean it.'

'Don't give me a hard time, little sister.' His smile was flat and counterfeit. 'The harder you make it on me, the harder I can make it on you.'

She didn't answer.

'Come on. Call it practice for later.'

'I don't need to practice.'

'Are you gonna keep pushing it?' Michael leaned forward. 'What do you care if we know what they're thinking. They won't know it. Come on.'

Her eyes narrowed. Michael watched her eagerly. He was expecting her to tell him out loud. She waited several seconds until she saw a hint of impatience in his face and then sent a stream of thought at him, directly instead of speaking. *—telephone-call-from-the-sitter-one-of-the-kids-is-sick-she-wants-to-check-out-and-go-home-and-he-doesn't-and—*

Michael fell against the padded back of the booth, shutting himself off from her. His face reddened with the effort. She had a sudden feeling that if she had persisted, she could have forced her way through his barrier and stayed inside him whether he liked it or not. But she let him break the contact.

'You little . . .' Michael sat up straight and pointed a finger at her. 'I oughta . . .'

'Sorry,' she said coolly. 'Just practicing for tonight.'

He reached for his beer. 'You just better do me right, little sister. You just better.'

'I will.' She looked over at the couple again. They were still staring unhappily at the table. She actually had no idea what their problem was; she had just made the whole thing up.


She insisted on buying another bag of pistachio nuts before she and Michael drove across town to a dark, rundown neighborhood and a bar that seemed to be nothing more than a hole in the wall. Michael parked the car on the street and told her to wait in it with the doors locked and the windows rolled up while he went in. A minute later he came out and took her around the corner to a side entrance.

'They run the game in the store-room,' he told her. But she was already listening, thoughts from several different people jumbling together in her mind. She followed Michael through a dim hallway and into a small room full of boxes and crates. Under a bare, hanging bulb, a round table had been set up and four men were already seated at it. Cigar and cigarette smoke slithered in the air over their heads. They looked up from their cards and one of them, a sandy-haired man with a florid complexion said, 'You're late, Mr, ah, Jones.' Then all the men caught sight of her.

'What the hell is this?' asked the sandy-haired man. 'You think this is some kinda tea party we're having here?'

Michael spread his hands. 'Hey, what can I do? At the last minute, my sister comes over and dumps the kid on my doorstep. She's going to the Ozarks for a week with her boyfriend and somebody's got to keep an eye on Sarah Jane.' Michael looked around at the stony faces of the men. Standing behind him, she clutched the *Vogue* and the bag of pistachios to her chest. The men's thoughts jabbered like an open telephone switchboard. *Guy's crazy what the hell does he think bring a kid here busted we all take a fall how old is she* and then Michael cutting through everything: *Do they believe me, Sarah Jane? Answer me! Are they buying it?*

She trembled. *They think you're nuts bringing me here.*

Michael seemed to relax. 'Hey, you guys. Really. What could I do?'

The sandy-haired man walked around Michael to have a look at her. She hunched her shoulders and tried to make herself smaller. 'Thought you were new in town,' he said to Michael but staring at her.

'I am. But my sister lives here. Moved here with her boyfriend.'

'Kid looks old enough to stay home alone.'

'Yeah, but she's afraid to,' Michael said and shrugged. 'She's kind of a big baby, you know what I mean?'

The man gave Michael a disgusted look. *Sleazeball scumbag dragging a kid to a place like this some people no decency—*

She couldn't help smiling.

'Something funny?' the man asked her.

She put her hand to her mouth as Michael turned to look at her. 'Sarah Jane's kinda, hey, you know. Sometimes she smiles at nothing, sometimes she laughs. You know?'

'So what are you saying here? Is she gonna create a disturbance or something?'

'Nah, nah, she's okay. She'll be real quiet, won't make a sound. She can sit on those boxes over there, look at her magazine, eat her nuts, she won't bother anyone. Right, Sarah Jane? You won't bother your Uncle Mike while he plays cards with his friends, will you, honey?'

She gave him a moron's stare with her mouth hanging open before she wandered over to some boxes against the far wall and sat down. The men's thoughts babbled as their eyes followed her. *—a hundred pounds stripped crazy or dumb call my kid tomorrow throw him out and her too christ are we babysitters or what no meat on her big girl—*

'She reads magazines?' the sandy-haired man said to Michael suspiciously.

'She looks at the pictures, big deal. Look, you don't want me here, fine, I'm out. But I came a long way for a good game and I got friends in this town. They like me to have a good time.'

The man gave a sharp little laugh. 'So take a seat, who's stopping you?'

Michael looked at her and nodded almost imperceptibly before seating himself at the table. Now it began, the worst part of living with Michael. She tore open the bag of pistachios, pretending to be absorbed in the pictures of the improbable models. She knew them all by heart now. The men's thoughts rumbled and churned in her head under the sound of the cards being shuffled and she began sorting them out. The man to Michael's right was some kind of repairman, he didn't trust Michael, didn't like him and wished he hadn't come. His thoughts were like heavy persistent drumbeats. The man next to him had trouble concentrating. Memories of insignificant things constantly rolled through his thoughts, interrupting them or enhancing them as though he couldn't stop free-associating. He cared the least about Michael having brought her but she recognized him as the one who was going to call his kid the next day. Now he was thinking about food.

The man with his back to her didn't like the idea of her sitting directly behind him. It meant he wouldn't know when she was looking at him. He was the one who kept wondering how old she was.

And the sandy-haired man with the red face. He showed flashes of concern for her but it was the kind he had for dumb, not particularly useful animals: don't hurt them but keep them well out of the way.

The circle came back to Michael, who was grinning at the cards piling up in front of him. The harsh overhead light threw strange shadows on to his face. She put a pistachio nut to her mouth and pushed out, touching Michael's mind.

*Let's go, little sister. What's the story?*

She sighed. A thousand ways they could have used their respective abilities and Michael insisted on using them to cheat at poker. She directed her attention around the table, listening in as each man evaluated his hand and then dutifully reported to Michael.

*Three nines; pair of eights and possible straight, seven low, ten high; one seven and possible straight ace through four; pair of fives and an ace, queen, jack.* Michael had taught her everything, coaching her over and over until she sounded to herself like she thought a Vegas croupier must sound. Michael's own hand had only a pair of threes. *So far, not so good*, she thought at him.

*Just report on their cards, little sister.*

She paid close attention as each player asked for one or two or three cards. Michael ended up with a pair of kings along with the pair of threes, but the three nines took the pot. Michael's disappointment oozed through her like the taste of something rancid.

*See, Michael? Even cheating can't help, sometimes.*

*Just you do what you're supposed to do and let me play. I'm getting the feel of them.*

Miraculously, during the third hand, Michael was dealt a straight, seven through jack. He stood pat while the others took two or three cards from the sandy-haired man – Harvey, they were calling him – and then began to bet. Michael's triumph thrummed in her, making her hand shake as she reached into the bag for another pistachio. The money in the center of the table increased.

*This is ideal, little sister. They'll believe every bluff I lay on them from now on.*

She squirmed. *The heavy man across from you doesn't believe you have anything, Michael. He doesn't trust you. He thinks you're cheating.*

*Chill out, little sister, and let me play it.*

Agitated, she cracked a nut between her teeth. The heavy man who thought Michael was cheating twisted around to glare at her.

'Does she have to do that? It's driving me bugfuck!' He turned to Michael but his anger pounded incoherently in her mind like a jackhammer; she passed that on to Michael. His mouth twisted down at the corners.

'Knock it off, Sarah Jane. No more nuts. We can't concentrate here.'

She set the bag quietly aside and listened as the betting continued. The angry man held a pair of kings; the rest of the hands were cold. Only Harvey attempted to stay in for awhile. Then he, too, folded his cards and sat back to observe the duel between Michael and the man opposite. Sarah Jane's head began to throb.

'Ten bucks,' said the man.

'See you and raise you another five,' *Bluff his ass out of the water. How far will he go, Sarah Jane?*

*He's thinking about cutting your throat.*

*That's why they call it cutthroat, babe.*
*For real, Michael. With a knife.*

The man – Klemmer was the name he identified himself with, not Albert, which was his first name – folded his five-dollar bill in half the long way and then set it like a tent on top of the other bills. 'Call,' he said.

'You first,' Michael told him.

The man wagged his graying head from side to side. 'I paid for 'em, I get to see 'em.'

*Don't show off, Michael*, she begged. But he laid his cards down showily, one at a time in descending order, until he came to the seven. He appeared to hesitate and then put it on the table face down.

'How much you bet it's a seven, Klemmer?'

A jolt of terror almost loosened Sarah Jane's bowels. *You're not supposed to know his name, Michael! He never told you!*

Michael smiled defiantly at the man, whose thoughts had flattened into a low hum of suspicion. But mercifully, he hadn't noticed Michael's use of his name.

*It's too early to pull this, Michael! Stop it!*

'How much?' Michael prodded.

The other man was about to answer – *twenty* – when Harvey leaned forward and turned the seven over. Michael's thoughts flared angrily but before he could say anything, the sandy-haired man just laughed.

'You even had me going there for awhile, Slick, but I knew that had to be a seven. Forget it, the pot's big enough for anyone. Right?'

Michael's anger died; he picked his winnings up bill by bill. 'Yeah. Sure. Big enough for anyone. I play sincere poker.'

*Don't be a big shot, Michael. That man saved you.*

*Lay off, little sister. They'd take me for everything in a minute if they could.*

*You're the stranger, they don't trust you!*

'Hey, Sarah Jane,' Michael said aloud. 'Go ahead. Have a few nuts. We concentrate just fine, don't we?'

The heavy man's anger seared her mind and brought tears to her eyes. She sat with her head bent, pretending to be in a light doze.

Michael's cards went dead for the next few hands but the tension between him and the heavy man increased steadily. The sandy-haired man, Harvey, kept watching him, undecided as to whether Michael was honest.

Sarah Jane felt herself settle into a weird calm. Michael bought the table a round of beer, brought in to them by a fat, bored bartender whose mind seemed to be on automatic pilot. The sight of her stirred no new thoughts, as though she were just a blurry photograph to him.

The game continued, the cards running cold almost without a break. Someone produced a new deck, which was examined and pronounced acceptable. It didn't do any of them much good. She ceased to pay attention to anything except the contents of each man's hand, reporting the information mechanically to Michael. Sometimes it helped, sometimes not. The heavy man's anger had subsided but remained ready. The others were nondescript in her mind, colorless entities who neither lost nor won large amounts of money, players Michael referred to as chairwarmers, there only to fill out the pot.

The time crawled past, leaving her with a feeling of weighty exhaustion. The smoke in the air turned her stomach and hurt her eyes. In front of Michael, the pile of money increased and then decreased but he continued to run ahead, consulting her as though she were just another part of his mind. And she seemed to be just that. In her inner eye, she could see the cards he held; she could taste the alcoholic maltiness of beer in his mouth, feel the air going in and out of his lungs. She slid in further, wincing at the ache in his back and the hardness of the chair. Michael's gaze flickered to her and she saw herself sitting on the boxes with her head bowed and her hair hanging down. Then she was all the way inside him and she saw her body go limp. There was a roaring in her/Michael's ears and the sensation of something about to give way. She began to topple over.

'Sarah Jane!'

The faces of the other men flashed before her dizzyingly and then the floor was rushing at her.

Moments later, she was blinking up at Michael who was bending over her, his face white with fury.

'I'd say it's past your little mascot's bedtime,' said the sandy-haired man. 'Either that or she's pitching a fit. Which is it?'

'Get up,' Michael growled at her, 'and don't pull that shit again, Sarah Jane.'

'Being a little hard on her, aren't you?' said the heavy man sarcastically.

Michael looked at him. 'What's it to you? She's just a dumb kid.'

'Yeah. Sure. Your sister's kid, right?'

Sarah Jane sat up with her back against the boxes. *Michael, let's get out of here.*

'That's what I said.' Michael straightened up slowly. 'What about it?'

*Michael, please! Something's going to happen!*

'She always faint when you're about to lose big?'

'What are you trying to say?' Michael asked.

'What is it you got going, some kind of signaling system maybe?'

'Hey, come on . . .' said the sandy-haired man stepping forward but the heavy man shoved him back.

*Michael, we have to run. Now!*

'Yeah, that's what it is, isn't it? Your little mascot signals to you and you signal back what you've got, right?'

'Bullshit in a bag, man, she's been sitting right over here on these boxes all night reading her goddam magazine and eating her nuts.'

'Eating *my* nuts, pal, looking over my shoulder and telling you what I got!'

Sarah Jane pushed away from them, crawling toward the corner.

'She can't see what you got from where she's sitting,' Michael said. 'And she sure as hell couldn't see what the other guys were holding. You're crazy.'

'Don't call me that, buddy.'

Michael sneered at him. 'Oh, *sorry*, Klemmer.'

*Michael, don't! I told you, you're not supposed to know his name!* Sarah Jane thought at him just as he turned to her and yelled, 'Will you shut up, you little bitch!'

The men looked at Sarah Jane and then at Michael. 'You're the one who's crazy,' said the sandy-haired man to Michael. 'The kid hasn't said a word.'

'It's their signaling system!' said Klemmer furiously. 'That's how she talks to him without saying a word! Isn't it, little girl?' He lunged for her but the other two men caught him and held him back.

'Hey, come on, now,' said one of them, the man who was going to call his kid. 'You don't want to hurt her.'

'I wanna *kill* her!' said the heavy man. 'I'm down three bills because of her!'

'Forget it, she's just a kid,' said the sandy-haired man. 'Who knows where he got her. I bet if we let her out right now, we'd probably never see her again. Would we, kid?'

Michael looked around at the men just as the sandy-haired man took hold of his upper arm. *Sarah Jane? What's going on, they can't believe that shit, can they? Sarah Jane? Answer me, goddamit!*

Sarah Jane pulled herself up and stood facing them all with her arms clutching herself. *It's too late, Michael. I tried to warn you. They know there's something going on, they just don't know what. But they don't like you because you were winning all their money and now—*

The sandy-haired man jerked his head at the door. 'Get out. And keep going.'

She opened her mouth to say something.

'I mean *now*, kid!' said the sandy-haired man. 'Beat it. And don't ever come around here again.'

'What are you going to do?' Michael said as she backed around the table. 'Hey, come on, we weren't cheating—'

' "We" weren't, huh?' said the heavy man. 'Sure, buddy.'

*Oh, Michael—*

*Get the cops, Sarah Jane. Go get them right now!*

'Out!' yelled the sandy-haired man and she fled out the door into the hallway.

'Hey, Klemmer, Harvey, come on . . .' came Michael's voice through the door.

'And how the hell do you know our names?' the heavy man said. 'We never told you our names!'

'Hey, come on, now,' Michael said desperately, 'you don't want to do anything—'

'We're just going to check your honesty a little,' said the sandy-haired man. 'Make sure it's still there.'

The men's thoughts rose to an incoherent roar in her head and over it all was Michael screaming to her to get help. Then the pain came, so white-hot and overpowering that she never heard the blows.

She was unable to think of anything except getting out of range of the agony pounding in her skull.


She came to herself crouched in an alleyway behind a trash dumpster, her forehead pressed against her knees. The awful noise in her mind had faded away a long time before and something like general background babble had rushed in to fill the void. She had been resting open, like a microphone that had been left on and forgotten. Distant thoughts faded in and out of her mind, mixing together unintelligibly.

Slowly, she lifted her head, forcing the mind-babble down into silence. It was like trying to close an enormous, heavy steel door that had been stuck open. She concentrated, pressing her own thoughts against the others, filling her mind with her own awareness until there wasn't room for anything else.

Peace. For a few moments. And then she remembered Michael.

*Michael?*

For the first time in months, there was no answer.

She stood up unsteadily and found her way around the dumpster to the mouth of the alley. The street was unfamiliar, dingy under the yellowish streetlamps. She had no idea where she was in relation to the bar or the hotel and she couldn't feel Michael at all. Feeling suddenly weary and light all at once, she leaned against a brick-walled building and looked up at the night sky. This was it. She was free. She hadn't been out of range of Michael since she'd found him and now she was. She could go now if she wanted to, just go, and not look back.

And then it came, so faintly she almost thought she was imagining it: *Sarah Jane. Sarah Jane . . .'*

She wiped her hands over her face. No, she could never be out of range of Michael. Not while he lived.


They had tossed him out of a car into the shadow of an abandoned warehouse on the other side of the freeway, perhaps a mile away from where she'd come to. She found him without any awareness of where she was going, only that she was going to him. Weak at first, his thoughts grew stronger as they hooked on to her, drawing her to him. The pain was curiously remote to her; she could feel it but she could keep it fenced off so it wouldn't take her over. She could also feel Michael's relief and joy at having found her but that, too, was fenced off with the pain. It was peculiar. She'd never done that before with Michael.

*Sarah Jane.*

He was lying on the broken pavement of what had once been a parking lot. She closed her eyes, not wanting to see the gleam of blood in the faint light of a streetlamp a block away. She got it from him all at once: they had not intended to kill him, just to beat him badly, teach him a lesson. Except they'd beaten him too badly and he was dying after all.

*Won't they freak when they hear about it on the news, how my body was found here. They'll shit their frigging pants over it.*

She crouched down a few feet away from his head, still not looking at him. *Yeah, Michael. They'll freak. They'll shit their frigging pants.*

*And they'll be worried about you, Sarah Jane. They'll be afraid you'll go to the cops about it.*

*Yeah, Michael. They sure will.*

*So we'll have to hide for awhile. And then, when they think they're secure, we'll go to the cops and nail their asses.*

Her mind stopped cold for a moment. *We?*

*Yeah. We. You and me, Sarah Jane. The way you always wanted it.*

*But you—*

And then she saw what he meant to do as clearly as a movie in her head. She could even see him as though in a waking dream, standing before her with his arms open, ready to catch her up in a big, never-ending hug.

*Come to me now, Sarah Jane. It's the only way. You can*

*save me and I'll be with you for good, the way you always wanted me to be with you.*

She felt herself moving toward him in her mind.

*Just reach down and put your hand on my head, Sarah Jane. Just touch me. You were always wanting to touch me. Touch me now, Sarah Jane. I know you still want to.*

She could see it — Michael wrapping himself around her, stepping out of the painful, dying body on the ground and into her young one, living with her, melding with her the way she had known he would have to someday. Either meld or — not.

*Come on, Sarah Jane. Touch me and we'll have it made. I'm not strong enough to come to you now, you have to bring me in. Save me, Sarah Jane, save me for yourself. Remember what you said about how maybe we weren't really two people but one that got split up somehow? That's the way it'll be for us, for always, if you'll just touch me now.*

Her hand trembled in the air. Horrifed, she snatched it back and pressed it to her chest. In her mind, Michael's image receded a little.

*Sarah Jane?* Underneath his hurt and confusion, she could sense the undertone of the old anger. *What's the matter?*

*You are, Michael,* she thought wearily. *How can we be sure you'd come into me and I wouldn't come into you instead and die with you?*

He didn't even hesitate. *Because you're the one with the power, Sarah Jane — the real power. I was always just your receiver. Right? You've got the power. You can keep us both alive.*

He was reaching for her now with his last bit of strength. She imagined the fence that kept out his pain growing up higher between them. Chicken wire, she imagined, like so many fences she'd seen. Chicken wire and barbed wire.

*Sarah Jane? What are you doing?*

*I can't, Michael.*
*Can't what?*
*Can't take you.*
*You always wanted this!*
*When you were alive.* The fence thickened, chicken wire criss-crossing barbed wire; he was disappearing behind the snarls. *When there was no alternative.*
*There's no alternative now!*
*Not for you.*
The fence shut him completely out of sight. *Sarah Jane! I thought you loved me!*
*I love you, Michael,* she thought miserably. *But I don't want to be you.*
His thoughts became a howl of outrage and betrayal. *I'll haunt you, little sister, if I can find a way, I swear I'll come after you, I swear I'll get you, you'll be cursed all your life and I'll be waiting for you when you die—*
The most amazing thing, she thought, was that he'd called her *little sister* at the end instead of something like *you bitch.*

She didn't take much from the hotel room, just one small bag of clothes and Michael's emergency stash of money. The clerk sitting alone at the desk in the lobby gave her an odd look as she passed him on the way in and on the way out again. The lateness of the hour. It was so late even the little store was closed. No more fashion magazines or pistachio nuts tonight.

Amazingly, she found a cab sitting a little ways from the hotel entrance, the driver dozing behind the wheel. She got in and told him to take her to the airport, ignoring his sleepy curiosity about her. There was enough cash to get her a one-way ticket to the coast. After that – well, there was the ability. She'd be able to listen in so she'd know when she could lift an unguarded purse or a few small food items. She'd get by. She'd done it before.

It was a long ride to the airport. She sat back and let her mind drift. She hadn't even felt him die. So strange; she'd have thought she'd have felt something that marked the ending of Michael's life but there'd been nothing. Was that all there was to it?

'Huh? What'd you say?'

Sarah Jane sat up with a start. 'What?'

'Did you just say something to me?' asked the cab-driver.

She swallowed, forcing herself to breathe normally. 'No. I didn't say a word. Nothing.'

'Oh. Musta been the radio I heard.'

She sat back again and smiled. 'Yeah. It must have been.'

The man picked up the microphone and murmured something in cab-driver to it. 'So, what's a young girl like you doing going to the airport so late at night?' he asked as he put the microphone back in its holder.

'I'm going home,' she said. 'Death in the family.'

'Oh,' the cab-driver said. She let his thoughts ramble lazily through her mind. He was wondering what she could have been doing here and families today, Jesus, how could they let their kids go traveling by themselves, didn't they know awful things could happen, especially to the really sweet ones, didn't they care . . .

And then, without warning, she was in.

The contact lasted barely half a second but it was dizzying; his name was Tom Cheney and he had a wife and three sons, he was working long hours for the oldest boy's college tuition and it wasn't the greatest life but at least they all had a home to go to and—

Sarah Jane wrenched away from him, shaking. They rode a mile on the highway in silence and then the cab-driver gave a long sigh. 'Jeez, I'm tireder than I thought. After I drop you off, I better call it a night.'

She sank against the seat cushions. Of course, he wouldn't know what it was. How could he? She wanted to laugh and cry with relief and dismay. Of all the crazy things, to find another receiver so soon after Michael . . .

Except he wasn't another receiver. She could tell by the aftertaste in her mind. He was just a normal person. It was her ability that had changed.

After all those months with Michael, pushing out to him, getting into him, it had been like exercising a muscle. It had strengthened the ability so that now, she could make anyone her receiver.

Anyone.

'Huh? Did you just say something?' asked the cab-driver.

'No, I – no. I didn't.'

'Damn. Sorry. I guess I must be going nuts or something, hearing voices.'

'The radio,' she said, smiling.

'No, it wasn't the radio,' the man said, troubled. 'It was real weird. I thought I heard someone say, "little sister." '

Sarah Jane's smile faded. ' "Little sister." '

'Yeah. Just like that. "Little sister." '

She wiped her hands over her face. 'Did you – did you hear anything else?'

The man shrugged. 'I dunno. Why? You hearin' the same voices or something?' He laughed. 'You psychic?'

Sarah Jane hesitated. 'I think everyone is. Just a little, I mean.'

'I don't much believe in that stuff. My wife does, though. She reads her horoscope every day in the paper, says she knows when one of the kids is in some kinda trouble. Me, I figure that's part of being a good parent. Intuition, you know. Say, what about your parents? They must be nuts, letting you run around in the middle of the night so far from home.'

'They're okay,' she said noncommittally. She pushed out with her mind. *Michael?*

Nothing. He could reach someone receiving her but he wasn't quite strong enough to reach her. Yet. How long before he was?

It didn't matter, she decided. Because she would find someone before then, and together, they'd keep him out. Two live people would be stronger than one dead Michael.

'Huh?' said the cab-driver. 'I *swear* you said something that time.'

'Like what?' she asked.

'I swear I heard you say "better hurry."'

'Oh,' said Sarah Jane. 'Yeah. I guess we should. I don't want to miss the last flight out. I want to find my family as fast as possible.'

'Find them?'

'You know, at the airport.'

'Oh, yeah.' The cab sped up slightly. 'Don't worry, little sister. I'll get you there.'

'You'll try,' she muttered, but the cab-driver didn't hear her.

# betsy tobin

## *the clockmaster*

My mother is dead. She died that I might live, they tell me, though I have no way of knowing. I have no memory of her. She is all hearsay, conjecture – nothing but other people's pictures painted on my brain. I think of her too often, and she is fluid, mysterious, ever-changing – not one but many people parading through my mind.

I have a likeness of her. It too seems oddly transient, as if it might alter itself or even disappear altogether. In the portrait she wears velvet brocade of deepest blue and her mass of dark hair is pinned loosely above her shoulders. Her eyes are large and black and serious; her expression borders on defiance. She does not trust the painter, perhaps, or does not wish to be painted. Does she sit of her own accord or has she been made to do so? I asked my father once but he only frowned and turned away. They say that as a young man he was obsessed with her beauty; driven crazy by desire, and desperate for an heir. Perhaps it was he who killed her, then, with his urgent need to sow the seed. Perhaps she died to spite him. He wanted an heir, a male heir, but instead he got me. An act of double vengeance, then: her death, and my birth.

This afternoon we will go by carriage to the clocktower, my father and I. We will don our best clothes, our most opulent silks and rosaries, all that which sets us apart from the others, and join the rest of Prague to gaze in wonder at the clockmaster's creation. They say it will have moving figures, and that the figures themselves will strike the bell upon the hour, even in the dead of night. I do not know how this will be achieved, only that he has laboured long and hard to make it so. I envy him, the clockmaster. I know nothing of him but his name, and that he has worked four long years to rebuild the clock. But I think he must be fortunate. I have no such labour of my own, only a deep and desperate yearning, though for what I do not know.

Silva, my handmaiden, helps me to prepare. It is barely mid-morning but already the sun is high and bright and menacingly hot. I overdress, knowing that if I do not my father will accuse me of undermining his authority. The sweat gathers under my arms almost as soon as the gown envelops me. Silva purses her wrinkled lips but says nothing and proceeds to tighten the underbodice. When she is through, she hands me a fan, an ornately carved wooden one, a gift from my father. I look her in the eye before taking it, and she meets my gaze briefly, knowingly. We are complicit, she and I, both in our hatred of him and in our unspoken acknowledgement of what is necessary to live under his roof. Silva was my mother's handmaiden before she was mine, though she alone of all the remaining servants in the house refuses to speak of her: Silva has long-held secrets that I can only guess at, but it is not my privilege to share them.

When we are finished, I stand in front of the mirror. I do not have my mother's beauty but I am not without her likeness, and today I have chosen a dark-blue gown which neatly resembles the one she wears in the portrait. When Silva looks at my reflection, I catch a fleeting glimpse of recognition in her eyes, as if for an instant we are both transported to another place and time, and I savour the sensation until long after she has turned away. At night, just before I go to sleep, I sometimes try to recreate these moments, to inhabit my mother's life and discard my own, an exercise which is pointless yet oddly satisfying. Silva clears her throat and I turn to see her standing by the door, her hands clasped tightly in front of her. My father waits for us below.

He is dressed in dark green velvet and wears the ceremonial burgher's cloak reserved for occasions of state. As head of the city council, he oversaw the clockmaster's commission and today will make a speech of dedication, together with the archbishop who will consecrate the clock in the church's name. He watches me now as I descend the stairs, Silva a few steps behind me, and as usual I find his gaze disquieting. He remains handsome despite his forty-four years. His forehead is broad and high, his hair is thick and the colour of burnished silver, and his eyes are almost an inhumanly pale blue. It is these that distinguish him – and I suppose they are what first attracted her. They must have made an oddly striking couple, my mother with her darkly sensual beauty and he with his icily noble good looks. My father defied his family to marry her, for she had no name, no fortune of her own. Her father (my maternal grandfather) was a commoner, and when my father looks at me I sometimes think that he is searching for some betrayal of this fact. If he finds it now, I cannot tell. I see him take in the dark-blue dress, the ornamental fan, but his eyes divulge nothing. This is not a house of disclosure but one of concealment.

He nods almost imperceptibly and offers me his arm, and

together we descend the last few steps to the carriage. My father's corpulent secretary, Johann, waits for us at the door. He bows to us, already sweating profusely in the heat. 'There's been talk of unrest in the square, your excellency,' he declares nervously, climbing in behind us. My father shrugs. Johann mops his brow repeatedly as the carriage rumbles slowly through the narrow streets. It rained last night, a summer shower, and the road is muddy and pockmarked under our wheels. Walking would be faster but my father would not consider soiling his feet.

As we approach the square the road becomes more and more crowded with those on foot. The driver shouts at them to clear the way, and they turn and offer us a curious mixture of envy, indifference and contempt. The carriage jerks forward in a painfully slow crawl as we pass within inches of their faces. I look at them one by one, unable to stop the silent correspondence which occurs with each. My father glances up from his papers and, seeing me transfixed, reaches over to snap the window shade closed, plunging the interior of the carriage into a hot and stifling darkness. He folds his notes with a sigh and leans back, closing his eyes. Johann shoots a reproachful look in my direction. He does this often, whenever I irritate my father. I raise my eyebrows to taunt him, and he looks away in disgust.

We stop at last. My father adjusts his clothing before stepping from the carriage and without thinking so do I. The square is jammed with hundreds of people crowded shoulder to shoulder, and dozens more lean from windows in the surrounding buildings. The heat and the stench of sweat are almost unbearable and my father, Johann and I lower our faces as we thread our way to the platform beneath the clocktower. The archbishop and curates have already arrived and are seated on the platform, fanning themselves furiously. We climb the steps of the platform and take our seats next to the others. My father looks around expectantly for Hanus, the clockmaster, as everyone is anxious to proceed. He dispatches Johann to search for him while we wait, eyeing the restless sea of faces in front of us. Some of the crowd are drunk though it is not yet midday, and an old man clothed in rags shouts garbled accusations of blasphemy before he is roughly shoved aside amidst roars of laughter. The archbishop, red-faced and eyes bulging, begins to cough uncontrollably and eventually spits what appears to be blood into a handkerchief. It is rumoured he has syphillis and will not survive the summer.

The crowd grows edgy; a small scuffle breaks out among a handful of drunken peasants, but guards from the palace move quickly to subdue them. My father frowns and turns towards the tower, just as Johann emerges, followed by the clockmaster. Hanus is dressed all in black and wipes his hands distractedly on a greasy rag, as if he has been interrupted in his work. He is not at all what I expected; for one thing he is young, not more than five or six years my senior, though his bearing is that of someone much older. Everything about him – his hair, his eyes, his expression – is purposeful and when he climbs the platform to face my father he gives us a look of such swift intensity that I look away. My father stands and offers his hand, which Hanus accepts after a split second's hesitation. 'I trust we're ready to proceed,' says my father in clipped tones.

'When you are,' says Hanus evenly, and I look from one to the other, wondering what has already transpired between them. My father motions for Hanus to be seated in the empty chair next to mine, and approaches the lectern, preparing to speak to the crowd. He raises a hand authoritatively, and the crowd grows quiet. My father opens his notes, clears his throat, and begins to address the crowd in Latin, a language unintelligible to all but a few of the nobility who line the front. They regard him earnestly, mindful of their example, but those behind begin to shift and stamp their feet impatiently as my father continues speaking. A shout of protest goes up from the rear of the crowd and the archbishop glances nervously at my father, who carries on, unmoved. After another minute he finishes and steps aside, making room for the archbishop, who rises hurriedly, anxious to be done with the ceremony. He carries a large marble cross which he raises up toward heaven, and kisses before placing it on the lectern. He genuflects and begins hurriedly to recite a prayer in Latin. Some of the more devout members of the crowd lower their eyes, as if joining him in silent prayer, but most gaze expectantly, impatiently, at the clock. The archbishop finishes with a flourish and returns to his seat and my father nods to Hanus, who turns and signals discreetly to an unseen assistant in the tower. Within a moment the sound of metal scraping metal can be heard, and the face of the clock begins to move.

It is a curious display: a tiny door opens and the figure of a cock appears and crows. Another door directly below opens and a succession of carved wooden figures emerge. One by one they face us, then journey across the face of the clock and disappear inside another door: Death, Vanity, Greed and the Pagan Invader all appear in turn; below them perch a Chronicler, an Angel, an Astronomer, and a Philosopher. The crowd is silent at first, but as the figures on the clock start to move the hush gives way to murmurings and cries of astonishment. Death nods towards the Invader, who shakes his head no, and an old peasant woman points and wails loudly before collapsing in the arms of her companions. From the rear of the crowd a burly farmer raises a fist and shouts, 'Who moves the clock?'

'Who else but God?' shouts someone else, unseen.

'It's the Devil!' comes the reply, this time from an old man holding a staff which he lifts and points at the podium. The archbishop glances uneasily at Hanus, whose eyes narrow slightly. Apart from this he gives no outward sign of emotion – neither disappointment nor disgust. More shouts ensue and a scuffle breaks out in the middle of the square. The crowd, a great mass of bodies, begins to move slowly towards the podium like a giant wave as it tries to make room for those fighting at the centre. We freeze for a moment, those of us on the podium, fascinated by the spectacle being played out in front of us. Then just as quickly we are scrambling for our lives as the crowd gathers pace and comes crashing towards us.

Like the others I clamber down from the podium, stumbling over my gown, and cross quickly to the base of the tower, flattening myself against the wall. The crowd is churning now. I see my father and Johann push towards the carriage, surrounded by guards from the palace. My father glances round for me and I ease myself into the shadows. Around the corner is a door and I pull it open and slip inside the base of the tower. It is dark inside and I sit on the cool stone steps for a moment, catching my breath and allowing my eyes to adjust to the darkness. The staircase winds steeply upwards and after a minute I begin the ascent. Eventually I reach a landing with a tiny wooden doorway half my size. I open the door and crouch down, crawling through on my hands and knees. The chamber inside holds the answer to the crowd's ignorance. Black metal gears the size of wagon wheels turn slowly, resolutely. And the figurines whose grotesque movements wrought havoc only moments before wait silently, benignly, along one wall.

I move closer to the machinery, run my hands along it, touch the centre of the gears as they spin, and marvel at the ease with which their grooved tongues come together, then separate. Enormous lead weights strain against thick cords, and deep within the machinery a pendulum swings slowly, resolutely. The movement seduces me and for a moment I lose myself in the precise mating of the machinery. Finally I cross over to the figurines and allow my hands to drift across each one, fingering their roughly hewn faces, searching for their secrets. Suddenly a noise startles me and I turn to see Hanus standing behind me, the ghost of a smile forming on his lips. 'What are you looking for?' he asks. I study him for a moment before replying.

'The truth,' I say, and then I turn to go.


A minute later, when Hanus and I emerge, blinking, into the sunlight, my father is standing in the centre of the square surrounded by guards. The crowds have been dispersed, and when my father sees me he frowns and crosses quickly to my side.

'Where were you?' he demands proprietarily.

'In the tower,' I reply. He looks from me to Hanus, who still wears his half-smile. For a split second my father's anger is so tangible I can almost touch it, and then just as quickly it is gone, hidden, banished. He gestures towards the clock, then raises his eyebrows archly at Hanus.

'Your clock not only moves, it moves those around it,' he says.

'That was not my intent,' replies Hanus with a shrug.

'No doubt they'll grow accustomed to it,' says my father, surveying the square.

'It is simple enough to alter, if you desire,' says Hanus. My father whips around to face him.

'No,' he says quickly. 'It is they who must alter.'

'As you wish,' says Hanus, perhaps a little too casually. I peer at him. Does it really mean so little to him? My father motions to his driver and the carriage makes its way across the cobblestones towards where we are standing. A footman opens the door and my father guides me towards it. I climb inside and seat myself by the window where I can see Hanus watching us. My eyes lock on his as my father and Johann settle themselves, and then the carriage is moving.

Once out of sight, I turn towards my father. 'The clock pleases you?' I ask ingenuously.

'Of course,' he says. 'It is a superior instrument, the finest of its kind in northern Europe.'

'And a testament to our municipal power,' adds Johann a little conspiratorially.

'And the clockmaster?' I say, ignoring Johann's comment.

'What of him?' says my father.

'He is very young to have accomplished such a thing.'

'He is old enough to build clocks,' replies my father.

'We are fortunate to have him,' I say.

'He was fortunate to get the commission,' says my father, a little irritated.

'Why? Are there others who could build such a clock?' My father shrugs evasively but says nothing. 'They say he's a genius. Or a sorcerer,' I add provocatively. Johann's eyes narrow.

'He is neither,' says my father crisply. 'He has talents. But he is insolent and naïve.' I lower my head so they will not see the corners of my smile. My father detests those who do not show proper deference. He also hates the competence of commoners.

'You do not like him then,' I say. My father turns to me with a quizzical expression.

'Why should I?' he asks.

Gratitude was not a part of my upbringing.

My grandfather was a blacksmith. A very skilled one, who was known for miles around as the most accomplished metalworker of his generation. As a young girl I used to sneak away and watch him work, entranced by the searing beauty of the furnace and the melodic beating of metal upon metal. I did not know him as a man. After they were married my father forbade any contact between my mother and her family, and for a long time I believed them dead. Indeed, it was only by accident that I discovered my grandfather's existence. One afternoon when I accompanied Silva to the market, we were nearly run over by a runaway horse and carriage. Silva shoved me aside but in doing so fell to the ground and twisted her ankle. A burly man with silver-white hair stepped out of the crowd and helped her to her feet. As she struggled to rise, she looked into his face for a long, knowing moment, and then he immediately turned to me. Out of the corner of my eye I saw Silva shake her head imperceptibly. The man stared at me for a few seconds, then turned and disappeared into the crowd. I asked her if she knew him, but she held her gaze and said nothing. Later, when we returned home, I rushed to my room to find my mother's portrait. When I opened it I saw the white-haired stranger staring back at me through my mother's eyes.

It took me almost two years to find him again. I was nearly eight by then, and old enough to slip away unaccompanied. Each time, I returned to the scene of our meeting, hoping to find him there. I imagined that he searched for me too, and that God would eventually enable us to meet when the time was right. Ironically, it was my father who found him for me in the end. One afternoon he insisted on my accompanying him to the other side of Prague to visit friends. It was spring and many of the city's roads were flooded and impassable. We took a route unknown to me and eventually found ourselves by the river, which was swollen from the rains. As we rounded a bend I saw the white-haired stranger hauling water from the river in wooden buckets. I watched as he carried the water to a shed not twenty metres from the river's edge. It was surrounded by many others, each with a roaring fire in front. I quickly took my bearings, desperately trying to remember the way we had come. My father never once looked up from his reading.

A few days later I returned to the river. Unsure of the exact location, I started at the top and made my way along the bank until at last I came to the line of blacksmiths' sheds. I walked slowly past each one, straining to see inside. When I had passed maybe a dozen I began to despair when suddenly he emerged directly in front of me, brandishing a large hammer and a red-hot iron. He stopped short when he saw me and I felt the blood thunder in my ears. Without thinking I planted myself firmly on a nearby log, afraid he might send me away. After a moment he shook his head and smiled. I then watched him work for nearly two hours, never once daring to move or speak. At the end of the day, he presented me with a tiny metal bird which he had fashioned from a thread of iron. For the next three years, I escaped as often as I could to the river, where I would sit in silence watching my grandfather hammer out horseshoes, weapons, candlesticks, cooking pots and tools of all shapes and kinds. We spoke very little, but we came to understand each other, and though I longed to feel his burly arms round me, we never touched.

And then one fine spring day as I threaded my way along the riverfront, I felt increasingly uneasy as I approached my grandfather's shed. The other blacksmiths stopped their work as I passed, and rather than return my greetings, their eyes clouded over as they wiped the soot from their hands with greasy rags. By the time I reached my grandfather's shed I knew something was amiss: his fire was cold and almost all his tools had disappeared. I stared at the empty shed in disbelief, then turned toward the first person I saw, an aging contemporary of my grandfather's who worked in the shed next to his. He stood silently, his face heavy with sorrow, and before he could say a word I had flung myself sobbing into his arms. I felt his hands stroke my hair in a gesture of affection that my grandfather and I had never once allowed ourselves. When I was through crying he sat me down and presented me with a small, tightly wrapped bundle which he explained was my grandfather's personal effects. I was his closest remaining relative, he said, a fact of which I had previously been unaware. My fingers caressed the coarse cloth and hemp that had been used to secure the items inside the bundle, and clutching it tightly to my chest, I stumbled towards home. When I drew near to my father's villa I hid the bundle inside my skirts and entered through the servants' doorway, climbed the steeply winding back stairs to my bedchamber and locked the door behind me.

Inside the bundle I found a goblet fashioned of burnished metal and decorated with birds of prey; my grandfather's spoon, which I had seen him use once or twice when he had taken a meal while working; two heavily worn leatherbound volumes, one a Bible in Latin and the other some sort of scientific journal with detailed drawings of the moon and stars; and a silver chain with a round medal depicting a saint slaying a dragon. As I laid the items carefully out on my bed, one final thing slipped from the wrapping and fell to the floor: a tiny, gilt-framed engraving of a middle-aged woman who I knew in an instant was my grandmother. Though her face was a different shape, she had the same chin as my mother, and the same look of defiance in her eyes. I took my mother's portrait out from its hiding place under my mattress and laid the two side by side. Then I made myself very small and curled up next to them, clutching my grandfather's silver chain and medal. I lay that way for as long as I dared, until the sun had all but vanished from my window, then I carefully wrapped all the items in the bundle and stowed it under my bed.

When I came downstairs a few minutes later, the first person I met in the hallway was Silva. One glance told me that she already knew of my grandfather's death, but as was her custom she said nothing. As she turned to leave, my father entered the room and demanded to know why I'd been crying. I stared at the floor, unable to reply, then heard Silva tell him she had punished me for some wrongdoing. I heard him grumble his approval, then leave the room. But when I raised my head to thank Silva, she was gone.


My father has always loved to entertain on a grand scale. Not from any desire for company, but because hospitality is the yardstick by which he and others measure his success. His villa is among the city's newly built, and it was constructed in a manner which would enable him to entertain on the scale he chose. The banqueting hall is large and ornately decorated, with gilded cornices along the ceiling and richly embroidered tapestries on every wall. The dining table spans almost the entire length of the room and is large enough to seat sixty, which it does whenever a suitable occasion presents itself. At the far end of the room stands a massive cupboard with seven shelves upon which is displayed my father's collection of ornamental silver, a collection he has spent a lifetime amassing. As a child I was forbidden to touch the silver, as it was always kept perfectly polished. That is why I touch it now from time to time; it pleases me to see the faint trace of human grease left by my fingertips.

Since I came of age five years ago, I have joined this display of my father's possessions. In my bedchamber are no fewer than three trunkfuls of clothing suitable for such occasions, a fact which means I am the envy of many of

Prague's young women. When I was younger I took pleasure in adorning myself and in securing my father's approving glances. Now I do so because it is expected, and because I am at a loss for an alternative. Tonight, however, for the clockmaster's banquet, I select my gown and head-dress with the utmost care. The former is of dark-red silk, embroidered with tiny gold threads, and the neckline is perhaps the most revealing in my wardrobe. My hair is freshly washed and scented, and I wear only a tiny gold cross round my neck to offset the effects of the neckline, and ward off my father's suspicion.

I delay my entrance on purpose, so my father will be otherwise engaged and I will not have to speak with him. When I enter the hall the musicians have begun to play and many of the town's nobilty have already arrived. Hanus has not, however, as the seat of honour below my father's remains empty. I take my own place at the opposite side of the table and accept the wine that is immediately offered. The steward who fills my glass is called Jurgen and his family have served mine for some generations. As children we played together under the stairs, and it was Jurgen whose lips first touched mine, when I was barely ten. Now he serves me wine, but as he does so his eyes brush my bodice in a knowing way. I catch Jurgen's eye just as he turns away and raise my chin a little defiantly, but the twinkle in his eye mocks me.

To my left sit the archdeacon and his consorts, the nearest thing to an archbishop that Rome allows us. To my right sit the wives of the council leaders, all older than I by some years. They are engaged in a heated discussion about the clock and its likely influence over the populace. The discussion is dominated by the mayor's wife, a distant cousin of my father's whom I have always disliked. Her emerald-green gown shimmers in the candlelight and, together with her oversized blue head-dress, reminds me of the peacocks which roam my father's courtyard.

I raise my glass and drink deeply of the sweet red wine, watered down for an occasion as grand as this, before I realize that she has fixed her beady gaze on me.

'And you, my dear Helen, what do you think of the clock?' The councillors' wives turn to me in unison, like an obedient flock of peahens.

'I think it very accomplished.'

'The clock or its maker, my dear?' She raises an eyebrow and the ladies of the flock titter in obsequious appreciation.

'The latter, of course,' I reply. Despite her ridiculous demeanour, this woman has always intimidated me. They say the mayor is no match for her behind closed doors.

'Perhaps,' she says, glancing sideways at her companions. 'But I fear there is some trickery involved.'

'Or sorcery,' chimes a hen.

'No,' I say. 'It is all gears and wheels and springs inside.'

'He told you this?'

'I saw it myself.' Heads turn and in an instant I am somehow implicated. The musicians begin playing once again, just as Hanus enters the hall. My father rises and crosses to greet him and I see Hanus bow. They speak for a few moments, then my father escorts him to his place at the table, pausing on the way to introduce him to the mayor, the archdeacon and other council members. When they arrive at our end of the table, the mayor's wife rises.

'Here he is at last, the subject of your deliberations,' says my father archly to his cousin.

'We are honoured,' she says, one eyebrow raised. Hanus bows to her and she acknowledges this with a benevolent nod. 'I trust your clock is working well,' she inquires. Hanus regards her closely.

'Yes, my lady,' he says.

'So well, in fact, that you lost track of time,' she says with a smile.

'Please accept my apologies,' says Hanus. He bows again to her, then turns to me.

'Lady Helen,' he says.

'Clockmaster,' I reply, but something in my tone catches my father's attention. He throws me a penetrating look and steers Hanus to his seat. More wine is poured and my father signals to the steward to begin serving the first course. The music continues and the noise and laughter fill my ears so much that after a time it all blends together and I hear nothing at all. I watch as Hanus answers questions from the council members. Now and then he glances over in my direction. The meal is served by a bevy of stewards and though the courses seem endless I eat almost nothing.

Instead I drink deeply of the wine. My mind returns to the clocktower, to the grinding gears, shifting weights and silent figurines, and then it leaps further back in time to my grandfather's furnace. One of the council members' wives attempts to engage me in conversation. I smile and nod as she speaks, but the sounds I hear are of metal beating metal. A bell rings, startling me, and the entertainments begin. A curious pageant of masked figures enters the room and performs a ritual dance whose significance I cannot fathom. Out of the corner of my eye I steal glimpses of Hanus as he watches the dancers. What does he make of such pompous displays? I wonder, but his face remains impassive. When the entertainers withdraw, the final course of fruit and sweetmeats is served, together with more wine. Thankfully the musicians do not resume their playing and the noise in the room is more subdued. I struggle to concentrate on the conversation at my father's end of the table, but the wine has gone to my head. The mayor's wife is holding forth once again, commanding the attention of all those around her, including Hanus.

'Bells, bells and more bells,' she declares. 'Bells to begin work, bells to eat, bells to pray, bells to open the market, bells to assemble. I fear we shall forget the sound of silence, and its sanctity.' At this last she turns to the archdeacon and nods piously. He returns her nod.

'Ah, but my dear cousin,' says my father, 'city dwellers need such guidance. Nature does not beckon at our doorstep as it does for the farmer. Without the ringing of the clock, how would we organize ourselves?'

'Precisely,' says the mayor. 'Everything depends upon the clock.'

'Vienna, Strasbourg, Nuremberg,' says another council member, 'they all have moving clocks.'

'I still think it is unnatural, all this interest in time,' says my father's cousin. 'We have created a demon.' She turns to Hanus and I am suddenly reminded of my grandfather's astrological journal, with its detailed drawings of the moon and the stars.

'My good lady, clocks did not create our interest in time – it was man's desire to harness time that led him to create clocks,' says Hanus.

'Perhaps your desire, not mine,' she counters. She turns to her flock. 'A demon,' she proclaims decisively, to a chorus of vigorous nods.

'Time stands above the ills of men,' says Hanus slowly. 'The moon, the sun, the movements of the stars – these things are truly sacred, and worthy of our study.'

'Young man,' says the archdeacon, 'these things you speak of, God alone controls.'

'God or science,' Hanus shrugs. 'I do not know which. I only seek to know the truth,' he replies, and our eyes lock for a moment.

For once there is silence. My father clears his throat and rises, signalling an end to the meal. He nods to the musicians, who resume their playing in the corner. A space is cleared for dancing, a fashion only recently imported from the west. The peacock and her flock rise in unison and make their way towards the floor, leaving Hanus and me alone at our end of the table. Hanus picks up his glass and moves to the seat next to mine.

'What does your silence indicate?' he asks. 'Approval or disapproval?'

'Of you?' I ask. He nods.

'I am not in a position to pass judgment,' I say ingenuously. He raises his eyebrows.

'Surely you are entitled to an opinion,' he says. I hesitate, choosing my words with care.

'I think that all science contains some mystery, that which is unknowable. Some choose to call that mystery God. But I prefer to think of it as nature.'

'So you disapprove of my quest?' he asks.

'I think the quest for knowledge is always worthy,' I say. 'So long as one continues to revere the mystery.'

A long, slow smile spreads across his face, gripping me. And then I feel a hand upon my shoulder and I turn to see my father. He offers me his arm, and I rise obediently, leaving Hanus once again.

Over the next few weeks I return several times to the clocktower, but each time the door is locked. At night, I dream of clocks and giant gears and moving figurines, only the faces on the figures are those of my family: my father, my grandfather and my mother all rotate round the belltower in endless succession. In the dream, I stand below them, watching, and each time my mother appears I open my mouth to speak to her, but the figure raises a finger to its lips and silences me. By day, I continue to visit the clocktower, craving the sight of smoothly meshing iron tongues, the smell of grease, the sound of metal scraping metal, but to no avail.

One day upon my return my father confronts me in the doorway.

'I've been looking for you,' he says.

'And here I am,' I reply.

We are both lying.


Two days later I am crossing the square on my way to see a friend when I catch a brief glimpse of someone entering the clocktower. I hurry quickly to the base, glancing around furtively, and try the door. To my surprise it opens and I duck inside, my chest heaving with relief. My heart races as I climb the stairs and I pause for a moment on the landing, outside the tiny doorway. I know now that it is not the gears nor the iron tongues nor the figures I am craving, but the flesh and blood of their creator. I crouch down and crawl through the opening, and as I rise to my feet, Hanus emerges from behind the vast machinery. Our eyes meet and Hanus sees, in an instant, all the things I have concealed for a lifetime. The giant gears continue to move and I feel myself step forward, the sound of metal upon metal surrounding me, surrounding Hanus, swallowing us. I take another step forward, then another, and soon I am so close that I can see the tiny beads of perspiration which have formed above his lips. 'Hanus,' I say, and in the next instant my own lips have found the salt of his. His arms encircle me and I feel his hands upon me, tearing at me, searching for the parts I have kept hidden for so long.

# amy bloom

## *sleepwalking*

I was born smart and had been lucky my whole life, so I didn't even know that what I thought was careful planning was nothing more than being in the right place at the right time, missing the avalanche that I didn't even hear.

After the funeral was over and the cold turkey and the glazed ham were demolished and some very good jazz was played and some very good musicians went home drunk on bourbon poured in Lionel's honor, it was just me, my mother-in-law, Ruth, and the two boys, Lionel Junior from Lionel's second marriage and our little boy, Buster.

Ruth pushed herself up out of the couch, her black taffeta dress rustling reproachfully. I couldn't stand for her to start the dishes, sighing, praising the Lord, clucking her tongue over the state of my kitchen, in which the windows are not washed regularly and I do not scrub behind the refrigerator.

'Ruth, let them sit. I'll do them later tonight.'

'No need to put off 'til tomorrow what we can do today. I'll do them right now, and then Lionel Junior can run me home.' Ruth does not believe that the good Lord intended ladies to drive; she'd drive, eyes closed, with her drunk son or her accident-prone grandson before she'd set foot in my car.

'Ruth, please, I'd just as soon have something to do later.

Please. Let me make us a cup of tea, and then we'll take you home.'

Tea, Buster, and Lionel's relative sobriety were the three major contributions I'd made to Ruth's life; the tea and Buster accounted for all of our truces and the few good times we'd had together.

'I ought to be going along now, let you get on with things.'

'Earl Grey? Darjeeling? Constant Comment? I've got some rosehip tea in here too, it's light, sort of lemony.' I don't know why I was urging her to stay, I'd never be rid of her as long as I had the boys. If Ruth no longer thought I was trash, she certainly made it clear that I hadn't lived up to her notion of the perfect daughter-in-law, a cross between Marian Anderson and Florence Nightingale.

'You have Earl Grey?' Ruth was wavering, half a smile on her sad mouth, her going-to-church lipstick faded to a blurry pink line on her upper lip.

When I really needed Ruth on my side, I'd set out an English tea: Spode teapot, linen place mats, scones, and three kinds of jam. And for half an hour, we'd sip and chew, happy to be so civilized.

'Earl Grey it is.' I got up to put on the water, stepping on Buster who was sitting on the floor by my chair, practically on my feet.

'Jesus, Buster, are you all right?' I hugged him before he could start crying and lifted him out of my way.

'The Lord's name,' Ruth murmured, rolling her eyes up to apologize to Jesus personally. I felt like smacking her one, right in her soft dark face, and pointing out that since the Lord had not treated us especially well in the last year, during which we had both lost husbands, perhaps we didn't have to be overly concerned with His hurt feelings. Ruth made me want to become a spectacularly dissolute pagan.

'Sorry, Ruth. Buster, sit down by your grandmother, honey, and I'll make us all some tea.'

'No, really, don't trouble yourself, Julia. Lionel Junior, please take me home. Gabriel, come kiss your grandma goodbye. You boys be good, now, and think of how your daddy would want you to act. I'll see you all for dinner tomorrow.'

She was determined to leave, martyred and tea-less, so I got on line to kiss her. Ruth put her hands on my shoulders, her only gesture of affection toward me, which also allowed her to pretend that she was a little taller, rather than a little shorter, than I am.

She left with the Lion, and Buster and I cuddled on the couch, his full face squashed against my chest, my skin resting on his soft hair. I felt almost whole.

'Sing, Mama.'

Lionel always wanted me to record with him and I always said no, because I don't like performing and I didn't want to be a blues-singing Marion Davies to Lionel's William Randolph Hearst. But I loved to sing and he loved to play and I'm sorry we didn't record just one song together.

I was trying to think of something that would soothe Buster but not break my heart.

I sang 'Amazing Grace,' even though I can't quite hit that note, and I sang bits and pieces of a few more songs, and then Buster was asleep and practically drowning in my tears.

I heard Lionel Junior's footsteps and blotted my face on my sleeve.

'Hey, Lion, let's put this little boy to bed.'

'He's out, huh? You look tired too. Why don't you go to bed and I'll do the dishes?'

That's my Lion. I think because I chose to love him, chose to be a mother and not just his father's wife, Lion gave me back everything he could. He was my table setter, car washer, garden weeder; in twelve years, I might've raised my voice to him twice. When Lionel brought him to meet me the first time, I looked into those wary eyes, hope pouring out of them despite himself, and I knew that I had found someone else to love.

I carried Buster to his room and laid him on the bed, slipping off his loafers. I pulled up the comforter with the long-legged basketball players running all over it and kissed his damp little face. I thought about how lucky I was to have Buster and Lion and even Ruth, who might torture me for ever but would never abandon me, and I thought about how cold and lonely my poor Lionel must be, with no bourbon and no music and no audience, and I went into the bathroom to dry my face again. Lion got frantic when he saw me crying.

He was lying on the couch, his shoes off, his face turned toward the cushions.

'Want a soda or a beer? Maybe some music?'

'Nope. Maybe some music, but not Pop's.'

'No, no, not your father's. How about Billie Holiday, Sarah Vaughan?'

'How about something a little more up? How about Luther Vandross?' He had turned around to face me.

'I don't have any – as you know.' Lionel and I both hated bubble-gum music, so of course Lion had the world's largest collection of whipped-cream soul; if it was insipid, he bought it.

'I'll get my tapes,' he said, and sat halfway up to see if I would let him. We used to make him play them in his room so we wouldn't have to listen, but Lionel wasn't here to grumble at the boy and I just didn't care.

'Play what you want, honey,' I said, sitting in Lionel's brown velvet recliner. Copies of *Downbeat* and packs of Trident were still stuffed between the cushion and the arm. Lion bounded off to his room and came back with an armful of tapes.

'Luther Vandross, Whitney Houston . . . what would you like to hear?'

'You pick.' Even talking felt like too much work. He put on one of the tapes and I shut my eyes.

I hadn't expected to miss Lionel so much. We'd had twelve years together, eleven of them sober; we'd had Buster and raised the Lion, and we'd gone to the Grammys together when he was nominated and he'd stayed sober when he lost, and we'd made love, with more interest some years than others; we'd been through a few other women for him, a few blondes that he couldn't pass up, and one other man for me, so I'm not criticizing him. We knew each other so well that when I wrote a piece on another jazz musician, he'd find the one phrase and say, 'You meant that about me,' and he'd be right. He was a better father than your average musician; he'd bring us with him whenever he went to Europe, and no matter how late he played on Saturday, he got up and made breakfast on Sunday.

Maybe we weren't a perfect match, in age, or temperament, or color, but we did try and we were willing to stick it out and then we didn't get a chance.

Lion came and sat by me, putting his head against my knee. Just like Buster, I thought. Lion's mother was half Italian, like me, so the two boys look alike: creamier, silkier versions of their father.

I patted his hair and ran my thumb up and down his neck, feeling the muscles bunched up. When he was little, he couldn't fall asleep without his nightly back rub, and he only gave it up when he was fifteen and Lionel just wouldn't let me anymore.

'It's midnight, honey. It's been a long day, a long week. Go to bed.'

He pushed his head against my leg and cried, the way men do, like it's being torn out of them. His tears ran down my bare leg, and I felt the strings holding me together just snap. One, two, three, and there was no more center.

'Go to bed, Lion.'

'How about you?'

'I'm not really ready for bed yet, honey. Go ahead.' Please, go to bed.

'Okay. Good night, Ma.'

'Good night, baby.' Nineteen-year-old baby.

He pulled himself up and went off to his room. I peered into the kitchen, looked at all the dishes, and closed my eyes again. After a while, I got up and finished off the little bit of Jim Beam left in the bottle. With all Lionel's efforts at sobriety, we didn't keep the stuff around, and I choked on it. But the burning in my throat was comforting, like old times, and it was a distraction.

I walked down the hall to the bedroom, I used to call it the Lionel Sampson Celebrity Shrine. It wasn't just his framed album covers, but all of his favorite reviews, including the ones I wrote before I met him; one of Billie's gardenias mounted on velvet, pressed behind glass; photos of Lionel playing with equally famous or more famous musicians or with famous fans. In some ways, it's easier to marry a man with a big ego; you're not always fretting over him, worrying about whether or not he needs fluffing up.

I threw my black dress on the floor, my worst habit, and got into bed. I woke up at around four, waiting for something. A minute later, Buster wandered in, eyes half shut, blue blankie resurrected and hung around his neck, like a little boxer.

'Gonna stay with you, Mama.' Truculent even in his sleep, knowing that if his father had been there, he'd have been sent back to his own room.

'Come in, then, Bus. Let's try and get some sleep.'

He curled up next to me, silently, an arm flung over me, the other arm thrust into his pajama bottoms, between his legs.

I had just shut my eyes again when I felt something out of place. Lion was standing in the doorway, his briefs hanging off his high skinny hips. He needed new underwear, I thought. He looked about a year older than Buster.

'I thought I heard Buster prowling around, y'know, sleepwalking.'

The only one who ever sleepwalked in our family was Lion, but I didn't say so. 'It's okay, he just wanted company. Lonely in this house tonight.'

'Yeah. Ma?'

I was tired of thinking, and I didn't want to send him away, and I didn't want to talk anymore to anyone so I said, 'Come on, honey, it's a big bed.'

He crawled in next to his brother and fell asleep in a few minutes. I watched the digital clock flip through a lot of numbers and finally I got up and read.

The boys woke early, and I made them what Lionel called a Jersey City breakfast: eggs, sweet Italian sausage, grits, biscuits, and a quart of milk for each of them.

'Buster, soccer camp starts today. Do you feel up to going?'

I didn't see any reason for him to sit at home; he could catch up on his grieving for the rest of his life.

'I guess so. Is it okay, Mama?'

'Yes, honey, it's fine. I'm glad you're going. I'll pick you up at five, and then we'll drive straight over to Grandma's for dinner. You go get ready when you're done eating. Don't forget your cleats, they're in the hall.'

Lion swallowed his milk and stood up, like a brown flamingo, balancing on one foot while he put on his sneaker. 'Come on, Buster, I'm taking you, I have to go into town anyway. Do we need anything?'

I hadn't been to the grocery store in about a week. 'Get milk and o.j. and English muffins and American cheese. I'll do a real shop tomorrow.' If I could just get to the store and the cleaners, then I could get to work, and then my life would move forward.

Finally they were ready to go, and I kissed them both and gave Lion some money for the groceries.

'I'll be back by lunchtime,' he said. It was already eight-thirty. Since his father got sick, he'd been giving me hourly bulletins on his whereabouts. That summer, he was house-painting and was home constantly, leaving late, back early, stopping by for lunch.

'If you like,' I said. I didn't want him to feel that he had to keep me company. I was planning on going back to work tomorrow or the day after.

While the boys were gone, I straightened the house, went for a walk, and made curried tuna fish sandwiches for Lion. I watched out the window for him, and when I saw my car turn up the road, I remembered all the things I hadn't done and started making a list. He came in, sweating and shirtless, drops of white paint on his hands and shoulders and sneakers.

Lion ate and I watched him and smiled. Feeding them was the easiest and clearest way of loving them, holding them.

'I'm going to shower. Then we could play a little tennis or work on the porch.' He finished both sandwiches in about a minute and got that wistful look that teenage boys get when they want you to fix them something more to eat. I made two peanut butter and jelly sandwiches and put them on his plate.

'Great. I don't have to work this afternoon. I told Joe I might not be back, he said okay.'

'Well, I'm just going to mouse around, do laundry, answer some mail. I'm glad to have your company, you know I am, but you don't have to stay here with me. You might want to be with your friends.'

'I don't. I'm gonna shower.' Like his father, he only put his love out once, and God help you if you didn't take the hint.

I sat at the table, looking out at the morning glories climbing up the trellis Lionel had built me the summer he stopped drinking. In addition to the trellis, I had two flower boxes, a magazine rack, and a footstool so ugly even Ruth wouldn't have it.

'Ma, no towels,' Lion shouted from the bathroom. I thought that was nice, as if real life might continue.

'All right,' I called, getting one of the big, rough white ones that he liked.

I went into the bathroom and put it on the rack just as he stepped out of the shower. I hadn't seen him naked since he was fourteen and spent the year parading around the house topless, so that we could admire his underarm hair and the little black wisps between his nipples.

All I could see in the mist was a dark caramel column and two patches of dark curls, inky against his skin. I expected him to look away, embarrassed, but instead he looked right at me as he took the towel, and I was the one who turned away.

'Sorry,' we both said, and I backed out of the bathroom and went straight down to the basement so we wouldn't bump into each other for a while.

I washed, dried, and folded everything that couldn't get away from me, listening for Lion's footsteps upstairs. I couldn't hear anything while the machines were going, so after about an hour I came up and found a note on the kitchen table.

'Taking a nap. Wake me when it's time to get Buster. L.'

'L.' is how his father used to sign his notes. And their handwriting was the same too: the awkward careful printing of men who know that their script is illegible.

I took a shower and dried my hair and looked in the mirror for a while, noticing the gray at the temples. I wondered what Lion would have seen if he'd walked in on me, and I decided not to ever think like that again.

I woke Lion by calling him from the hall, then I went into my room while he dressed to go to his grandmother's. I found a skirt that was somber and ill-fitting enough to meet Ruth's standard of widowhood and thought about topping it off with my 'Eight to the Bar Volleyball Champs' T-shirt, but didn't. Even pulling Ruth's chain wasn't fun. I put on a yellow shirt that made me look like one of the Neapolitan cholera victims, and Lion and I went to get Buster. He was bubbling over the goal he had made in the last quarter, and that filled the car until we got to Ruth's house, and then she took over.

'Come in, come in. Gabriel, you are too dirty to be my grandson. You go wash up right now. Lionel Junior, you're looking a little peaked. You must be working too hard or playing too hard. Does he eat, Julia? Come sit down here and have a glass of nice iced tea with mint from my garden. Julia, guess who I heard from this afternoon? Loretta, Lionel's first wife? She called to say how sorry she was. I told her she could call upon you, if she wished.'

'Fine.' I didn't have the energy to be annoyed. My muscles felt like butter, I'd had a headache for six days, and my eyes were so sore that even when I closed them, they ached. If Ruth wanted to sick Loretta McVay Sampson de Guzman de God-knows-who-else on me, I guessed I'd get through that little hell too.

Ruth looked at me, probably disappointed; I knew from Lionel that she couldn't stand Loretta, but since she was the only black woman he'd married, Ruth felt obliged to find something positive about her. She was a lousy singer, a whore, and a terrible housekeeper, so Ruth really had to search. Anita, wife number two, was a rich, pretty flake with a fragile air and a serious drug problem that killed her when the Lion was five. I was the only normal, functioning person he was ever involved with: I worked, I cooked, I balanced our checkbook, I did what had to be done, just like Ruth. And I irritated her no end.

'Why'd you do that, Grandma? Loretta's so nasty. She probably just wants to find out if Pop left her something in his will, which I'm sure he did not.' Loretta and Lionel had a little thing going when Anita was in one of her rehab centers, and I think the Lion found out and of course blamed Loretta.

'It's all right, Lion,' I said, and stopped myself from patting his hand as if he was Buster.

Ruth was offended. 'Really, young man, it was very decent, just common courtesy, for Loretta to pay her respects, and I'm sure that your stepmother appreciates that.' Ruth thought it disrespectful to call me Julia when talking to Lion, but she couldn't stand the fact that he called me Ma after the four years she put in raising him while Anita killed herself and Lionel toured. So she'd refer to me as 'your stepmother,' which always made me feel like the coachmen and pumpkins couldn't be far behind. Lion used to look at me and smile when she said it.

We got through dinner, with Buster bragging about soccer and giving us a minute-by-minute account of the soccer training movie he had seen. Ruth criticized their table manners, asked me how long I was going to wallow at home, and then expressed horror when I told her I was going to work on Monday. Generally, she was her usual self, just a little worse, which was true of the rest of us too. She also served the best smothered pork chops ever made and her usual first-rate trimmings. She brightened up when the boys both asked for seconds and I praised her pork chops and the sweet potato soufflé for a solid minute.

After dinner, I cleared and the two of us washed and dried while the boys watched TV. I never knew how to talk to Ruth; my father-in-law was the easy one, and when Alfred died I lost my biggest fan. I looked over at Ruth, scrubbing neatly stacked pots with her pink rubber gloves, which matched her pink and white apron, which had nothing cute or whimsical about it. She hadn't raised Lionel to be a good husband; she'd raised him to be a warrior, a god, a genius surrounded by courtiers. But I married him anyway, when he was too old to be a warrior, too tired to be a god, and smart enough to know the limits of his talent.

I thought about life without my boys, and I gave Ruth a little hug as she was tugging off her gloves. She humphed and wiped her hands on her apron.

'You take care of yourself, now. Those boys need you more than ever.' She walked into the living room and announced that it was time for us to go, since she had a church meeting.

We all thanked her, and I drove home with three pink Tupperware containers beside me, making the car smell like a pork chop.

I wanted to put Buster to bed, but it was only eight o'clock. I let him watch some sitcoms and changed out of my clothes into my bathrobe. Lion came into the hall in a fresh shirt.

'Going out?' He looked so pretty in his clean white shirt.

'Yeah, some of the guys want to go down to the Navigator. I said I'd stop by, see who's there. Don't wait up.'

I was surprised but delighted. I tossed him the keys. 'Okay, drive carefully.'

Buster got himself into pajamas and even brushed his teeth without my nagging him. He had obviously figured out that I was not operating at full speed. I tucked him in, trying to give him enough hugs and kisses to help him get settled, not so many that he'd hang on my neck for an extra fifteen minutes. I went to sit in the kitchen, staring at the moths smacking themselves against the screen door. I could relate to that.

I read a few magazines, plucked my eyebrows, thought about plucking the gray hairs at my temples, and decided not to bother. Who'd look? Who'd mind, except me?

Finally, I got into bed, and got out about twenty minutes later. I poured myself some bourbon and tried to go to sleep again, thinking that I hadn't ever really appreciated what it took Lionel to get through life sober. I woke up at around four, anticipating Buster. But there, leaning against the doorway, was Lion.

'Ma.' He sounded congested

'Are you all right?'

'Yeah. No. Can I come in?'

'Of course, come in. What is it, honey?'

He sat on the bed and plucked at my blanket, and I could smell the beer and the sweat coming off him. I sat up so we could talk, and he threw his arms around me like a drowning man. He was crying and gasping into my neck, and then he stopped and just rested his head against my shoulder. I kept on patting his back, rubbing the long muscles under the satiny skin. My hands were cold against his back.

Lion lifted his head and looked into my eyes, his own eyes like pools of coffee, shining in the moonlight. He put his hand up to my cheek, and then he kissed me and my brain stopped. I shut my eyes.

His kisses were sweet and slow; he pushed his tongue into my mouth just a little at a time, getting more confident every time. He began to rub my nipples through my nightgown, spreading the fingers on one big hand wide apart just as his father used to, and I pulled away, forcing my eyes open.

'No, Lion. You have to go back to your room now.' But I was asking him, I wasn't telling him, and I knew he wouldn't move.

'No.' And he put his soft plummy mouth on my breast,

soaking the nightgown. 'Please don't send me away.' The right words.

I couldn't send my little boy away, so I wrapped my arms around him and pulled him to me, out of the darkness.

It had been a long time since I was in bed with a young man. Lionel was forty-two when I met him and, before that I'd been living with a sax player eight years older than I was. I hadn't made love to anyone this young since I was seventeen and too young myself to appreciate it.

His body was so smooth and supple, and the flesh clung to the bone; when he was above me, he looked like an athlete working out; below me, he looked like an angel spread out for the world's adoration. His shoulders had clefts so deep I could lay a finger in each one, and each of his ribs stuck out just a little. He hadn't been eating enough at school. I couldn't move forward or backward, and so I shut my eyes again, so as not to see and not to have to think the same sad, tired thoughts.

He rose and fell between my hips and it reminded me of Buster's birth; heaving and sliding and then an explosive push. Lion apologized the way men do when they come too soon, and I hugged him and felt almost like myself, comforting him. I couldn't speak at all; I didn't know if I'd ever have a voice again.

He was whispering, 'I love you, I love you, I love you.' And I put my hand over his mouth until he became quiet. He tried to cradle me, pulling my head to his shoulder. I couldn't lie with him like that, so I wriggled away in the dark, my arms around my pillow. I heard him sigh, and then he laid his head on my back. He fell asleep in a minute.

I got up before either of them, made a few nice-neighbor phone calls, and got Buster a morning play date, lunch included, and a ride to soccer camp. He was up, dressed, fed, and over to the Bergs' before Lion opened his eyes.

Lion's boss called and said he was so sorry for our loss but could Lionel Junior please come to work this morning.

I put my hand on Lion's shoulder to wake him, and I could see the shock and the pleasure in his eyes. I told him he was late for work and laid his clothes out on his bed. He kept opening his mouth to say something, but I gave him toast and coffee and threw him my keys.

'You're late, Lion. We'll talk when you get home.'

'I'm not sorry,' he said, and I almost smiled. Good, I thought, spend the day not being sorry, because sometime after that you're gonna feel like shit. I was already sorrier than I'd ever been in my whole life, sorry enough for this life and the next. Lion looked at me and then at the keys in his hand.

'I guess I'll go. Ma . . . Julia . . .'

I was suddenly, ridiculously angry at being called Julia. 'Go, Lion.'

He was out the door. I started breathing again, trying to figure out how to save us both. Obviously, I couldn't be trusted to take care of him, I'd have to send him away. I thought about sending Buster away too, but I didn't think I could. And maybe my insanity was limited to the Lion, maybe I could still act like a normal mother to Buster.

I called my friend Jeffrey in Falmouth and told him Lion needed a change of scene. He said Lion could start house-painting tomorrow and could stay with him since his kids were away. The whole time I was talking, I cradled the bottle of bourbon in my left arm, knowing that if I couldn't get through the phone call, or the afternoon, or the rest of my life, I had some help. I think I was so good at helping Lionel quit drinking because I didn't have the faintest idea why he, or anybody, drank. If I met him now, I'd be a better wife but not better for him. I packed Lion's suitcase and put it under his bed.

When I was a lifeguard at camp, they taught us how to

save panicky swimmers. The swimmers don't realize that they have to let you save them, that their terror will drown you both, and so sometimes, they taught us, you have to knock the person out to bring him in to shore.

I practiced my speech in the mirror and on the porch and while making the beds. I thought if I said it clearly and quietly he would understand, and I could deliver him to Jeffrey, ready to start his summer over again. I went to the grocery store and bought weird, disconnected items: marinated artichoke hearts for Lionel, who was dead; red caviar to make into dip for his son, whose life I had just ruined; peanut butter with the grape jelly already striped into it for Buster, as a special treat that he would probably have outgrown by the time I got home; a pack of Kools for me, who stopped smoking fifteen years ago. I also bought a wood-refinishing kit, a jar of car wax, a six-pack of Michelob Light, five TV dinners, some hamburger but no buns, and a box of Pop-Tarts. Clearly the cart of a woman at the end of her rope.

Lion came home at three, and I could see him trying of figure out how to tackle me. He sat down at the kitchen table and frowned when I didn't say anything.

I sat down across from him, poured us each a glass of bourbon, and lit a cigarette, which startled him. All the props said 'Important Moment.'

'Let me say what I have to say and then you can tell me whatever you want to. Lion, I love you very much and I have felt blessed to be your mother and I have probably ruined that for both of us. Just sit there. What happened was not your fault, you were upset, you didn't know ... Nothing would have happened if I had been my regular self. But anyway ...' This was going so badly I just wanted to finish my cigarette and take him to the train station, whether he understood or not. 'I think you'd feel a lot better and clearer if you had some time away, so I talked to Jeffrey . . .'

'No. No, goddamnit, I am not leaving and I wasn't upset, it was what I wanted. You can't send me away, I'm not a kid anymore. You can leave me, but you can't make me leave.' He was charging around the kitchen, bumping into the chairs, blind.

I just sat there. All of a sudden, he was finding his voice, the one I had always tried to nurture, to find a place for, between his father's roar and his brother's contented hum. I was hearing his début as a man, and now I had to keep him down and raise him up at the same time.

'How can it be so easy for you to send me away? Don't you love me at all?'

I jumped up, glad to have a reason to move. 'Not love you? It's because I love you, because I want you to have a happy, normal life. I owe it to you and I owe it to your father.'

He folded his arms. 'You don't owe Pop anything. He had everything he wanted, he had everything.' The words rained down like little blades.

I ignored what he said. 'It can't be, honey. You can't stay.'

'I could if you wanted me to.'

He was right. Who would know? I could take my two boys to the movies, away for weekends, play tennis with my step-son. I would be the object of a little pity and some admiration. Who would know? Who would have such monstrous thoughts, except Ruth, and she would never allow them to surface. I saw us together and saw it unfolding, leaves of shame and pity and anger, neither of us getting what we wanted. I wanted to hug him, console him for his loss.

'No, Lion.'

I reached across the table but he shrugged me off, grabbing my keys and heading out the door.

I sat for a long time, sipping, watching the sunlight move around the kitchen. When it was almost five, I took the keys from Lionel's side of the dresser and drove his van to soccer camp. Buster felt like being quiet, so we just held hands and listened to the radio. I offered to take him to Burger King, figuring that the automated monkeys and video games would be a good substitute for a fully present and competent mother. He was happy, and we killed an hour and a half there. Three hours to bedtime.

We watched some TV, sitting on the couch, his feet in my lap. Every few minutes, I'd look at the clock on the mantel and then promise myself I wouldn't look until the next commercial. Every time I started to move, I'd get tears in my eyes, so I concentrated on sitting very still, waiting for time to pass. Finally, I got Buster through his nightly routine and into bed, kissing his cupcake face, fluffing his Dr J pillow.

'Where's Lion? He said he'd kiss me good night.'

'Honey, he's out. He'll come in and kiss you while you're sleeping.'

'Where is he?'

I dug my nails into my palms; with Buster, this could go on for half an hour. 'He's out with some friends, Bus. I promise he'll kiss you in your sleep.'

'Okay. I'm glad he's home, Mama.'

How had I managed to do so much harm so fast? 'I know. Go to sleep, Gabriel Tyner Sampson.'

'G'night, Mama. Say my full name again.'

'Gabriel Tyner Sampson, beautiful name for a beautiful boy. 'Night.'

And I thought about the morning we named him, holding him in the delivery room, his boneless brown body covered with white goop and clots of blood, and Lionel tearing off his green mask to kiss me and then to kiss the baby, rubbing his face all over Gabriel's little body.

I got into my kimono and sat in the rocking chair, waiting for Lion. I watched the guests on the talk shows, none of whom seemed like people I'd want to know. After a while, I turned off the sound but kept the picture on for company. I watered my plants, then realized I had just done it yesterday and watched as the water cascaded out of the pots on to the wood floor, drops bouncing on to the wall, streaking the white paint. I thought about giving away the plants, or maybe moving somewhere where people didn't keep plants. Around here, it's like a law. The mopping up took me about eight minutes, and I tried to think of something else to do. I looked for a dish to break.

Stupid, inconsiderate boy. Around now, his father would have been pacing, threatening to beat him senseless when he walked in, and I would have been calming him down, trying to get him to come to bed.

At about three, when I was thinking of calling the hospital, I heard my car coming up the street slowly. I looked out the kitchen window and saw him pull into the drive, minus the right front fender.

He came inside quietly, pale gray around his mouth and eyes. There was blood on his shirt, but he was walking okay. I grabbed him by the shoulders and he winced and I dug my hands into him in the dark of the hallway.

'What is wrong with you? I don't have enough to contend with? Do you know it's three o'clock in the morning? There were no phones where you were, or what? It was too inconvenient to call home, to tell me you weren't lying dead somewhere? Am I talking to myself, goddamnit?'

I was shaking him hard, wanting him to talk back so I could slap his face, and he was crying, turning his face away from me. I pulled him into the light of the kitchen and saw the purple bruise, the shiny puff of skin above his right eyebrow. There was a cut in his upper lip, making it lift and twist like a harelip.

'What the hell happened to you?'

'I got into a little fight at the Navigator and then I had sort of an accident, nothing serious. I just hit a little tree and bumped my head.'

'You are an asshole.'

'I know, Ma. I'm sorry, I'll pay you back for the car so your insurance won't go up. I'm really sorry.'

I put my hands in my pockets and waited for my adrenaline to subside.

I steered him into the bathroom and sat him down on the toilet while I got some ice cubes and wrapped them in a dish towel; that year I was always making compresses for Buster's skinned knees, busted lips, black eyes. Lion sat there holding the ice to his forehead. The lip was too far gone.

I wasn't angry anymore and I said so. He smiled lopsidedly and leaned against me for a second. I moved away and told him to wash up.

'All right, I'll be out in a minute.'

'Take your time.'

I sat on the couch, thinking about his going away and whether or not Jeffrey would be good company for him. Lion came out of the bathroom without his bloody shirt, the dish towel in his hand. He stood in the middle of the room, like he didn't know where to sit, and then he eased down on to the couch, tossing the towel from hand to hand.

'Don't send me away. I don't want to go away from you and Grandma and Buster. I just can't leave home this summer. Please, Ma, it won't . . . what happened won't happen again. Please let me stay home.' He kept looking at his hands, smoothing the towel over his knees and then balling it up.

How could I do that to him?

'All right, let's not talk about it anymore tonight.'

He put his head back on the couch and sighed, sliding over so his cheek was on my shoulder. I patted his good cheek and went to sit in the brown chair.

I started to say more, to explain to him how it was going to be, but then I thought I shouldn't. I would tell him that we were looking at wreckage and he would not want to know.

I said good night and went to my bedroom. He was still on the couch in the morning.

We tried for a few weeks, but toward the end of the summer Lion got so obnoxious I could barely speak to him. Ruth kept an uncertain peace for the first two weeks and then blew up at him. 'Where have your manners gone, young man? After all she did for you, this is the thanks she gets? And Julia, when did you get so mush-mouthed that you can't tell him to behave himself?' Lion and I looked at our plates, and Ruth stared at us, puzzled and cross. I came home from work on a Friday and found a note on the kitchen table: 'Friends called with a housepainting job in Nantucket. Will call before I go to Paris. Will still do junior year abroad, if that's okay. L.' 'If that's okay' meant that he wanted me to foot the bill, and I did. I would have done more if I had known how.

It's almost summer again. Buster and I do pretty well, and we have dinner every Sunday with Ruth, and more often than not, we drive her over to bingo on Thursday evenings and play a few games ourselves. I see my husband everywhere; in the deft hands of the man handing out the bingo cards, in the black olive eyes of the boy sitting next to me on the bench, in the thick, curved back of the man moving my new piano. I am starting to play again and I'm teaching Buster.

Most nights, after I have gone to bed, I find myself in the living room or standing on the porch in the cold night air. I tell myself that I am not waiting, it's just that I'm not yet awake.

# claire calman
.............................
## *the secret voyager*

The ship was a talisman, a totem, moored in perfect calm in the year-round harbour of the windowsill of no. 32. He passed it as often as he could. And sometimes more often, detouring along the narrow back street – walking sideways ever-so-slowly as he neared the ship's window, watching it with lighthouse eyes, scuffling backwards a few steps to keep it in sight, then turning, running, cutting through the graveyard to make up for lost time.

It was a totally first-rate, excellent, ship-shape sort of ship. Its sails were crisp white triangles, stiff as the hotel napkins that time Uncle Arthur and Auntie Val took them for tea to celebrate their silver wedding four years ago. The sails were stretched by threads so fine you could only see them when you peeked at them out of the corner of your eye, then moved very slowly until they caught the light. The ship's hull was wood, dark and gleaming, dusted daily by loving hands, its sails blown softly by gentle breath.

One day, he would sail away in such a ship, sneak on board as they loaded their provisions before they set sail for Tahiti or the Caribbean, South America or to discover some secret island not marked on any map. A stowaway, creeping into the galley at night to steal a chicken drumstick, a dry cracker, an orange. Maybe they'd discover him and make him their mascot, or a lookout. He could clamber up the rigging faster than a monkey, his fingers alive and stinging at the roughness of the rope. He would have a brass telescope, heavy and smooth, the smell of metal glinting in his nostrils, cutting through the salt-washed air. At night, the ship would sail on, watched over by a thousand stars. He'd sleep in a hammock, swinging in the dark to the creaking chords of straining timbers, hearing the waves slapping against the hollow hull, swaying through his dreams.

He *is* late, he knows, and grasping the ship in a final glance, he turns for home, sprinting along the paving stones, no time to avoid the cracks, praying: 'Don't make me late. Don't make me late. Please, God. Please.'

He swoops round the corner, swerving as sharply as a speedboat and pushes himself for the final stretch. His heart is thudding now, his throat hot and tight, a stitch in his side stabbing at him, a promise of pain.

He goes round to the back door, wipes his shoes on the metal scraper, pulls his socks up slowly, too late to hurry now. One more moment. He turns the knob silent as a thief, holding his breath.

His father sits at the kitchen table. Doesn't look up when the boy enters but points to the space on the floor next to him. Grinds his chair back with a jerk from the table, the chair legs screeching on the stone flags.

The boy braces himself, then he closes his eyes to see the silent blue of the sky and, all around him, the sparkling of the sea.

# claire calman

........................

## *a restricted view*

Cathy sits in the window seat, knees up, feet flat against one wall, head pressed against the other, as if squashed between two bookends.

'That's right, love. Keep your feet out of the way while I do the floor.' Mum gets out the squeegee mop, plunges it into the bucket, pushes the handle to scoosh out the water, then skates the sponge head back and forth on the floor. The chequered lino goes wet in stripes, the white more white, the black more black as the mop glides past.

Sometimes, when Mum has to do cleaning in the school holidays, Cathy comes too. She can have a comic and a quarter of pear drops to suck. The outsides are all gritty sugar at first, then smooth, filling her nostrils with their nail-polish taste, clicking against her teeth. She likes it here in the window seat, with the mop squishing and splashing, Mum half humming, half singing, mopping in rhythm: 'Oh, soldier, soldier, won't you marry me, with your musket, fife and drum? Oh, no, pretty maid, I cannot marry thee, for a-dum-dah dee diddy-dum . . .'

There is a creak on the stair. Mr Barwood must be coming down. He is allowed to stay home all day. He has a room upstairs with a big computer and lots of books and a telephone just for him in it.

'Ah, Helen, hello. How are you? I was going to take a break now if you wanted to do my study?'

'That's fine, of course. Now you just stay there, Catherine, and keep off my nice clean floor.'

Mr Barwood is standing on the forbidden floor. He has dark hair that flops over to one side, like Daddy's did.

Upstairs, the vacuum roars alive and settles into a whine.

'So then, Catherine. Cathy. Enjoying your comic?' He smiles at her nervously, as if she might suddenly bite him or wet herself.

'Yes,' says Cathy, bulging her pear drop into one cheek.

Mr Barwood nods. 'Good. Good. Well.' He pushes his hair back from his eyes. 'I'll just make some coffee.'

Cathy wonders if he will give her a glass of orange. She knows she is not to ask for one.

Mr Barwood pours himself a mug of coffee from the glass jug in the machine on the tiled counter. He smiles at Cathy, then looks down at his shoes, apparently studying the floor. Puts his hand in his pocket and chinks the change up and down, up and down, then pulls out a coin.

'Here' – he thrusts it at her, nodding – 'for sweets.'

She quickly looks down at the coin in her hand before she can stop herself. It is a pound. A whole pound.

'Thank you,' she says politely, slurping the final sliver of her pear drop.

Mr Barwood smiles again and she hears the creak as he pads softly upstairs.

The whine of the vacuum stops.

Cathy holds her coin tight in her hand. She thinks of all the things she could buy with it: lots and lots of swizzle lollies and flying saucers and candy shrimps, or a proper big bar of chocolate and a bottle of cherryade, or two comics and some smoky bacon crisps. Or she could save it, save it for something really special.

She turns to look out of the window, her cheek cold against the glass. Above her, at street level, people rush past. Here, imprisoned in the window seat by the still-glistening floor, she has a restricted view: two pairs of grey trousers flapping above black, shiny shoes; a blue, swirly skirt and sandals the colour of sky; slow, shuffling feet in brown slippers and a little dog, shaggy as the bathmat at home, only dirty white not pink. She rubs the glass with the flats of her fingers, wiping at the breath-cloud to make everything clear.

Helen comes down the stairs, her backless sandals slapping softly against her bare feet on each step.

'Okay there, love? I'll just put the mop away and we can be off.' She clacks carefully across the almost dry checks, rinses the mop under the tap, empties the bucket. She bends down to stow the bucket under the sink. Straightening up, she tugs at her waistband, smooths down her skirt with her hands.

'Right then. All done.'

In the hallway, Helen calls up the stairs, 'We're just off, Andrew. See you next Wednesday.'

Mr Barwood's head appears over the bannister on the landing.

'Righto. See you then.' He pushes his hair back. 'Thank you. Bye, bye, Cathy.' He nods and waves.

Cathy waves back politely, before Mum has to nudge her.

On the way home, they stop off at the corner shop.

'Let's be naughty and have a treat,' says Mum, girls together, conspirators.

She chooses a box of Meltis New Berry Fruits, the ones that go all liquid in the middle when you bite them.

'You can get a drink as well. Go on, pick one from the fridge.'

Mum opens her purse to pay. Peeping out from its soft pocket is a £10 note, her cleaning money. In the deeper pocket, half-hidden behind, are two £20 notes. They are crisp and new, unused.

She pays and takes Cathy's hand as they leave the shop.

'Here,' she says, handing the sweets to Cathy, 'Hold these a sec.' And she reaches her hands up behind her neck, fumbling as she refastens the button at the back of her blouse.

# gill horitz

## *about time*

It is Saturday night, yet it is Thursday lunchtime. How can both these statements be true? I've turned on the tape for the first time, kneel beside the speaker through which my mother's breath passes and move my head from side to side to catch her words, which float in a soup of night sounds. Gradually, they congeal and become momentous speech.

'These are the great circles of time that hold the months together.'

Pages turn. 'In this *Book of the Universe* are all the episodes that link the days and the months. As the wheels turn, see how the curves of the planets echo our thoughts. In this model of circular symmetry you will see our beginnings.'

A gentle voice asks, 'Why don't you get back into bed now, Myrtle?'

She replies, 'Is this *anybody's* bed?' and the sheets shush and crackle in my ear. Into her bed she steps, into the adventurer's galleon, and sets sail.

'What is the exact time?' she asks.

'Quarter past five.'

'Is that *exactly*?' Electric silence. She answers herself,

'This is Saturday night. All the days of our lives join up . . .'

A journey begins.

Myrtle was a science teacher and my mother, born seven years into the new century. When she was five she discovered a picture of Sir Isaac Newton floating in a river, which thrilled her father, Henry, for he had once proved that the family were Newton's descendants.

Myrtle's father taught himself Latin and Greek. And he made cabinets and chests, and within each he carpentered a secret drawer. Myrtle's favourite game was to discover how to release the drawer: each had a different, intricate mechanism but her fingers always solved the conundrum, for uncharted regions were a joy to her.

Some people have a need to get to the truth, draw things into the open.

Some nights, Henry woke her, led her up the steep stairway into the attic to look at the moon and the stars through his home-made telescope.

Everything that could be revealed, would be.

One day, he eased open the secret drawer in the mahogany chest in his bedroom and took out a folded paper.

He led Myrtle down the winding path to the garden shed hidden behind borders and the vegetable garden; there lay more uncharted territory, woody and perfumed with pipe tobacco where light came to life, suffused with motes. Seeds and dust orbited their heads. In that impressionable atmosphere the rules of the home had no place: things were not put away but opened out. Myrtle was shown the insides of things, the wheels of watches, the lenses of a telescope. She handled intricacies, interior workings.

She watched Henry's fingers unfold the paper, saw

soil-encrusted whorls, and wondered about the things in life he might yet bring to her attention.

On the page were lines and words plotted like a puzzle; the whole sheet was covered with them and he called it a family tree. Its branches were a canopy of names: Myrtle, Edith, Wilhemina, Henry, Muriel, Edwina, George, Elizabeth, William, Joseph, Alexander, Hannah . . . In the tree's crown sat the eagle roosting: Isaac in the year 1642.


When things went missing, when her car was stolen from outside the supermarket, when the fridge filled up with the same goods, when the man across the road entered her house at night, then I knew our lives were changing.

There is a space in the cranium, I imagine at the base, where protein amyloid begins the unsettling of the universe. It is a silent, painless working. But nothing ever again can be relied upon. My mother has Alzheimer's disease; once it was diagnosed, no one ever again asked her to play bridge.

I was forty years younger, yet I had to stop her driving her white Morris Minor, which was a chariot of sorts that took her out of the doldrums. For sixty years she drove off whenever she wanted, her prerogative most certainly; we should all have that much control over our lives.

Mother said I was out of my mind; she said she would step under a lorry in Commercial Road if I took away her car. Every afternoon she drove to the sea. It was the last vestige of independence. A way out into the world. Turn right, left, to the roundabout and straight over, on for about five miles, past the garage, then left at the hotel and park at the sea front. There the light stipples the sea, its moods flood over the watchers in their cars. They stare and stare. Always their eyes are held by its constancy. It doses them with elemental calm.

When she failed an eye test and it became illegal to drive,

it could be avoided no longer. Still she made me follow her the five miles to the sea to observe her driving, and never once lost her way.

It was like a mother telling her daughter what to do. I practised in bed the words I would use and they made me cry.

I forced her to give me the keys for ever. She sat huddled on the edge of her bed, holding them like a dagger. I heard the tone of my voice, subtlety was not possible. The words sounded like someone who always plays by the book, who never takes risks.

She said, rising up, the dagger close to my chest, 'The trouble with you, Caitlin, is that you're so dull, you always play things by the book, always try to do things for the best. You always mean well.'

'Mean well' is ditch water, low and stagnant – there is no reflection of self there. Mother was fighting me.

Fierce voice, eyes ablaze, she gathered herself up, all strength, status, dignity into her right arm, and I felt the sword enter. Oh sad day. Between Mother and me there had always been so many different ways to look at things.

Outside the room hovered Mr and Mrs Evans, the Rest Home proprietors; they made me do it, for the best. Always for the best in the long run. The doctor made me do it – she told me that I could not live with myself if my mother caused an accident.

That night I cried, sought refuge in the dark's desert, soared up into the heavens and down into the earth's core, but could only go so far. Once I felt my mouth slacken into an O as the owl sang in the wood opposite. Its note entered my head, or the owl itself flew into my cochlea, spiralling me and Myrtle into other dimensions.

We sailed on a liner in the Aegean Sea and Myrtle sat at

the captain's table discussing brain haemorrhages. Her hands lay like shells in her lap all through dinner and I longed to hold them.

And while I dreamed, Mother, lying in her bed, would see her car and daughter and keys hover on the lip of a black hole, about to be swallowed.

And under her skin, molecules continued their work, suffusing clusters of memory. Although I didn't realize it then, as one life came to an end another was being revealed. In those regions, cranium dark as galaxies, something was germinating. No brain scan can show the secrets I now surmise and intuit.

In the morning, as she woke, she felt the wound in her palm where I had forced the keys from her hand.

---

It takes time to realize how much people are changing.

Myrtle was no actress yet she became addled with voices: slow, philosophical soundings of self-knowledge. She was her old self yet not so, speaking about things she knew but had never spoken about. Context and language seemed to slide away from each other.

She told me, 'There is a universal belief that I shall die before my next birthday. There is no point now in taking interest in what's happening around me. I see only too clearly it won't lead anywhere. For one thing, I have no responsibilities; it's no longer necessary to make decisions for other people. I may as well leave.'

She was unable to go anywhere. Over the two years since the Home had become her home, her body had grown heavier, noticeably so each week as though the food piled up inside and needed movement to shift it. She was like a frail dormouse, soft and round, tottering on hind legs. It was for the best to sit all day, and all the other underling mice, Wally, Emily and Dorothy, were happy to sew and snooze beside her from breakfast to tea.

One autumn afternoon, I arrived and she was rising from her chair when I entered the room, on the move. She looked slimmer: recently there had been a change, less of a totter when she walked, less softness when we hugged.

Up she got, full of vitality, and began to climb the forbidden stairs. I hovered behind her in case she fell. She and I sat in her room to rest.

'Be a bit braver, Caitlin, you've got to get out of yourself, see your own potential. You're missing something.'

The thrill of my own name; it was like being nursed with a mother's soft croon, a lullaby in my ear.

'You seem different today. What have you been doing?' I asked.

'What on earth would I do? I am fixed here, fixed with a bloody great anchor. You get used to sitting all day in one chair. Falling asleep is our salvation.'

Then she fell asleep and I watched her eyes dart beneath their shining lids. Behind her, the curtains were open and outside in the darkening sky I saw us both sitting in the bright room.

For a woman like Myrtle, the ache of apathy was too much to bear. Something occurred, some physiological change to mind and body. We must not be deterred by what we cannot understand. Watching my mother, I realized I was finding out about the workings of the universe.

With anchor weighed, she rose up out of her chair into the night: her arms become wings and eased her over the town centre towards the north. As she flew away, I realized the present need not constrain us. It was no apparition, a journey began there although I didn't that time see where she went.

When she was almost out of sight, I leaned over and covered her with a rug.

At about that time, the night sitter reported that Myrtle woke frequently, sat up and spoke aloud as though people from her own past came to life before her eyes. To understand how senility was liberating her, letting her slip between layers of memory, I began to study physics. Newton's laws of motion became my everyday reading:

'Every body continues in its state of rest or uniform motion in a straight line unless it is compelled to change that state by forces impressed upon it.'

Soon, she was in the present less and less. Once, the family photograph album had been a catalyst, being so full of evidence. On many occasions we turned the pages over and over; there was a sensory magic which conjured smells and sounds out of the silver granules.

One day I pointed again to my daughters, Rachael and Alice, and their cousins, all climbing rocks, spellbound in youth. And I pointed to myself wearing the same bright woollen jumper that we both could see on my arms holding the album.

My mother turned to look at me, and asked, 'Did *I* have any daughters?'

Speech lay mute in my chest, all the words piling up around my heart. For a moment I was in jeopardy.

The album became a closed book and slid off her knees. A book full of unborns. Who is to say we are happening now? Were we both in a coma or out of one? No one can tell.

When I spoke, the words, never before spoken, sounded unreasonable in the bright lounge light.

'I'm your daughter – Caitlin.'

Then I remembered that nuclides have daughters, formed from other nuclides, caused by radioactive decay.

I had became unrecognizable, seen as I was from such great distances.

*Where are you, Mother? Can I go with you?*

She closed her eyes. Her head fell to one side and in the orifice of an ear, I saw her hurtling through dark midland tunnels, felt the rhythms of the steel pulse and scents of the journey, saw the word 'Darlington' on the platform.

I no longer existed. I had not yet been born, no one could see me.

I decided to eavesdrop on Myrtle's nights, record her awakenings into the past. I gave a small tape recorder to the night nurse, who agreed to switch it on when Mother began to speak.

'This is Saturday night. All the days of our lives join up the months and I have reached a mid-January far from now. We can go forwards or backwards like the proverbial arrow: it depends which way you face. We have always known that space has no preferred directional characteristics and I have found from my own experience that this is also true of time.

'Take out your books and we shall look at ways to measure time. The lunar cycle has twenty-nine point five days between crescent moons. Numbers are merely coherent sounds to help us visualize our measurements. Now, I've found a crevice in this understanding, a high-up cranny, where you can go either way.

'To move into the past is not cumbersome or weird. Rethink, all of you, begin to rethink the dimensions you know.'

For several minutes she said nothing, yet I was bound to go on listening to the surfeit of rustles, the breathing.

'I am entering the tunnel, here I go; pack up your books and I'll see you again another day. I am going home to visit my parents.'

My face was inches from the black gauze pulled taut over the speaker. I leaned closer and through the cloth's fibres saw her pass down the platform; her parents were waiting by the ticket barrier, as they waved to her, she began to run towards them, her thick, dark hair spread like a cape on her back.

They took her to their home at 47 The Mead. I saw inside the back room; there was a domestic vapour; the hearth was a nugget of heat and the dark corners of the room were frozen. A meal was laid out on a white cloth on the table in the room's centre, a dish of white cod, baked, steaming. They were about to sit down to eat.

At first their voices were indecipherable but as I played the tape over and over and watched their mouths move, words became distinguishable.

Then click. The night sitter turned off the machine. Myrtle's voice was trapped. It was Thursday afternoon again in Dorset.


Apart from that tape, I have four others wound up tight: 'Myrtle watching the night skies with her father from the attic', 'Myrtle playing with friends on a railway embankment', 'Myrtle watching her father carpenter in the garden shed' and 'Myrtle working in a laboratory at Birmingham University'.

No one except the night sitter knows what I have done.

The tapes, coiled in their plastic cases, contain time before I was born. That's how I know about the family tree and the atmosphere of the shed. I saw Henry take the folded paper from the secret drawer in the chest in which I now keep my jumpers. As Myrtle's voice relives the day, the place comes into view and I follow them out of the house, down the garden path into the shed. I notice shade and sun slice the rhubarb leaves in the vegetable plot. There is no sign of my grandmother, Wilhemina.

They stay in the shed making calculations from birth and death dates. Eventually, Wilhemina must call them, although I don't hear her. Henry hurriedly folds the paper and puts it into his waistcoat pocket. Myrtle speaks about tea, how they will be in trouble if they are late. Just as they are about to step out into the garden, my mother's voice stops as she falls asleep. The scene diminishes at that very moment, in the shed doorway.

In the university laboratory tape she talks indistinguishably to herself about measuring chemicals and I am there standing against the dark wood bench. Then two friends enter, Vera and Kathleen, and they speak about a plan to go skiing in Austria. Vera's hair falls over one eye just as it did when I knew her as my godmother twenty years later. Myrtle puts away the equipment, and they go outside, chattering all the time. I am behind and above them, following them through the morning. In spite of the realism, I notice it has limitations. Not everything is visible. As we walk down the street, the windows of houses are opaque and we pass no one.

On the railway embankment she is about eight. Six children slide down to the tracks until they hear them hum and crackle.

'There's no time to lose', my mother calls, and I see rather than hear them scream and shout as they clamber to safety. When the train has passed, they walk on the iron lines and speak about the presence left in the air by the furious engine.

The attic tape starts on the landing. Myrtle is about fourteen. Her father has woken her and they climb the almost vertical steps into the attic. As I follow, I look down at the blue woollen dressing-gown and glimpse her ankle, my mother's unswollen and smooth ankle. They talk knowledgeably about the moon's surface until the night sitter tries to make Myrtle settle down and sleep.

One day she may relive the years in which our lives coincide. But I expect nothing.

Her ancestor unfolded a verbiage of mathematical

equations: *time runing forwards is replaced by time running backwards; the numbers do not alter, for the sum of two negative numbers, like the sum of two positive numbers, is always positive.*

Now I believe that Newton's mechanics cannot distinguish between the two different directions of time. Myrtle and I have no way of knowing whether we are growing older or younger.

# janette turner hospital
## *flight*

'Yes, I'm coming,' Cecily promises, breathless, hearing Robert's urgent voice above the wind. She runs barefoot, tripping on something in the early morning dusk. The wind beats against the bedroom window and beyond she can see thousands of dead leaves whipped into squalls, no, not leaves, she sees with astonishment, not leaves but birds, wheeling galaxies of small brown birds. The air is thick with them. The air sways and tilts with the soft spirals of their flight, a Milky Way of migration so dense she can see nothing but wings. She can hear Robert, she can hear the edge of panic in his voice, but she cannot see him. She can hear the other man, the passenger, the one they have brought with them. 'I'm coming!' she promises, fumbling with the lock on the window.

The birds spin like a nebula. Through the glass, the riff of beating wings is like the chant of monks, a low nervy hum. It must be winter that drives them like this: the sudden onset of frosts and the sharp unseasonable plummeting of the mercury; it must be panic.

The velvet folds of the birdswarm brush the glass. The sash window is old and heavy, she cannot lift it. Robert calls her name again, his alarm transposed up to a higher key. 'I'm *trying*,' she cries, almost sobbing. She hears the passenger, the man they do not know. The window is impossibly heavy. 'I'm coming!' she promises, but very likely years have passed since the sash was last opened, and it will not budge. She hammers on the glass with her fists, a stammer of rage, because it is pointless, she will not be in time, she is never going to be in time, she will always be a second too late, there will always be the sickening thump, the shower of glass . . .

The sound, when it comes, is like gunshot.

She will not look.

There is blood on her arms from the glass but she ignores that, she crawls back into bed, she tosses, she wakes – she *wakes*! *Oh, thank God* – but the waking brings no more than a second's relief. Her days come and go like birds, her dreams like days.

She shivers and reaches for her robe.

What time is it? What day? What week?

In the refrigerator she finds a loaf of bread flecked with blue and green and whitish circles, rather interesting, she thinks. The bread gives off the dense, yeasty smell of a forest floor. There is also a tomato delicately slumping into one corner of the vegetable drawer and leaking pale-red fluid. I have to buy food, she thinks. I have to walk into the village to buy food. She frowns, concentrating. First I have to get dressed, she remembers. She concentrates again. Which language, which country? English, she remembers. England. I am in old farm house near the Channel coast.

'This one's been round a bit,' the man in the general store and post office says, proffering a postcard. 'Crossed a few oceans. They ought to call you the Artful Dodger.'

Cecily smiles and slips into her flippant voice. Nothing in her wardrobe fits well any more, but she can always make do with flippancy, a hitch here, a tuck there, the lightness is all. 'Fleeing the scene of a crime,' she says. 'Got to cover my tracks.'

'You Australians.' But he has no complaints with her shopping list, cans of this and that, Sussex cheese that smells like old socks, a jug of cider. 'Don't you want to know what it says?' he prods. 'The postcard, I mean.' She smiles at him. She is tempted to ask who it's from. Of course he has read it. Of course the whole village is involved in exegetical debate at this very hour in the Brewers' Arms. 'Came five days ago,' he says with a hint of reproach. 'Is it dust you're looking for?'

'Pardon?'

'Why d'you always run your fingers along the sides of my shelves like that?'

'Oh,' Cecily says, embarrassed. 'Do I?' She studies the pink cushions of her fingertips vaguely.

'They've been asking about you down at the pub. We thought you must have moved on already.'

'No. Not yet.' She tucks the vegetables into her knapsack, between the cans, and starts putting the apples on top. 'But maybe now that my mail has found me.'

The old man throws his hands up in mock despair and laughs.

*Dear Cec,* (says the back of the postcard, in scrawl) *This photograph seemed appropriate. If I didn't know better, I'd say it was you. Bought it in Sydney on a back street in the Glebe. Actually it leaped out from a rack in a bookstore and assaulted me, clobbered me, made me go weak at the knees, but since the setting's France and you're in south-east Asia (aren't you?), it seems unlikely. If you steam off the airmail sticker (didn't want to waste valuable space), the fine print will tell you the staircase is in Château Chambord. You have a doppelgänger in the Loire Valley, and what is she doing on the racks of a bookstore in*

*Sydney? you may well ask – the jackpot answer being that some graphics company in Paris, bunch of art students, has cornered a niche market worldwide. Seriously. I read it somewhere. Artsy photo-cards selling like hot cakes from New York to New South Wales. Anyway, the symbolism seems just right.*

*FLIGHT OF FOLLY. WOMAN TRAPPED IN CAGE OF OPEN DOORS. Hope this finds you. Hope you have a magnifying glass to read my wingèd words. Hope no one else is not missing you as much as I don't miss you. Hope your life is as shitty as the bottom of a birdcage, like mine. Hope somebody clips your wings. Hope the brakes fail in all your nightmares. As for myself, I'm down to one car-crash dream per month. Sorry, sorry, sorry, that is really below the belt, but that's what you get for running away. Hope you rot in the jungle, and afterwards I hope you come back. Love, Robert.*

Cecily does not believe in the postcard, in spite of the apparent external evidence of the old man in the general store. She knows the mind is a very queer bird and an artful dodger of exceptional skill. There are, for example, highly intelligent people who believe they can fly, there are others, well read and well travelled, who see revenants in doorways and under stairwells and tell no one, there are those who believe they receive messages from the dead, there are crazy people who read coded information in raindrops on a window or in the migratory patterns of birds.

She pins the trick photograph to her bulletin board, and stares at it. What is shown is a luminous corkscrew of nothingness, an arrangement of delicate openings in a curved limestone wall. Through the openings, she sees stairs fanning upwards into light. In the upper left corner of the photograph, a bird is poised on a blur of wings. In the lower right foreground, framed by one of the openings, is the face of a woman, startled, her lips parted, caught in the act of turning towards – or perhaps away from – the camera.

At first the bird had seemed to Cecily to be there by design, well aware of the complicated updrafts of air and the whorls of light. There are complicated people, though Cecily is not one of them, who can step back inside the frames they once inhabited and decode the whirling updrafts of design. There are others who can step out of photographs to haunt us, and still others who are not so free to leave. (The wind changed, perhaps, as the shutter clicked, and the subject was stuck for ever in the blink of a particular minute.) At first, it had seemed to Cecily, the bird was not at all stuck but was there by design, she remembers that, she remembers thinking that. She remembers thinking that the bird knew the stairwell intimately.

She remembers wondering who could be following her so relentlessly, watching so closely, sending (out of malice or desire?) such heavy messages. She remembers fearing that her paranoia was out of hand.

She remembers thinking of the Venerable Bede, his monkish Latin winging by, *Talis mihi videtur, rex . . .* feathered words from the eighth century, a quick flash of history, King Edwin in his mead hall with his pagan thanes, *This life of man, O King, is like the flight of a sparrow through a lighted hall,* and there is nothing like a well-shaped line to move through time, so Cecily thinks, as Bede keeps flapping his elegant prose, *and outside it hails and snows and storms . . . and the bird flyeth in one door, and while it hovers inside the hearth-bright wine-heated hall it knows nothing of winter, and it is warmed by the fire, and its wings are bright in the torchlight, but then it flyeth out through another door and the winter night swalloweth it again and we know not whither it goeth . . .* and where does it come from, all this arcane knowledge, where does Cecily keep all this gilded bric-a-brac?

This is her problem precisely; she remembers too much,

she cannot jettison knowledge, she has a brainful of junk, and what use is King Edwin? Of what possible use are his thanes in his lighted hall? With respect to her present situation, Cecily is unable to list a single advantage springing from her intimacy with assorted medieval manuscripts, and therefore King Edwin's sparrow, O grab-bag memory, should put itself back in its venerable bead-box, where it belongs as far as she is concerned, yes, it should fold itself quietly away like a good little *bibelot* in its Bedebox, because there is much that Cecily would like to forget. This freefall into photographs is for the birds, and she does not want to be there again, with the bird again, in the stairwell, *here*, at Château Chambord again, because in fact, O tourists, this life of birds is like the short ridiculous flicker of kings in vast palaces.

The limestone, cunningly lit, is the colour of butter. Against it, the bird is like a quick black thought of death, and Cecily notes that it is bloody marvellous the way forbidden words will come winging in without any provocation whatsoever. Give them an opening in a stairwell and they stage a stunt-flying display at the moult of a feather.

*Excusez-moi, excusez-moi,* a man says, and that must be a Portuguese accent, or Basque maybe, or at any rate from somewhere south of the Pyrenees, and Cecily must be making progress after all if she is detecting these finer linguistic shadings, or thinks she is, and please, she says, think nothing of it, *ça ne me gêne pas*, something I've always dreamed of, catapulting down a few hundred corkscrew stairs into the Latin arms of a stranger. No, really, it's nothing, monsieur, it's nothing... Pedro then, *enchantée*, really Pedro, don't give it a thought, *Cécélie, je m'apelle Cécélie*, Cecilia, Cecily, Cec, Cess (and Cesspool during certain early years in school), though Cecily embarrasses herself beyond endurance when she babbles on like this, and she does not think her ankle is twisted, at least not badly, and in any case accidents arrive, and the crowds are *affreux, schrecklich,* whatever, isn't it? she is sorry, she is afraid she doesn't know a single word of Portuguese, she's just recently arrived in France herself, from Malaya as a matter of fact, but this business of daily living, O pushers and shovers, is like wading through a cesspool, is it not? and this life, this life, O Pedro, is for the birds.

The bird brushes her cheek. From outer darkness to outer darkness, a feathered meteor through a moment of light, what a daredevil, Cecily thinks. What tenacity. *What comes before and after, we know not.*

*François I,* says a guide in too-careful English, and Cecily has to flatten herself against the luminous shell of the hollow core to let the group pass, *was bringing Leonardo to France for this express purpose ... the design of the staircase, it is his, Leonardo's, of the double spiral around the nothingness.*

The bird is flirting with the nothingness now. It drops in odd little freefalls, hovers, flutters, plummets another metre or so, a plumbline down the pale-gold windpipe of the double stair. It is level, now, with Cecily's eyes and she sees, with sudden anguish, that this has nothing to do with the sport of tormenting *her*. 'You poor little thing,' she whispers, and leans out into the core, a precipitous and dangerous and altogether pointless move. 'Here,' she murmurs urgently, 'here, baby,' straining across the limestone sill, offering her hand, her wrist – and sees the man at the opposite opening, on the opposite arm of the stair. Watchful. Watching. More than watching. Is it surveillance? No. She has no word for the meaning of his gaze or for its intensity.

His eyes, her eyes ... she feels as helpless as the bird, and what is strange, what is frightening, what is as exhilarating and terrifying as a brush with death, is this weird sense of fusion, this sense that they have entered the same tailspin, she and the man, that it is not his freefall, not hers, not the bird's, but *theirs*, the same one, same delirium, same shock, same euphoria, same express trip to unknown end.

*What comes before and after, we know not . . .*

Days and months later she spins theories. It is possible, for example, that random arrangements of certain objects constitute some kind of magnetic field. It is possible that currents pass through the poles of such a field. It is possible that shifts occur, earthquakes, upheavals of the magnetic poles, irreversible changes . . . Or it is possible, yes, it certainly could be possible, why not? as good an explanation as any, didn't Leonardo himself, after all, believe in potent alignments, in perfect symmetries and numerologies and arcane geometrical powers, so yes it is possible that spells are generated spontaneously from certain precise mathematical configurations, for example from the axis that begins with Cecily's eyes and passes through the hovering bird to the eyes of the man.

Cecily's wings shiver; her heart jumps against her breast feathers. She can feel giddy air pockets opening into nothing.

The man seems to be there by design. He seems to know her, and for a moment it seems to her that she knows him, that it is all happening again, that he is the passenger, that he was the man that she and Robert had brought with them, but no, no, actually he does not resemble the passenger at all, she does not know why she thought that stupid thought.

The man in Leonardo's staircase continues to stare at her with a slightly stunned look, the look perhaps of a man who has loved a woman passionately, lost her, and is stupefied to see her again after many years. Cecily has the lunatic sensation that he must indeed know her. She has the impression that he comes here often, that he returns, just as she herself seems to return, for reasons private and dangerous, much as wanton boys on rollerblades will return to the concrete underpass of an autoroute.

But she is sure she has never seen the man before. She has never been to Chambord, nor indeed to the valley of the Loire, before. Her mouth is dry. She swallows.

*Excusez-moi, excusez-moi,* someone says, and she feels faint, gripping the limestone sill because there is shuffling, pushing, there are people behind him, behind her, there is a swarm of languages, cameras, flashbulbs, *flashbulbs,* yes, and collisions occur between particles of light and bewilderment. He too has a camera in his hands. She blinks and sees white circles, lightning, the quick black spark of the bird.

*Oh, the bird!* someone says, and talk ricochets off the walls. *Got it, I think. Good shot... What shutter speed...? Do you think the light...?*

Distressed, Cecily brushes the voices off like flies.

'Don't move,' the man says softly, urgently, in French, no... in English, no, she feels the words as feathers against her skin. But she is drowning in a river of people and the rising tide of the tour groups on the opposite stair is lapping and pulling at the man.

'Don't go,' she pleads silently.

He smiles very slightly, a half-smile, the shadow of a smile, and points upwards. Like a sleepwalker, she nods. She begins to climb. He is on the other coil of the double stair. The two flights twist round and round each other, but never meet. At each turn of the twinned whorls, at each matched pair of openings, the current of sightseers pauses and the man and the woman seem to float, suspended, for ten seconds, twenty, sometimes thirty. At several openings they almost smile. The air is heavier and heavier. Cecily can feel the drugged weight of it in her lungs, on her eyelids, between her legs. When we get to the top, she thinks, we will meet on the balcony. It seems certain to her that afterwards nothing will be the same.

But nothing can be counted on except uncertainty, there is always constant interference in the lines of flight, a man and a woman may meet in Sydney or in Paris or wherever, signals may be exchanged, heat of various kinds given off, future possibilities intimated... but then... But then a bird and a car may meet without warning and all flight paths are in drastic disarray. There are never any guarantees that desired effect will follow the cause or the course of desire.

Near the top of the double staircase, the flotsam of tour groups is impassable. Americans, Cecily thinks with exasperation, already breathing French attitudes and air. There should be certain hours for American groups, and other hours for contemplatives, she thinks, then she sees the Australian flags on several backpacks. Once, before she became so flighty, she would have felt a leap of pleasure. She would have tapped the traveller on the shoulder, *G'day, mate*, just to hear the dear diphthongs again, the muddy vowels. Now she makes herself invisible. Swimming against the current, slipping sleekly through hollows in the tide, she slithers through to the labyrinth of outdoor galleries and the pinnacle-forested roof.

There is no further sign of the bird.

The man has flown.

Cecily leans against the outer wall of Leonardo's lantern, breathing raggedly, and stares across parklands and parterres into the dark wood of François I. She feels weak with relief. I must run, she thinks. I must move on before I see that man again.

'Excuse me,' he says, touching her shoulder, and Cecily startles violently and turns and their eyes meet.

She cannot breathe for sheer panic. No, she says, tries to say. No, it's too dangerous.

She runs toward the stairs and keeps running.

In a farmhouse in the rural south of England, Cecily stares at the postcard on her wall. For some reason, she is shivering. She takes the quilt from the bed and wraps herself in it and huddles in a chair, but she still feels cold. Then she pulls the suitcase out from under her bed.

For a whole minute, maybe two, she kneels there, indecisive, her hand in the pocket on the inner side of the suitcase lid. Her fingers read the large brown envelope like Braille – the grainy outside, the gummed flap, the smooth lining. *It's shock, that's all*, she hears Robert say. *It wears off with time.* She extracts the envelope, and for a long time sits with it unopened in her lap. Then she takes out the 8 × 10 inch black-and-white photograph, the one from the inquest, the one the lawyer gave her. She pins it to the wall beside Robert's card.

A tree is growing through the middle of a car, and the car has split open like a well-charred seed. The tree grows through the place where a front passenger might have sat. No photograph exists of the passenger, the man to whom they had offered a ride.

It is dark, but Cecily lights a candle and stares through the two photographs all night.

In the morning, she takes pen and paper.

*Dear Robert*, she writes. *You think I am running from misplaced guilt about the accident. You think that I think I caused it because of the birds, because I distracted you. I did cause it. I am guilty of manslaughter. But not in any way you could know . . .*


The sheer randomness of desire, its casual ruthlessness, is what frightens Cecily. She did not know the man. She heard that he came with the friend of a friend of someone, not that she would ask. He is in Political Science, she has overheard, or maybe it is the History Department, a new appointment freshly arrived in Sydney from somewhere else, Melbourne, Brisbane, nobody seems quite sure. There is such a crush at the party, such a thick fog of bodies and smoke, people flattened against walls, people falling over coats in the hall, people pressing up against one another (sometimes by design, sometimes not), people spilling champagne or good Australian beer.

But no one has introduced Cecily and the man from Brisbane or wherever, and they have not yet brushed up against each other. In fact she has been going to absurd lengths to avoid him, she has no idea why. There is something about the soft skin at the back of his neck, just above his jacket collar, and something about the way a curl falls across his forehead, which affects her breathing. With whom has he come to the party? With which woman? She cannot believe she is asking herself these ridiculous questions.

If she stands by the tub of ice from which spiky bottles jut like porcupine quills, she can swap small talk with the bartender, behind whom is a wall of mirrored tiles. From somewhere near the windows, Robert waves to her reflection. She smiles and raises her glass. Robert blows her a kiss. In the mirror, she sees a woman, laughing, lean in close to the man from somewhere else and brush invisible lint from his shoulder. Cecily turns away.

People come and go. Into the brief spaces of monologues, Cecily releases small sounds of approval and they rise like tiny trial balloons. 'It's so refreshing,' a man tells her, slurring his words a little, 'to talk to someone who's so interested in the kind of research I do.' *Yes?* she murmurs. Through the crook of the researcher's drinking arm, she watches the man from Brisbane – she has decided it must be Brisbane because of the tan – she sees him move away from the woman who touched his jacket. He is watching someone in the mirror, watching with an intense, demanding, look-at-me look. Not that this is any concern of Cecily's, or of any interest to her whatsoever. Still. Out of simple curiosity, she turns.

And who knows how long they stood like that, reflecting, and did he cast the spell, or did she, her heart jumping like a fish on a hook? His eyes, her eyes: how could movements so tiny throw so many lives off course? She feels dizzy. She has to catch hold of something, the bookcase behind her. She concentrates on setting her champagne flute delicately on one of the shelves. Everything is in slow motion now, the way the man walks through the mirror and takes her glass from the bookshelf and tips his head back and drinks, watching her, watching her.

'That is a dangerous thing to do,' she says in a small voice, and now Robert is waving from the mirror, signalling, and the man says: 'Ah, you belong to someone then,' and she says, breathless: 'Well, uh, we've been together a long time . . .' and everything speeds up, everything goes to Fast Forward, Robert is explaining that it's two in the morning and they have the trip ' . . . but I don't *belong* to anyone,' she says, and now suddenly it's flight she wants, yes, yes, she agrees with Robert, we have to leave, but Robert is saying, 'You're Joe's friend. From Brisbane, right? Good to have you here, can we give you a lift, are we heading in the same direction?' and as a matter of fact, what do you know? they are indeed, but there's absolutely no need, no need, except that Robert of course is his always generous jovial self and insists, he *insists*, no problem. And then Cecily says, well in that case the passenger should take the front seat, yes, this time it is she who puts her foot down. Absolutely. Because, because. So the two men can talk.

'Oh look!' she says, as they leave the city behind and skim along the shore road north of Manly. To their right are the dunes, and beyond them the curl of Pacific surf. Cecily leans forward, pushing slightly between the bucket seats, pressing against the passenger a little from the sway of the car. 'Look at the nightbirds!'

'Where?' Robert asks, and swerves, and the birds come at them like leaves. Instinctively Robert puts his hands in front of his face. 'Cec!' he shouts, and she lunges forward between the seats and she tries, she tries, to reach the wheel.

*Dear Robert*, she writes. *Accidents are accidents, as the inquest said, and as you have said a thousand times. They are nobody's fault. Nevertheless there is something I've never told you . . .*

She crushes the sheet of paper into a ball and takes another.

*Dear Robert*, she writes. *I have a confession to make. It is* desire, *that careless predator, that outlaw, I am running from . . . My crime was that of desire . . .*

She tears the page neatly and precisely into shreds and begins again.

*Dear Robert*, she writes. She leaves the sheet blank and signs her name at the bottom. *P.S.*, she writes. *Thank you for the card. You are dear to me, and always will be, but I cannot come back. I am so so sorry. As you'll see from the stamp, I'm in England at present, but please don't try to write as I'm moving on. Love, Cecily.*

Yes, she has the right street. She takes the postcard from her pocket: the luminous staircase, the bird, the woman's face. She checks the back of the card again: yes, right street, right number. And there is the place, Graphique de Paris. But perhaps I will come again another day, she thinks, turning back to the Métro entrance. Her hands are shaking. Then again, maybe it is better to get this over and done with. People are looking at her strangely. She leans against the staircase wall in a kind of trance and watches them pass up and down, whole flocks of them, like birds in an aviary.

What have I got to lose? she asks herself.

And in fact it is all very brisk and businesslike in Graphique de Paris. An elegant young woman studies the postcard, turns it over to find the title of the photograph, and then types *Flight* on a keyboard. Her computer hums thoughtfully for several seconds. She looks from the screen to Cecily and back again. She swivels the monitor round so that Cecily can see the image, enlarged, in digital clarity. 'Is it you?' the young woman asks curiously.

'I think so,' Cecily says, feeling a pulse at her temples quicken.

The young woman swings the monitor back to herself and presses another key. 'Hmm. The photographer's one of our freelancers. Lives in the Marais. Here.' She swivels the monitor again. 'You can copy down his address and phone number if you like.'


Cecily sits in a coffee shop near the Place des Vosges in the Marais, watching the building across the street. If she were to push open its large wooden door, and cross its courtyard, and climb Staircase B, and ring the bell on the second floor, what would she say?

She pays for her coffee. She crosses the street and pushes open the great wooden door. She walks through the courtyard, she climbs Staircase B, she rings the bell. But when he opens the door, she is unable to say a word.

'Ah,' he says, nodding. Seconds pass. He is smiling slightly. He scarcely even seems surprised. 'So you got my message,' he says, and words come back to her then.

'Why did you look at me like that, at Chambord?'

He shrugs. 'I don't know. You reminded me of someone I used to know.' He rakes a hand through his hair. 'I don't know why I say that. You don't really look like her at all. It was just something... I don't know, something fugitive about you.'

They stand there staring at each other.

'I'll confess something,' he says. 'I willed you to come back. I planned it. I've been waiting.'

'That's crazy,' she says shakily. 'The odds were overwhelmingly against you.'

'Yes, they were, weren't they? Just the same, I believed you would come.'

'I have to warn you,' she says, and there is something the matter with her voice, she has to struggle to make herself heard. 'I have a dangerous record. I'm a very bad risk.'

'The worst risk is never to take any,' he says gravely.

And she feels, suddenly, a rush of warmth and radiance, like a bird that has accidentally, miraculously, flown into a lighted hall. *What comes before and after we know not* ... Oh, almost certainly there will be another door, and some future current of air will push her, or suck her, into darkness again. But she doesn't care.

# alyson hallett

## *bone song*

Small town, we pull into some small town with a name too long to remember. It's hot and still. Heat runs in rivers down the street. Midday shadows crush in on themselves. Like a fist.

I wonder how many others have passed through here. Drifted across this vast continent like ash.

We park the car and leave the engine running. Listen to Kurt Cobain singing 'No Denial', over and over, the thrash of guitars like storm waves pounding on a tin hut. He's got the call of the wild in him. Makes my hair stand on end.

– I'm tired, Mark says. He slumps over the wheel. Forehead resting on his knuckles.

– Hang in there, I say.

Just yesterday we were the other way around. Me down him up. People are seesaws. Not people, but whatever it is that goes on between them. Relationships.

We've been going out for two months, two days. Nonstop crazy loving. Feel like I've found a part of myself that's been missing for ever. And the mad thing is, I didn't know it was missing until I found it.

I've known Mark all my life. Even knew him before we were born, if you can believe that. We played together when we were toddlers. Sat next to each other in school. Spent as much time in his back yard as my own. He went away for a few years when I was thirteen. His dad was in real estate and thought going north would make him his fortune. I missed Mark like mad when he was gone, but when they came back, everything was different. His father was broke. Took a job delivering papers and cleaning the local bar. Mark acted like a stranger. He was moody and wouldn't speak to me. He avoided me whenever he could.

I thought Mark hated me. I slammed doors and shouted at my mother. She told me God worked in mysterious ways. That there were plenty of other boys who were just as good as Mark if not better. I smashed her crystal glasses and she hit me with a stick.

Then everything changed.

The night before my seventeenth birthday I couldn't sleep. Or I'd slept for a while and then woken with this nutty idea that I should go down to the lake. It was a quarter past two. I closed my eyes. Counted sheep, dogs, peppercorns. But these words kept going round in my head; go to the lake. So up I got because there was no peace or point in lying there any more. Didn't expect to find anyone there. Least of all him. We smiled at each other, then I don't know who made the first move – I swear it was me and he swears it was him – but we were kissing and rolling around in the damp grass until the sun came up.

Never imagined I'd leave the town I'm from. With its straight-line grid of streets, landsweet air that hasn't touched sea for days. The huge harvest moon that hangs over corn fields in August. Thought I'd get a job in one of the stores or marry a farmer. But here we are. Miles from home. Running to godknowswhere.

We didn't have a choice. The morning I got back from the lake, my mother was waiting by the gate for me. I told her what had happened. Had no reason not to. And she starts muttering and wailing and going off her head. Something about the bird with a broken wing that hopped into the yard the day she gave birth to me. Omens. Forebodings. I said, Mum, I've kissed a boy. That's all. But she ran into the house, locked herself in her room and wouldn't come out.

The next day I found her in the kitchen. She was sipping sweet potato wine at nine in the morning so I knew something serious was up. That the carry-on of the day before wasn't a random fuse blow. No good comes of bad love, she said. I told her I didn't know what she was on about. Of course you don't, she screamed. Then added, I don't know how to tell you. Tell me what? She emptied her glass, refilled it, emptied it again. Mark's your brother, she said.

I laughed. What else could I do? She told me he was my twin, put out for adoption at birth because she already had five boys, no husband and a car with a broken carburettor.

Well I'm not stupid and neither's Mark. We agreed not to see each other ever again. But every time I went to the store, to the dump, to the river, there he was. It was spooky. Like something bigger than the two of us was at work. Conspiring to bring us together. Whenever he was near, my belly filled with butterflies. The smell of him made me shiver.

I cried long and hard for three nights in a row not knowing what to do. Then I thought, Hell. I love him. He loves me. If we want it to be, it's simple.

There was no way we could stay at home. My mother made that perfectly clear. I'll get the police, she said. I'll break your legs with a baseball bat. I'll do anything to stop you seeing him. So we left. In a clapped-out car that we stole from Mark's father.

We haven't got much money but we find what we need. You can get most things for nothing if you look hard enough. Food from bins. Clothes dumped in unlikely places. Flowers from gardens. The only thing we're really missing out on is sleep. Two people on one back seat isn't easy. We stayed in a motel for a night but the sheets were creased and warm and there were long black hairs all over the pillowcase.

We've agreed to be careful in bed. Neither of us wants a baby with two heads or a brain short of cells. I might have my tubes tied one day. We don't want children. Just each other. We're both sure of that.

When the song ends, we get out of the car. I take a deep breath and the air burns down my throat. Mark locks his hands together and stretches them high above his head. His blue T-shirt lifts a little and exposes his pale belly skin and button. God he turns me on. His face is tanned and smooth, eyes black as tar. We walk up the street, small clouds of dust puffing at our feet.

A shadow cuts across the path. The sound of wings beating. We look up and there's a huge bird, maybe an eagle, lumbering into the distance. Mark takes my hand and squeezes it. We don't talk much. No need.

There's only one place open. An old metal sign hangs above the door. *Pat's Place*.

The counter is covered with small china dogs. Pictures of stick people are pinned to the walls. Sea-shells strung up with red cotton hang in the window. After a minute or two, a woman swishes through a stripy plastic curtain. She presses a button next to the till and an overhead fan creaks into action. Her face is round and shiny as a full moon. There are faint lines around her eyes that deepen when she smiles. She could be twenty or eighty years old.

– What can I get you?
– Two cold beers, please.

She nods towards the empty tables behind us. Mark leads the way and sits at the one furthest from the window. He gets nervous sometimes. Thinks my mother might be putting Wanted adverts out on the news channel. Transmitting our faces into every home in the country.

The woman comes over with three beers and three glasses. She turns the radio on. Sits down.

– Patty, she says, then stretches her hand out. Mark takes it and shakes it.

– Hello, he says.

I do the same. Careful not to give my name away either. Patty smiles. Takes a long drink of beer then wipes her mouth with the back of her hand. On the left of Mark, there's a shelf covered in old boots and shoes. Patty sees me looking at them.

– We don't have photographs in our family, she says. Just boots and shoes and stories. The bottom of your foot isn't called a sole for no reason. No sir. And what gets closer to your sole than a shoe? Never worn socks in all my life.

Mark starts to giggle. Patty ignores him, stands up and goes over to the counter. Comes back with rolls stuffed with cheese and salad. She puts the plate in the middle of the table. I go to take one then change my mind. We haven't got much money left and the car needs gas more than we need food.

– Eat, girl, Patty says. I look at Mark and Mark looks at me. Eat! she says again and there's no way I can refuse her. And you, she says, nodding in Mark's direction. I'm starving. Eat so fast it's rude. When we're done, Patty moves the plate to one side and reaches down a pair of old brown boots from the shelf.

– Granny Pat's, she says handing them to me. I run my fingers over the toe, tongue, eyelets. My hands start to shake so I pass them on to Mark.

– It's a powerful pair that, Patty says. Belonged to Granny Pat. She built this place. Alone. Worked herself to the bone, but that was the point. She said if you could hear the songs in your bones, you could do anything. Five feet tall she was, with the will of a giant. She burned sage, offered prayers, then put one brick on top of another. When the walls were high enough she added a roof. To begin with, people didn't trust a woman who'd done a man's work. Then they got wise to the beer, music and wine and came all the time.

Mark puts the boots back on the shelf and a young girl comes in with three more beers. She looks like Patty.

– I'm Melly, she says. She gives us the drinks. Walks over to the window and plays with the shells. Her back's straight as a ruler. Patty burps loudly, then lights a cigarette. Exhales slowly, smoke rising in grey-blue ribbons.

We drink slowly. Sweat. Relax.

When the time comes to leave Patty refuses the money we offer her.

– No need, she says.

– Sure?

– Sure.

As soon as we're out the door Mark stops. Steps to one side and glances over his shoulder. Peers back into the café. Then he grabs my arm and starts pulling me along the street.

– What is it? I ask.

– She's up to something, he says. I saw her at the counter, speaking to someone on the telephone.

We jump into the car. Mark turns the key. Nothing happens.

– Shit, he says, then tries again. The engine's dead. Not even a clunk. He gets out and kicks the front tyre like that's going to make a difference. Puts his hands on the bonnet then takes them quickly off again.

– Shit, shit, shit. He runs his hands through his hair and I wish he wouldn't because it's sexy and now's not the right time. He gets back in, locks his door. Ahead of us, we can see Patty strolling down the street. In our direction. Blood drains from Mark's face. I put my hand on his knee. Take a deep breath.

Patty knocks on the window. I wind it down slowly. Heart beating so hard I can hardly hear her.

– There's a caravan, she says, behind the café.
– We're just waiting for the engine to cool down, I say.
– And an alley to put the car in.
– No need, we'll be off soon.
– Suit yourselves, she says.

A three-legged dog limps after her as she walks back down the street.

The first night in the caravan we can't sleep. Every now and then Mark pulls the curtain to one side and looks out. Nothing but blackness. Pitch black punctured with stars. And a silence so loud I don't believe it. Keep thinking I hear footsteps. Voices. Branches snapping.

In the morning, Patty gets the man from the hardware store to help push the car into the alley.

– We'll fix it today, Mark says, then we'll be on our way.

He's never mended an engine in his life. But he sounds so sure of himself that even I believe him.

– Sure, Patty says, whatever you want.

Every couple of hours Melly comes out with food.

The next day, she brings cups and pans.

And the day after that, knives and a chopping board.

Mark doesn't like it. But even he has to be vaguely grateful for the towels and soap. Gunk-like stuff to get the grease off his hands and arms.

By day four I'm bored. Low threshold. Mind like a cricket. So I go for a walk. At the end of the town I take a path leading up a hill into a pine forest. It's good and cool and dark inside. Pine scent so strong it makes me sneeze. I find a couple of cones and some blue feathers. Put them in my pockets like I used to when I was a child.

When I get back, Mark's given up on the car altogether.

He's lounging around on the grass. Drinking beer. Strumming an old guitar that Patty must have lent him.

There's no TV and no radio in the caravan and we still can't sleep. By two in the morning we're building goalposts with cups and rolling the cones around on the red formica table. Loads of tiny seeds fall out, so Mark stumbles around in the dark and fills a bowl with soil. We plant the seeds. Water them. Then I stick the feathers in the top because a bowl of earth doesn't look too interesting.

– What d'you reckon's going to grow? Mark asks. A bird or a tree? He starts tickling me, so I tickle him back. Then we're kissing and getting into each other like it's the first time.

We wake late the next day. Tired because we've slept. Every time I open my eyes all I want to do is close them again. So I do. It's like everything is catching up. Until I haven't got a clue any more where we're going or why we're going or what day of the week it is.

There's a tray of food sitting on the step when we finally get round to getting up and opening the door. No one's about so we sit on the grass and eat. The car a couple of metres away.

– What the hell . . .? Mark says, getting up and going over to it. He yanks the door open and inside there's a family of dolls and stuffed toys. Melly, he says, grabbing the toys and throwing them on to the grass. When they've all been evicted, he sits back down. We must have fallen asleep again because the next thing we know all the toys are back in the car and Melly's kneeling on the front seat. Giving a lecture about how dead people go to the moon when they die.

I shut my eyes but I can feel Mark next to me, restless and tense. Suddenly he's up and storming over to the caravan. Comes out minutes later with something shiny in his hand. The bread knife. I jump to my feet. Thinking he's really lost it this time.

– Mark! I shout.

Melly stops talking and turns round. She doesn't flinch, even though there's a madman walking towards her with a knife and me mad and screaming running after him. Then he does it. Kneels down and stabs the knife into the tyre.

– Mark? I say, but he ignores me. Melly turns back to her dolls and carries on where she left off. I'm shaking all over, but he's totally cool, humming and sawing at the tyre until a large chunk of rubber comes away.

– Mark, what the hell are you doing?

He stands up and turns to face me.

– It's dead.

– What do you mean, dead?

– Kaput. Dead. Useless. Understand?

I slap Mark in the face and run to the caravan. Throw myself down on the bed and start to cry. Tears that come from the bottom of my belly and make my body convulse like I'm having some sort of fit.

Mark's never seen me like this before. He puts his arms round me. I push him away.

– Leave me alone! I scream.

As soon as he heads towards the door I want him back.

– Don't go, I say.

He sits on the edge of the bed. Takes my head in his hands. Looks me in the eyes. And I suddenly realize that it's going to take for ever. Knowing each other. Puzzling out the different pictures we see when we look at the same thing. Being brave enough not to run away from the monsters or the angels.

# erica wagner

## *haircut*

6.30. I slap off the alarm and it falls off the table, cheeping again like a chick out of the nest.

'Jim . . .'

Linda puts her head under the pillow and her blonde hair fans out on her back. I grope on the floor and shut the thing up.

'Morning, honey.' It's amazing. I know I sound just the same. I've discovered something about myself, something I can do. The consolation prize. I haul myself out of bed and into the shower, pushing the water hotter and hotter until I can't take it any more, and then one more notch, or two. The steam scours my lungs and fogs the mirror. I don't wipe it. I've discovered I like shaving this way, taking that little risk. Sometimes I close my eyes completely. It feels like skiing, those fast, steep slopes when you don't know what's around the next bend. Mysterious. My own face. Three days ago it occurred to me that maybe I just can't stand to look at myself anymore, but I put that thought out of my head completely.

I leave the house like I always did. Camel jacket, nice tie. A present from Linda. Smart but casual, something out of a window at Saks. 7.15 and Lin's just awake, a steaming cup of coffee by her bed, brought to her by me. I said to her five years ago, Nothing's too good for you, sweetheart, and I meant it. I still do. Her face is soft and floury from sleep, without her make-up, looking like anything might happen to it. It's a hard world out there. I lock the door behind me. I protect her. Not that she can't protect herself, believe me, she can, and she won't let you forget it. So I protect her, but I don't tell her. It's a secret between me and me.

I have a cup of coffee at Big Nick's round the corner. I buy the *Times* and read it, folded up into neat quarters, while I drink. I sit there for half an hour, maybe forty-five minutes. They don't mind. Stefano, he pours my second cup, he knows me. 'Mista Gol'man,' he says, and nods. I forget how he learned my name. I've been coming in here for years. I'm a good customer. Maybe I'll give him a tip at Christmas. Sometimes I think we're in a conspiracy, Stefano and me. But he doesn't know either. No one knows.

Eight o'clock and there's more than a buck shot. I have five, all ones. I keep them in my inside jacket pocket. A day's allowance.

It's getting cold now. I've got my tweed coat – Ralph Lauren – over the camel jacket and a dark cashmere scarf wrapped tight around my throat. The air has that rasping winter bite, like someone slapping your cheeks. Wake up! It says. It also says: Get to work! but I don't listen to that one. I walk. I tell you, I'm a healthy guy these days. It's a good thing I never let myself buy a cheap pair of shoes. I've got a lot of mileage ahead of me. I tuck the paper under my arm and I set off at a good clip across the park. The naked trees arch over my head, like cathedral spires.

I'm a student of human nature. That's my new job. The old one, well – I guess I knew it was coming. Who doesn't, these days? I'm leaner and meaner myself. I don't think about that revolving door, spinning and spinning behind me, the sidewalk a new, wide-open space.

Maybe I'll write a book someday. The things I could tell. I get across the park – I walk uptown, so I come out at 90th Street – and already they're lining up to get into the Guggenheim Museum. The first time I saw this, I thought they must all be foreigners, but they're not. They're mostly Americans, and they come from New York, too.

I get another coffee from the stand parked on the corner. Seventy-five cents, which is too much. But it's fucking cold this morning. The wind hits my head and I wish I had a hat.

'Sandy!' Somebody comes up behind me and shouts in my ear. I'm not Sandy. I turn around but the guy's not looking at me. Sandy's in line behind me, standing with her girlfriend. She's cute. She's got short dark hair and a lot of lipstick, and red woollen mittens. The girlfriend's pretty cute too. I know, I know. But like I said, I'm a student of human nature. I can't help it.

'Art?' I think Sandy hasn't seen Art in a while. I step away and turn my back to them so I can listen.

'Hey, Sand, what's up? Long *time* no see. Nice to meet you . . .' he says to the other girl.

'Uh, Art, this is Felicia. Felicia, Art.'

'Nice to meet you, too.' This is the girlfriend talking. She doesn't sound convinced. There's this negative vibe coming off Sandy: I can feel it from here. But I think Art is oblivious.

'Doing the culture-vulture thing, huh? I guess the early bird catches the worm.' Art, master of the English language.

'Well, you know. We didn't think there'd be a line this early. Looks like everyone thought that.' She laughs. She's stuck, standing in line. It's Art that has to walk away. The coffee's terrible. I take another sip.

'Looks like it. But hey, did you get my message over the holidays? I left a couple on your machine but there were so many fuckin beeps I thought maybe it was on the fritz or something. I wanted to ask you about this new project that Steve's got going.'

'Steve?'

'Hey! Come on! Steve, Steve Bassett! He used to work at Dano's, remember? I know you remember. Anyway, he's got this new thing going at a gallery down on Spring – Canal? – Spring, I think – anyway, you know, conceptual, video, virtual reality, all that shit. The up and coming. We were having a few drinks the other night and he was laying it on me and I thought, Sand! This is Sandy's kind of thing! She's got to hear about this! And look at that, I run right into you here. It's karma, right?'

'Um ... Art? I'm at law school now.' Her voice goes quiet. Lawyers, I guess, aren't into the conceptual shit.

'So I—you what? You're kidding.'

'No kidding. Columbia.' She's smiling now, I can hear it. She should be. She'll make a fucking ton.

'No shit. Hey, good for you.' He blows into his hands and stamps. He's stuck. 'Well – I'll tell Steve. Maybe you'll come to the opening or something?'

'Right, Art. Leave me a message.' The line shuffles forward and their voices move a little farther away.

'I will, I will. Yeah, well. Anyway, good to see you, Sandy. Nice to meet you, Felicity.' His voice is a popped balloon. No shit, Art. Good morning. I drink my awful coffee through my teeth because I'm grinning. Art walks away.

'Feli*city*.' Felicia says.

'Don't get me started. God, it's like shutting the vacuum cleaner off.'

'He's *your* friend. From under what rock?'

They're giggling like teenagers now. They're almost at the front of the line. I turn around and throw my cup in the trash. That Sandy has a cute ass on her, too. Nothing like cold weather to get you thinking about women's asses.

I walk down Fifth, puffing into my scarf. This wind's coming down from Canada, I can tell you. It sucks the warmth right out of you and blows your hair to pieces. I keep pushing my hair out of my eyes and it just blows right back again.

That's when I think, I need a haircut. And I turn into this side street and what do you know, there's this barber pole right there. Karma, like Art said.

It's a weird place. A tiny little building all on its own, squashed between two huge expensive buildings, like a pebble stuck in a cliff face. It has a tin roof. I've never seen a tin roof in New York. The place is about the size of a bus, long and thin with one wall all mirrors, one of them cracked, and a border all around of colored glass. I put my face on the cold glass and my breath steams the door. I can't see anyone. The floor is mottled black linoleum. It's seen better days, this place. But I like it. I rattle the door handle. The door's locked. I rattle it again and rap my knuckles on the glass.

An old man comes out of a door in the back. He's got a barber's smock on, snow-white hair combed back just so and thick Buddy Holly glasses. He's holding a cup of something that steams. He gestures to me, pulling me in with his arm and smiling, and saying something that I can't hear. I rattle the door again and point to the knob. I make a big shrug with my shoulders like a clown. Fuck it's cold out here. Standing still makes me feel I just want to get inside, haircut or no haircut.

The old guy unlocks the door and I practically fall inside. My hair's all over the place. I can see his eyes, like fish in bowls through the thick lenses of his glasses, peering at it.

'I need a haircut.' I'm panting. It's so warm in here. It's nice.

'I can see,' he says. 'Have a seat.' He snaps a cape off a big old leather barber chair with a ringmaster's flourish. His fat little finger has a thick gold ring on it. I go to sit down and then I remember.

'How much?'

'Cut and shave?'

'Just a cut.'

He's staring at my chin now. But there's nothing I can do.

'Twelve dollars fifty cents.' He's got this little accent. Italian, maybe. I read once that all the good barbers are Italian. I'm in luck. But twelve fifty. That's steep for me. And I've only got three and a quarter now. But I don't care. I've got to have this haircut. A man needs a haircut. What's Lin going to think if I start coming home with my hair all over my ears, curling down my collar like a dead man's?

'I've got to go get some cash,' I say. 'I'll be right back. Hold the chair.'

'Yes sir,' he says. He doesn't smile. He's what I guess you'd call grave, like he takes all this very seriously. I head out the door and the freezing wind attacks my head again.

There's a bank on the corner of Madison. I keep my cash card in the back of my wallet now, behind all the old receipts and dog-eared business cards ('Here – can I give you my card?') so I have to hunt for it in the wind. Someone stands behind me. A man in a suit, a man like me.

'Sorry.'

He grimaces at me and I assume it's a smile. The brotherhood of men. Don't look now, buddy, you're next, is what I think.

The card slips into the machine with a smooth, sexy click. I do everything the machine tells me to do but when it flashes my balance on the little screen I look away. Once a month I make myself look. But today I just ask for twenty dollars and the machine offers me two new tens. I slip them in my wallet, no big deal. I used to take out a hundred at a time, sometimes two. I wonder how much Smiler behind me takes. I walk away and we nod at each other, ships in the night. So long, pal.

The barber's waiting for me. Opens the door and ushers me in, reaches up to take my coat from my shoulders. He's really very short. But stocky, like you wouldn't want to mess with him. When I get in the chair he has to pump it right down so he can reach my head.

And there's my face in the big mirror right in front of me. Long time no see. I smile at myself. I stare. I forget that the little guy's watching me. I try to figure out how different I look. I'm looking for lines. I see them, but I'm sure they were there before. It's not so bad. I smile again. I've got good teeth. I've always been proud of my teeth.

'Mister.'

I jump like I've just woken up.

'What you want?'

Jesus, my heart is going in my chest. 'Short back and sides. Just short back and sides.' I talk to him in the mirror. He nods and pushes his heavy glasses up on his nose. There are long, skinny scissors on the cluttered shelf in front of me, the real old barber's kind with a tail coming off one of the loop handles, and he picks these up and shoots his cuff. His pinky, the one with the ring, rests on the tail. He takes up a thin black plastic comb. Then he takes my chin in his right hand, puts his left on the back of my head, tips my head forward and gets to work.

When I was a kid I used to hate to have my hair cut. My mother used to take me to her hairdresser, out in Brooklyn, where we lived, and one of the girls would cut my hair. Sitting with my neck bent over, staring at my shoes, I can still smell the hairspray stink of the place. The girls had sharp red fingernails that always seemed to catch in my ears and I hated the bright pink smock they wrapped around me. I used to keep my eyes shut the whole time. It was humiliating. 'Time for a cut, honey,' my mom would say, pushing my bangs out of my eyes, and my stomach would shrink right up inside me. What was I afraid of? That one of my friends would see me. And of course one of them did. Just once, but it was enough. *Jimmy goes to the beauty parlor.* I tell you, I never thought I'd live that down. It was why I grew my hair in college. I wasn't any kind of beatnik. It was just such a relief not to have my hair cut.

But I got over it. And this is okay. The barber puts his fingers under my chin again and lifts my head so I can look at myself again. I can't see any difference, he's just been going at the back. There's a Christmas card propped by the mirror, a big one, with green holly and red berries. It's a little open. To Frank, it says, Thanks and Happy New Year. Next to it there's an old framed photograph of a guy with swept-back black hair and Buddy Holly glasses and a serious face, standing outside a building, maybe a school. Is it the barber? Frank, the barber? I turn my eyes back and forth between the picture and Frank (maybe Frank is someone else, the barber's partner, but I'm pretty sure this is Frank behind me). It's hard to tell. You'd think it would be easy but the picture is like a thousand others from thirty years ago. It could be my dad. He had glasses like that. I think everybody did. I want to ask the barber if it's him but his serious face stops me. He's concentrating on my hair and that's good. He takes my hair between his fingers and frowns at it and snips, very fast, and the little hairs fall like rain on my shoulders.

There's a heater right by my feet and waves of hot air waft up the legs of my pants. A month ago I'd have asked him to turn it off – 'It cracks the leather of my shoes' – but a month is a longer time than you think. I settle into the heat and close my eyes and listen to the cheep, cheep of the scissors and the hum of Fifth and the heater like an ancient cat. He pulls a comb through my hair and snips, and pulls it through and snips, working back from my forehead and I can feel my head getting lighter and my mind clearer. It's a dead weight. When I'm gone he'll sweep my hair into a pan and throw it in the trash. He leaves me with only what I need. I open my eyes. He's watching my head in the mirror to see how I look. He's a student of human nature too.

'Okay?'

'Great.'

'This way, please.' He puts the scissors down, tips my head again, just this way – no, just that – and reaches into his pocket. Christ. I didn't think they made those things anymore. It's a straight razor. I stare ahead into the mirror. He adjusts his glasses on his nose and I hear a noise, whisht, whisht, whisht, as he sharpens the razor on a leather strop that hangs off the back of the chair and which I never noticed before. He blows on the blade and regards it in the dull white light like he's a surgeon.

'Just this way.' His fingers cup my chin and stretch the skin of my cheek. The cold razor rasps beside my ear, like a cat's tongue. I've never sat so still in my life before. I don't look in the mirror but at the cracked counter in front of me, which is all covered in little hairs of all different colours, like the linoleum below. It isn't very clean. I start to think about AIDS.

But then I remember it's Frank with the razor in his hand. Frank's an artist. I relax a little and he tips my head the other way and does the other sideburn, pressing on my face so I can feel my jawbone underneath. We both look at me in the mirror. It's a good haircut. It's sharp.

'Just natural, at the back?'

'Just natural, yeah.'

He tips me forward again and the razor catches the light, flashing in the mirror. It's so sharp that all I feel on my skin is cold, nothing else, while his left hand holds me steady. His fingers smell of flowers and are warm and dry, pressing gently on my forehead and holding me still and safe while the cut-throat brushes the tight skin over my spine. The thought I have at this moment is that I've never felt anything so good as his warm, sure fingers, that I never want to leave this shop. The thought is so strange and new that it makes me tremble, and for a second I'm afraid he'll cut me. But he won't. He won't.

# rosemary friedman

## *southern comfort*

I am well-travelled in all senses of the word. Five continents and four husbands. I don't make a big issue of either. I can go down with cramps, rashes, fevers, gnat bites, snake bites, stomach acid – anything that doesn't require major surgery – anywhere in the world and be my own physician. In my drugs bag I carry every pill known to man and then some, yet I haven't slept in twenty years. Twenty years is a long time.

I know you have panaceas. Hot milk. Cold milk. Hypnotism. Relaxation tapes. Sleep clinics. This therapy. That therapy. Leave me alone. I've swallowed the pharmacopoeia. I've heard your theories. I've tried them all. Twenty years is long enough. I get into bed. Or not. I fix my pillows. Goose-down, duck-down, feather, fibre, rubber, synthetic, non-allergic, orthopaedic, square, oblong, crib, air-filled, water-filled. Even hops. Hops! Sometimes I pick up a book. Then the whole damned pantomime begins. A blue pill, then a yellow, then a white. Like candies all night long. I drop off for an hour, two maybe, till my whole body shrieks out 'pill' and I fumble like a drunkard for the water carafe. Those to whom sleep is no problem, 'balm of hurt minds', 'sweet nature's second course' and all that garbage, cannot hope to understand. They will never know how long are the small hours or how empty though peopled with forgotten voices, fragmented places, familiar and recurring anxieties. They will never know the blind panic which comes with the first tongue of light as it identifies like an aching tooth the hairline cracks in the dense drapes, with the first note of the earliest bird signalling the utter desolation of yet another *nuit blanche*. They will not have yearned, prayed, wept for oblivion that will not, no matter what the pill nor the strength of it, descend. They will not know what it means to lie, more vigilant, more alert, than in the day, wide-eyed, the senses painfully aware, while the old snore and the young coil innocently like snakes round sleeping partners, and golden babes with flickering eyelids quietly breathe away the night plucking at the blankets with scaly fingers like those who are about to die.

At such times death would be welcome. Don't think I haven't considered it. Unconsciousness at any price. Anaesthesia, concussion, it doesn't need to be natural.

It comes, of course, sleep. If you can call it that. Ten minutes, twenty, before it's time to rise. Although there's nothing to rise for, 6.45 am is my wake-up time and that's when I wake up. Wake! Well I open my eyes from the few minutes' respite that was the night and wonder whether with my arid mouth, my reverberating head, the raw orbs that pass for eyes, my snarled-up nerves, it is possible to make it through another day. One way it is possible. Only one. Across the room is my lifeline, my life. Appraising the shape of the familiar bottle with its reassuring label, I know that only with its help will I manage to traverse that no man's land of time that lies between now and the next confrontation with the enemy.

There are doctors, you say. Doctors bore me. They agree I am an interesting case, although it's my money that interests them. Who can blame them? A wealthy widow with an art collection worth tens of millions of dollars (husband number four) and as much again in the bank. Old money.

Milward brought me to Jamaica the last Christmas before he passed away at the wheel of the Merc. An insulin-dependent diabetic, he succumbed to a coronary infarct. It was on the cards. Macabre as it may seem, Jamaica is the only place in the world to which I have remained faithful.

Jamaica, with its Blue Mountains and undulating fields of sugar cane, where the lukewarm waters of the Caribbean lick the white sands to reach the coconut palms and red-leaved almond trees. Jamaica, land of cloves, of cinnamon, of spice, with its yellow corato and hibiscus, its oleander and its jasmine and its fragrant jacaranda. It is for none of these that I return, as faithfully as the humming bird, the moment the Christmas trees appear in the windows of Park Avenue. It is not for my cottage where the bougainvillea and thunbergia hang sweetly from the pergola and tiny lizards drop on to my breakfast table with its moist bowl of papaya, water-melon and nazeberries. It is not for Agatha my maid, dark as night and golden of heart, who will be there waiting, nor for the daytime song of the blackbird, the chorus of the evening crickets with the solo call of the bullfrogs. It is neither the ever-changing colours of the mountains nor the rainbow curtain of the falls that brings me back to the island year after year. It is for oblivion. It does not come cheap.

The cottage Milward rented, and which I ultimately bought, was in a complex of privately owned hillside properties not too far from the facilities of the main hotel. It has no name. Only a number.

That first Christmas, the last we were to spend together (if you can call it that), there was an urgent message from New York waiting for us on our arrival. Milward said it was a crisis, but I guessed it was nothing more urgent than the charms of his latest PA – a raven-haired girl young enough to be his granddaughter – and without waiting to unpack, he headed straight back to JFK, saying he'd be back in a few days and leaving me in the care of Agatha.

I never take more than a cup of clear soup and a little cold chicken or beef at lunch. Agatha told me that if I was tired from the journey she would call room service and have it brought to the cottage. I wanted to take a look at the place however, and find out who was staying there – we never did the circuit without bumping into someone we knew – so I showered and changed and took the cinder path in my gold mules, through the soursops with their heavy prickly fruits and the giant flame trees towards the restaurant, which was set on stilts and open on all sides.

There was the usual mix of well-heeled travellers in exotic leisurewear lifted straight from the winter holiday pages of the women's magazines. It was the year of the sarong, which, cunningly tied and in bright colours, looked, according to the fashion gurus, particularly alluring in the crystalline light of the tropics. I recognised poor blank-eyed Poppy Wilmington whose elevator no longer quite reached the top storey, and the Hailey-Whites, my neighbours in the Hamptons, and waggled a couple of fingers in greeting as I was seated by the captain at a prime table overlooking the ocean from where I could see the vultures, or buzzards (I never know which is which), swooping then rising again over the coral reef.

I sat, gold linen napkin in my lap, fortified by the Southern Comfort I had imbibed before leaving the cottage, feeling only moderately self-conscious at my unaccompanied state, when a soft voice said, 'Good morning, Madame. My name is Carstairs. I'm the maitre d'. Today I can recommend the lobster and the red snapper papillot or you are welcome to help yourself from our luncheon buffet...'

I looked up.

Six foot three and dark as velvet. Bamboo slim with an exquisite head, flat ears, moist eyes, and a slow smile which revealed impeccable teeth, only one of which was gold. He stood motionless, his pale-blue tuxedo elegantly draped round his spare frame, his notebook poised, ready to take my order. He did not stir, yet I knew that when he did his movements would be fluid, effortless.

'Carstairs,' I said, as much to test the name out on my tongue as anything else.

'Madame?'

'You can bring me a little bouillon and some beef. Rare. I seldom take anything more at midday. And Carstairs . . .'

'Madame?'

'After lunch I should like to discuss my menu for tonight.'

Throughout lunch he did not come near me. Lithe, boneless, his lapis studs winking from his frilled shirt-front, he attended to his duties, conducted his orchestra, the darting eyes missing nothing, the commanding presence everywhere, gliding smoothly between the tables, greeting, directing with the merest wave of the menu. Coordination itself. And so beautiful.

Over the bouillon on which floated a green *julienne* of scallions, I laid my plans. I always got what I wanted. My four husbands had seen to that. There was nothing that did not have its price.

I only played with the beef, realizing that it was not going to be easy. I knew what I was up against in this part of the world where the white man no longer ruled and the destiny of the country had long been in the hands of the native population. I guessed how it would be with Carstairs, but I was not accustomed to being thwarted.

I refused coffee and dessert and waited until he came soft-footed to my side. I kept him waiting.

'Carstairs,' I said when I was ready. 'Tonight I should

like to have a lamb cutlet and a little green salad. French dressing. I am not a big eater. I don't care for fancy food...'

He inclined his head and made a note on his pad, the pale undersides of his hands gleaming.

'I shall have it in my cottage. Number fourteen. My husband is away on business.'

'No problem.'

'I would like you to bring it yourself.'

The pencil stopped and I could hear the clatter and chatter of the restaurant.

'That will not be possible, Madame.'

I placed my used napkin on my plate.

'Carstairs, in this world everything is possible. What time do you close the restaurant?'

'After the last guest has gone.'

'That will do very nicely.'

Signing the bill for my meagre lunch, and without looking at him, I returned to my cottage.

I suppose he checked me out. Mrs Milward Sandilands Burrows who could feed his entire family for a year on what she spent each week at the beauty parlour. Mrs Milward Sandilands Burrows to whom to say no was to risk losing a job for which the fight had been long and hard and which could never be regained.

I have said enough for you to have cottoned on to my secret. There had been men before (apart from my husbands), rough trade I suppose you'd call it, and there would be men again. It was part of my sickness and I could no more live without them than I could contemplate a day without my Southern Comfort. You would be surprised if I told you how many men are available to a pampered, bloated and grossly overweight 'blonde' crossing the frontiers of old age, even if they are not available.

Back in the cottage Agatha had unpacked. I passed the

afternoon between the percale sheets of the cool bed to dispel the fatigue of the long journey.

At six o'clock I went over to the hotel where a boy from Italy, who wasn't at all bad-looking, fixed my hair. I had my nails done too, mainly to pass the time.

Agatha helped me dress in a pale-blue *peignoir* with a matching Alice-band. She tidied the cottage and left a thermos of ice-water and some fruit and cookies in the icebox. She changed from her pink-checked overall into a cotton dress and armed with the inevitable umbrella against the tropical rains which came without warning, she bade me good night, telling me that she would see me in the morning.

It was nine o'clock and the steam heat of the evening swallowed every particle of air. I sat fanning myself on the lamp-lit patio and watched the limos ferrying the guests from the cottages to the restaurant. I thought of them at table, Carstairs waiting upon them. After a while I grew tired of looking at the dark palms and starry sky and listening to the cacophony of the night. I went inside and closed the shades and switched on the air-conditioning. I didn't much like the noise of that either.

The black-and-white ceramic tiled floor of the sitting room was strewn with cane mats woven in the intricate circular pattern indigenous to the island. On every table there were bowls of flowers – orchids, cups of gold, allamanda – freshly picked. They complemented the tones of the loose covers and the conch shells, open, obscenely pink, on the shelves.

I sat on the sofa holding an ancient copy of *Stories from the New Yorker* which someone had left behind, and settled down to wait.

It was not five minutes before there was a discreet knock on the door.

'Room service.'

It was not Carstairs.

Four boys carried in a round table, covered with a gold cloth, on which, beneath a silver dome, sat my solitary cutlet.

I ate slowly. Very slowly. I don't think anyone could have made a lamb cutlet last longer.

After a while they knocked again to clear away.

'Was there anything else, Mrs Burrows?'

No, there was nothing else.

It was ten forty-five. I eyed the Southern Comfort and it looked me straight back in the eye. Although there was ice in the ice-box I had no mind to struggle with it. I took it straight.

The light in the bathroom was fluorescent strip. I looked a hundred. I went back to the sitting room and the rapidly diminishing bottle.

Towards midnight I began to hear the cars returning along the roads and over the 'sleeping policemen', taking the first guests back to their cottages.

At one a.m. there was a knock at the shutters. More of a tap really.

'Who is it?'

I opened, knowing.

He wore a white tuxedo, black satin revers, onyx studs and links. He had to incline his head to step inside. I noticed the gold signet ring on his finger, matching the gold tooth.

'I came to see if you enjoyed your dinner, Mrs Burrows.'

'The cutlet was very good.'

I had turned down the lamps and hoped I didn't look too bad.

'Is there anything else I can get you?'

I looked at him, tall, thin, handsome. I looked at him directly and noticed that the lashes curled upwards over the gazelle-like eyes.

'Yes, Carstairs,' I said softly, 'as a matter of fact there is something else.'

I led the way unsteadily into the bedroom, where Agatha had prepared only one of the twin beds. He hesitated for only a second, wondering about his job although he had had plenty of time to think about it. For one dreadful moment I thought he was not going to follow me, then I heard the soft fall of his feet.

Carstairs, Carstairs. In the limpid mirror of your eyes I was young, beautiful, desirable, needed, loved, possessed. The vaulted ceiling with its fan turning like a huge propeller over our sweating bodies was lovelier than the velvet night, stars thrown in for good measure.

He did not speak, did not lose his dignity, but was aware of my needs as he was instantly aware of the needs of every diner in his restaurant. Carstairs the virtuoso, I his violin.

Milward was away three days. For three nights I had Carstairs. For three nights I slept. No pills, no potions, no alcohol. Slept like a log, a baby. Slept like I was comatose. Slept till Agatha woke me gently opening the blinds.

When Milward came back bright and breezy with dark rings beneath his eyes, he took one look at me and commented that the rest had done me good. Yes, Milward, I said, I like it here. Jamaica has done me good.

That night we ate in the restaurant. Milward gave Carstairs fifty dollars to look after us. He slipped it into his pocket. I did not raise my eyes above the wine-red tuxedo which skimmed the mobile hips.

It's five years now since Milward died. At Christmas time his wealthy widow can be found at her hillside cottage in Jamaica where, in the afternoons, she disappears, alone, and in a taxi, often for several hours. Although the other guests assume that she is visiting the Craft Market, they find it curious that she returns empty-handed, with neither the ubiquitous straw hat nor souvenirs of hand-dyed batik.

In between times she is to be found in her Park Avenue appartment where sometimes, in the small hours, she puts on a CD and with a far away look in her eyes moves rhythmically to the beat of a calypso: 'Annie Palmer' (she was a wicked witch), 'Tak' Him to Jamaica' (where the rum come from), 'Yellow Bird' and 'Island in the Sun'. Like many women of her size she is surprisingly light on her feet.

She knows that some day she will become old – old old – and that Carstairs will move on. Until then, as soon as the first flakes of snow fall on Park Avenue, she picks up the telephone and books her flight to Jamaica. It's a long way to go for a good night's sleep.

# lorna thorpe

## *the dead lie down*

Martha stands in the kitchen, her bare feet blue with cold against red-earth ceramic tiles. She slots her feet into fourth position, the way Sammy always did on Martha's linoleum floor only Sammy always did it easier with her spindly legs, her fine blonde hair fanning round her face as she spread open her arms and said, 'There, Mummy, it's easy. Easy-peasy.' But Martha had never found it easy, even when the muscles of her legs were sprung with elasticity, even when her flesh didn't crinkle like the loose skin of an old peach. And now. Now sharp pains strike at her thighs and she can almost hear the creaking of her rigid bones as she forces her feet into position. Breaking bones would be more bearable, she thinks, a clean snap, a plaster to mould the splintered pieces back together again. A few weeks or months to recuperate. You'd never walk exactly the same again but you would walk. And talk, and laugh and cry.

And cry.

When they walked into this kitchen six weeks ago, Martha and Giles both stopped at the doorway, held their breath and turned to one another. This was uncharacteristic of Sammy: the teetering piles of dirty dishes in the sink, the half-empty wine glasses sticky with fingerprints cluttering the draining board; the cut loaf of bread, hard and mouldy, its crumbs as brittle as crisps; the stench of rotting vegetables, rancid butter, stale booze.

Three days she'd been missing then and now it's six and a half weeks. Martha dampens the unused yellow J Cloth and wipes the work surface repetitively, back and forth, back and forth over the same mark of grease. No message, no reason. No bloody reason for God's sake. I mean, look at Sammy's life. The lead in a new production this winter, Richard who was completely in love with her, friends, family . . . Martha pulls open the drawers and rifles through their contents, slowly at first, then furiously, tumbling papers and knives and forks and loose matches on to the kitchen floor, ripping a fingernail on a sharp corner. She feels hot tears jabbing at her eyes and then they're loose and she's throwing everything on to the floor, kicking the cupboards and not caring where it all came from, not caring about replacing every item neatly, just the way she'd found them. Not caring at all, just looking. Looking for the one piece of paper missed by the detectives who pulled the place apart (until they'd ransacked all Sammy's private moments and Martha had turned her eyes away from the intimate corners that a mother dare not disturb and yet a stranger, yes a stranger, could be at home there). The one tiny piece that would yield up the evidence, the clue.

The future.

Different mirrors give you different faces. In this one Martha believes she's younger, the spring still in her skin, a sparkle still wetting the corner of her eyes. People tell her she looks young for her age but mostly they see her from a distance. It's only Martha who catches off-guard sideways glances or the unforgiving full frontal at the hairdresser's; chance encounters with brutal mirrors which remind her of her need to raise her chin, remind her of the encroaching looseness around her jowls. A slackness that causes her an itch of discomfort, a sharp wince of unwanted recognition.

Blinded by the harsh lights (professional lights, circular white bulbs planted evenly in the chrome border of the mirror), Martha wonders, for a moment, what she's doing here and then she remembers. She's here to bring her daughter back. She leans close to the mirror, expecting perhaps to see Sammy. But the bright lights obscure everything except the central reflection so that when you look into it you see nothing but yourself.

Nothing but yourself.

She has chosen her outfit. No more black, she won't wear black now unless ... and so, even though it's winter and she would normally wear black tights, her stockings are champagne. She glides the stockings over her legs, snaps the fastenings over the seamed tops and stretches out a leg. They may not bend as easily and the flesh may crumple a little around the knees but they're still shapely, you could still look at her legs and take her for thirty, maybe even younger, as young as they feel when she slides her palms over their sheer silkiness. And she has to admit that they'd been a surprise, the stockings, you never think. Too busy looking at the surface to worry about what lies beneath. And she'd blushed when the detective had pulled the stockings from her daughter's drawer like a magician drawing silk scarves from a hat.

Sitting at the dressing table in her underwear, Martha sips white wine, the glass beaded with cold. Once it would have been a cigarette too and she remembers the box of duty-free that fell out of the kitchen drawers earlier. She tosses the argument back and forth but it's only a game, she knows she has already made her decision and she takes her glass with her for a refill as she pads in stockinged feet to the kitchen.

What the hell.

This is not a time for caution, after all. There has been too much caution and tonight is not a night for it. For one, she doesn't have to drive. There's a taxi booked. What lightness, what freshness there is in this getting ready with no arguments about who's to drive; with no need to be the keeper of domestic knowledge, the guardian of cream linen suits that have lingered forgotten at the dry cleaners, of cuff links that disappear into dark crevices of the house, of shoes that contrive a dusty materialization in the garage. Giles tells her she remembers these things because she is a woman, because she has a mind for details and she imagines the machinery of her mind clogged with the grease and dirt of twenty-five years of household rubbish. And she pictures an intelligent thought trying to work its way through a sludge of rotting information (like how many cans of tomatoes they have, and what day the bin men call and which suit and tie Giles last wore to the Campbells'), but the thought gets stuck in a swamp of half-remembered tips for using leftover chicken, and she gives up.

Back at the dressing table Martha lights the cigarette. The smoke tastes acrid, like summer rain on hot dusty pavements. She inhales cautiously, the smoke grates like sandpaper against her throat and she coughs, holding her hand at her neck and glancing up at the mirror, her attention caught by the redness of her face blurred behind a fine splattering of saliva on the glass. Next time she holds the smoke in her mouth but the taste is of chemicals and the urge is to suck and the smoke she lets loose billows in front of her face in a grey riot. But the body soon adjusts, the body seems to take up its forgotten vices with an ease that makes you feel guilty for ever having deprived it. Her throat stops itching and her lungs, which had seemed to contract in fear with the first inhalation, gulp up the smoke as if they were hungry for it, starved of it. Martha remembers the very first cigarette; crouching behind the bushes on the rec, the nausea, the choking, but it was cool, so very cool, and then she remembers the way she used to practise. She faces the mirror, her elbow resting on the glass top of the dressing table: holds the cigarette between extended fingers, captures a mouthful of smoke, releases a small amount to suck through her nose and then inhales deeply, blowing the digested smoke out in a long stream which clouds her reflection.

And she grips the edge of the seat when the dizziness takes hold. Closes her eyes, just a little, as the room spins around her, tilts, spins again and her heart thumps as . . . Geoff Manning holds out a hot hand to steady her and later, as she scratches a coded entry in her diary and listens for the creak of the top stair, she stubs out her cigarette on the lid of an empty packet, throws the dog end in with the others and slides the smelling pack along with the diary beneath her rumpled pile of treasured pink and yellow angora sweaters.

The smallness of her had always made Sammy seem vulnerable. The thin legs, even though they were packed with dancer's muscles, never looked strong enough to hold her up. Martha always thought Sammy would snap, or be blown away in a strong wind. Not that she, Martha, was strong. Not thin like Sammy but soft, a layer of plump padding covering her bones. She squeezes the flesh on her arms and it creases, takes a moment to fall back into place after she lets go and she does it again, squeezing harder this time until she can feel the pressure pulsing through her fingers as they push against one another. It seems she can never hurt herself enough.

Although she is readily hurt. That coating of flesh has the delicacy of a baby's skin: soft, permeable, fragile. It's the same as her mother's and hasn't she always hated the way her mother can't fend off the world; doesn't she despise the seeping wounds that never heal, the pulpy, child's flesh that soaks up all the badness and then wrings it out in stale old tears? Sammy had – *has, goddam it* – Giles's flesh and Martha's glad for her because while his flesh will furrow and frown itself into old age, it is dry enough to form a barrier. Yes, strong as a suit of armour and while there may be chinks at least they might let in the light; at least they're not gaping great holes that let in every mote of dust carried on every passing wind.

The wine tastes good. She swirls it round her tongue and over her teeth, soaks it into her gums, trying to capture every last bit of flavour. *Savours* it. Free of guilt, packed only with the fruits of pleasure, she takes another intoxicating mouthful. Is it true that there are no cuff links to be found, no shirts to be ironed, no one to please but herself? All this and the anticipation of meeting someone later, no dragging the dead weight of that night's argument between you like a drunk beyond the stage of colour, beyond wit, beyond charm.

Then she pulls herself up, tells herself to remember, that this isn't about her, for God's sake, it's about Sammy.

But it's so difficult to *forget*. Why, here she is now at the hi-fi, seeking out something, she's not sure what but then she finds it and, good God, it could even be her copy, she remembers giving it to Sammy when she first left home. Martha blows the dust from the stylus and lowers the arm on to the record. 'Vinyl' they call it these days, as though what it's made of is more important than what it contains. With the volume jacked up so she can hear it in the bedroom, Martha dances back up the stairs.

Wicked woman, she thinks, you are a shameless, wicked woman.

She hadn't expected Richard to agree. Especially when she said she didn't intend to tell Giles. But he was as desperate as her, it seemed, and she had taken only a few minutes to persuade him. Of course, most of the clothes didn't fit but she'd found a loose silk shirt among the neat rows of beautiful clothes draped so perfectly on their padded hangers that you could almost believe they'd never been worn.

Now, as she eases her head into the shirt and raises her arms so that the silk slithers down her skin, she begins to feel the weight of Giles's probable argument, wonders whether she shouldn't have told him. It's a foolish idea, and she was a fool for thinking of it and no doubt Richard was simply humouring her, the half-crazed mother thinking she could dress up as her daughter and re-create something that might spark a hidden memory, a word or a look forgotten in the mathematical details of dates and times.

Foolish, mutton dressed up . . . but the shirt doesn't make her look like Sammy, she still looks like Martha . . . Martha who has already made the boys moan more than they should but who is interested only in the groans of one: the one who'll be tucking his white shirt into his jeans right now, the one who will one day terrify her parents with the roar of his motor bike and the creaking of his leather jacket. The one who knows all the words to 'Just Like a Woman' and who sings them to her in a transatlantic drawl that sends shivers up her spine.

'She makes love just' . . . so many hopes in those words and she sees them reflected in the young face that stares back at her, framed by a rectangle of white bulbs. Is that what Sammy saw when she looked in the mirror? A window of dreams. Or did she see something else that night, a shard that cut into her dreams, a pin that deflated her hopes? Her dressing table was littered with the signs of her getting ready: make-up scattered over the surface, a fine dusting of powder, a pair of earrings, a hair-dryer, a brush (with strands of her fair hair woven through the bristles), an empty glass. And even though Martha and Giles insisted that it was unlike Sammy to leave without tidying up behind her, the police said there were no signs of a break-in, or of her having been disturbed, and one of them suggested that people change their habits, once they leave home.

We can all change our habits, thinks Martha, although the older you get the more they cling to you, shooting out new tendrils to wrap themselves round you like ivy cladding a crumbling house. Sometimes they eat away at you and sometimes they're the only thing that keeps you standing but the old ones, the old ones are easily remembered. Friday nights, Saturday nights. A new dress, a new man, the night ahead holding so much promise. She strokes foundation on to her skin with a nugget of sponge and dusts on powder with a large soft brush. In those days she hadn't used foundation, just a strip of colour on her lids, a lining of black round the rims and a frosting of light pink lipstick. False eyelashes on special occasions.

Special occasions. Hadn't every Friday and Saturday night been blessed with the spark of a special occasion? Martha sprays perfume on to her wrists and behind her ears. She teases apart the neck of the shirt and sprays her cleavage. They're the nights you live for, the nights you sacrifice the rest of the week for. The week spent going over the details of the last weekend, preparing for the next.

Had Sammy enjoyed the rituals as much? Or was she more casual about it, having so much else in her life? Because Martha hadn't thought of a career back then, only enough money to buy the clothes and the records and the cost of getting into the dingy little basement club and a few drinks and fags while she was there. Now and then some speed or a tab of acid. That she has a career now is more by accident than design. Marketing. No, she had never dreamed of marketing, never dreamed of anything except of love. And passion. Drifted from one meaningless job to another, until she just found herself there. With the word executive tagged after her name and a company car and an expense account. And a secretary who expects Martha to make her fair share of the coffee.

But Sammy had always had dreams. From the first set of ballet pumps there was no doubt in her mind, and none in Martha's either who had known the pain of bending double with indecision. She slips her feet into Sammy's shoes. And they fit! Their feet, if nothing else, are the same size and she *will* go to the ... is this sick? Is it sick to wear your missing daughter's clothes to go out to dinner with her boyfriend? Or is it madness? Sheer madness to think she could inhabit the mind of her daughter, that the rituals and the clothes and the expectations would summon the spirit of Sammy, drag her old thoughts into this room until they were as clear as if she'd left a message in lipstick on the mirror.


Martha purses her lips to apply lipstick. In the end she'd chosen matt russet, feeling her green eyes and softening skin would look washed-out against shocking scarlet. She presses the lipstick against her lips and when she looks in the mirror and hears the music she sees her poster of Mick Jagger on the wall and hears her father shouting up the stairs for her to turn the music *down*. She pictures Geoff waiting for her at the bus stop or by the pier, his hair freshly washed, the smell of Patchouli that seems to seep from his every pore and that clings to her clothes for days after. It will never be the same thrill with Giles. She'll love him of course, but there will always be a calm, cool voice telling her what a good choice Giles is, that Geoff might make her feel the wind through her hair and the ground disappearing beneath her feet but that he'll only take her as far as the trimmed edges of suburbia. That Giles has a bigger vision, a vision that embraces the sharp click of heels on city streets; the curled, dusty voices of foreign lands.

Did – *does* – Sammy love Richard? Deep down, Martha hopes she does. For all that she wants her daughter to be successful in her career she wants her to have good love and Richard has something of Geoff in him. Something deep and passionate, something a little wild, something that didn't suffer a pause when she asked him if he'd re-enact the last night, the night Sammy went missing.

And now Martha stands before the full-length mirror and gazes critically at her reflection. She's far too early . . . she always gets ready far too early but what else is there to do once you've gulped down your dinner (and they always go on at her about it, 'You'll give yourself indigestion,' they say. 'What's the hurry?'). What's the hurry? What else is there to live for but this? and once she's ready she poses in front of the mirror: front, side, back, smoking a cigarette, drinking from the bottle of cider she sneaks home and hides under the bed each Friday.

She hears the clicking of a door downstairs, hushed voices, and she thinks no doubt they're moaning about me again and Dad'll bellow up the stairs for me to turn down the bloody music. That was Mrs Henderson from next door complaining about it, he'll yell, and you know her son works shifts and the stupid old cow doesn't miss any opportunity to get her foot inside our front door and if you don't turn it down *now*, I'll come up the stairs and switch it off myself and then you'll be sorry, then you'll wish you'd listened to me in the first place.

And he is coming up the stairs, both of them by the sound of it, and Martha plays with her earrings, jet black and shiny as beetles, waiting for the creaky floorboard at the top of the stairs and she pulls a tissue from the box by the bed and rubs off her lipstick because he says only tarts wear lipstick and they must have mended the floorboard because she didn't hear it creaking but now the door handle is turning and they're coming into the room, shadows first, long and dark . . .

When Giles and Richard walk into Sammy's bedroom they see clothes strewn across the bed and shoes scattered over the floor. Martha is crouching in the corner, brown lipstick smeared across her face. She is crying.

'Martha, Martha . . .' Giles reaches out for her and she shrinks away from him, hiding her face in a new silk shirt.

'Martha?' Richard squats beside her.

She looks at him angrily. 'You told him,' she spits.

'I . . . yes, I told him. I'm sorry. I thought he should know.'

Giles and Richard look at one another. They move to either side of her, place their arms under her shoulders and start to lift. Martha curls herself into a hard little ball, lashes out with her arms and kicks wildly at them, her shoes flung from her feet and scuttling beneath the bed.

'Leave me alone,' she screams, 'just leave me alone.'

The two men retreat, sit on the bed. Giles unfolds a scrap of newspaper from his jacket. 'Martha love, you have to listen. You can't bring her back. She's gone. Listen to this,' and he begins to read from the newspaper as slowly and clearly as if he were talking to a child. 'The parents of Samantha Willard were in court today as the coroner announced a verdict of suicide. The inquest, which had—'

'No! *No!*'

'The inquest, which had taken place . . .'

Martha crawls, reaching under the bed to retrieve Sammy's

shoes, then pushes herself to standing, holding out her arms to keep the two men at bay. She walks steadily towards the dressing table, like a drunk trying to balance on a straight line, and lowers herself slowly and gently on to the little stool. She sees a sprinkling of spilled ash on the glass surface and she tears off a wad of cotton wool, damps it with a drop of spittle and dabs up the ash. Then she takes a sip of wine and tears off more cotton wool. Not dead, she thinks, because the dead lie down; they don't sit before mirrors, they don't stroke their dry lashes with mascara. She looks into the mirror.

And sees nothing but herself.

Dear God, what a mess, what was she thinking of? All that time wasted and now she'll have to finish in a hurry. She hates to be late and Geoff hates it too. She spits on the cotton wool and then she draws it heavily across the tangled tracks of smeared lipstick and mascara, leaving small traces of fibre in their wake.

# joan diamond

## *the dowry*

Lucia sits in the courtyard of her grandmother's house. She embroiders the last pillowslip of her dowry. The fountain whispers to her as it plays low over broad green leaves. She listens and lets her soft back rest and seep into the thick stone walls. Her body is part of this house and cannot leave.

In the old Jewish quarter, the carved wooden door is bolted.

Outside, in another quarter of Córdoba, she knows that Rodrigo's mother is setting her table with the best silver. Tonight they are to celebrate.

Lucia's black hair rests on her shoulder, shining like a raven's wing.

Last night in her troubled sleep a grey cat entered her dreams. It perched on the high wall of the courtyard. As the full moon came closer, the cat turned to silver and began to wail. Soon the wailing changed into the deep, rounded voice of a contralto. The cat turned to her with tender longing in her eyes and Lucia knew this was her mother singing to her. All night she strained to understand the words and then finally, as she lifted out of her dream, she heard them clearly:

'We are sisters, sisters, sisters.'

How can my mother be my sister? Lucia wonders now as she stitches blue leaves round a pink sunflower. At seventeen she still has not given up her childlike habit of making nature over into her own colours.

Of course my mother can come to me, she thinks, because she is already dead and the dead can travel. Everyone knew that. The bell towers had no glass in their windows so the dead could come and go as they pleased. Lucia left her window ajar at night in the hope that her mother might visit.

But in all this time her mother had never come and now, just as she was about to be married, she came and sang to her.

'We are sisters, sisters, sisters.'


She takes a lilac thread and starts to make a fish in the sky above the pink sunflower. Yes, certainly it is a riddle, she thinks.

Lucia has been raised by her grandmother who is a Catholic.

'Your mother is with the angels, very safe, very safe,' she assured her granddaughter a long time ago.

Lucia's grandmother is a plump and practical Catholic who talks to God whenever she wishes, mostly while ironing. Inside the house through the open shutters, Lucia sees her grandmother ironing and by the constant movement of her mouth she knows that the late-afternoon conversation with God has begun.


As a small child, Lucia often watched her grandfather come into the courtyard at dawn. He started praying to God in a language she did not understand. The old man rocked back and forth on the stone bench in the courtyard.

The same stone bench that she is sitting on now. She rocks herself awhile.

But then her grandfather put his hands over his head and wept. Why did this have to happen? Later he stopped weeping and returned to his study. Simple food was brought to him there. He never ate with the rest of the household.

'Why does Grandfather weep and hold his head?' she asked her grandmother when she was still a child.

'Because God is telling him too many things at once,' her grandmother said.

'Why does he stay in his study all day and eat alone?' she asked.

'Because he is very busy writing down everything God said.'

Carved deep in the stone lintel above the door is a star of David. As a child Lucia thought that maybe God could see this star and it guided Him to the house and into the courtyard at dawn to speak to her grandfather.

She takes a yellow thread and begins to sew little eyes on the purple fish. She will never understand why her grandfather wept so much.

She remembers the one time she entered his study. Her grandmother was nowhere to be seen and Lucia followed the servant woman through the house, stepping quietly behind her skirts as she carried the tray of food to the furthest room in the courtyard.

Inside, the walls were lined with old books and her grandfather sat at his table, his long white hair brushing his shoulders.

He caught sight of her as she peered round from behind

the servant woman's skirts. His eyes were the palest green, like a cat's, and she saw that they had a fire in them.

He reached out one long, bony hand to her across his table covered in books and papers.

'My child, my child, you have come to me at last.' Then he wept and covered his head with his hands.

Not long after that her grandfather died. They buried the casket of his ashes under the stone bench in the courtyard.

Lucia feels better about her grandfather now he has stopped weeping.


The purple fish is covered in yellow eyes. She ties off the thread and cuts it. As she searches through her basket for a certain deep blue – she wants to make a raven in flight – she thinks of what she will wear tonight for the celebration. Deep blue for the sadness she feels at all she is to lose and amber for her trapped spirit. They will find her elegant in those colours but she will know their meaning. The amber belongs to her grandmother.

She puts down her sewing and walks into the cool house through the polished, tiled hallways to her grandmother's room. On the low mahogany dresser sits the carved jewellery box. It still smells of cedar. She picks it up and presses it to her face.

As she lifts off the lid of the casket she sees a folded letter under the little roof. That's something new.

The amber necklace lies sleeping and glinting in the deep velvet of the casket along with other treasures in ivory and silver. But she puts them all down and takes the letter.

Lucia sits on the edge of her grandmother's four-poster bed, careful not to rumple the lace counterpane.

On the letterhead are two angels intertwined and the heading: SISTERS OF MERCY.

## 182 *the dowry*

> My dearest Mother,
>
> Thank you for the news of Lucia's coming engagement. I praise the Mother of us all that we have so been absolved. I am fearful. They say that the children of incest bear offspring with tails. They say the sins of the fathers travel down unto the third generation. For my daughter's sake, tell her the truth.
>
> I trust in God for your judgment.
>
> Your ever-obedient daughter,
>
>         Rachael.

She folds the letter noticing an address in Granada. She puts the little roof back on the casket, returning the amber to the darkness.

Quietly, she walks back to the courtyard and sits down with her sewing. She takes up her small scissors and cuts an empty window into the sky above the purple fish with yellow eyes. Then she puts the scissors into her pocket and walks through the silent, tiled hallways to her room.

Below her window is the cedar chest with her dowry. She lifts the lid and takes out the first set of linens. She cuts an open window in each napkin and then in the table cloth. She continues through the pillow slips, the sheets, the counterpanes until the whole dowry lies like snowy mountains around her knees.

She puts the little scissors back into her pocket and takes the money saved in gold coins from underneath her carpet.

Empty-handed she walks through the house to where her grandmother stands ironing and talking to God. She is thanking Him for the fine match He has granted Lucia and is telling Him what a fine dowry she has made; the best in Córdoba.

'I have run out of black thread,' she interrupts her grandmother. 'I'll go quickly myself to the market.'

Her grandmother smiles and nods.

'You can wear my amber necklace tonight,' she promises.

Lucia walks into the bright street and down the hill to the open marketplace. She crosses the marketplace to the far end where the horses are sold.

'Is one of you returning to Granada?' she asks the traders.

The one with the beard up to his eyes nods to her in silence.

She takes a gold coin and holds it out to him.

'Will you conduct me safely to the Sisters of Mercy?'

He nods again.

Lucia rides behind the trader on a grey mare. In the fields the wheat has been harvested. Further along, silver oaks clasp the low-lying hills with their gnarled claws. Gradually the rising hills give way to mountains until finally she sees snow on the jagged peaks of the Sierras. Each night she cuts a little more of her raven hair off and buries it where she sleeps.

By the time she stands in front of the small door of the Sisters of Mercy, her head is as cropped as the wheat fields she left behind.

'I am Lucia, I have come to join my sister,' she says.

'Yes, we knew you would come.'

The old nun leads her into the cloister.

'They are all sleeping now. They have been praying,' the nun explains.

Lucia follows her along the stone corridors and into a room. They sit at a wooden table where a bowl of figs and a jug of water stand.

'Here.' The nun offers her figs. 'They come from our courtyard.'

Lucia dives deep into her pocket and takes out the scissors and the gold coins.

'I ruined my dowry,' she says.

'It was already ruined,' the old nun answers, 'but you can still sew.'

# catherine gammon

## *letter from an upstate prison*

*Dear Nita – ,* (the letter began) *I am told that you want to visit me here. This is not a good idea. I know why you want to come. I know what you are thinking. But your thinking is wrong in every way.*

It was written with flowing blue ink in a big round regular hand on the kind of lined yellow paper that comes in a pad, the top edges curled from being folded over the pad and frayed from being torn off it, and maybe from handling and rereading. There were many pages – the whole pad or more – and they had come, unfolded, in a big manila envelope with the return address of the state prison where Jimmy Rivers had been sent. The letter continued:

*I don't want you showing up here trying to save me. I don't want you saying what you think you know. I killed a woman I loved. I have to be where I have to be. I have to be here. So rest your heart easy on my account. Anything more that's bothering you, and I know what it is, you keep to yourself. You get on with things now. Get on with your life and don't give over to brooding.*

*That is all I have to tell you, for your sake, and I hope you will listen to what I tell you and take my advice.*

Here the handwriting changed slightly, as if he had

stopped writing, to think and maybe to read over his words. Then he began again:

I find I want to tell you about my life. Like this:

Profile: Jimmy Rivers. James. At twelve the owner of a gun. At seventeen thrown out of his mother's house to the streets, to hustle a while and then settle down, working here and there, illegal work at first, which was just as hard as work that was legal, if not harder, but paid better, then going to school one year and finding a talent and love for painting, working all the time – bike messenger, office boy, bouncer, bartender – strictly legit, except for not reporting the tips for taxes. He was popular and fast and slick. He let people teach him things, everyone, anything they wanted, white people, black people, Chinese people, Latino people, women and men, old and young, his mind was open to all of them and he took in whatever they offered, and sometimes he went back to school, although he was still without a vision for his future and loved wildness and sensual satisfactions and always seemed to crash on his bitterness against his mother, until eight years after she threw him out she dropped a dime and he went to jail and now to prison, fifteen to life.

Jimmy Rivers. Taller and older and stronger than you remember him, a stranger to you after so many years, driven by remorse now, and probably a little bit, in some unscientific old-fashioned sense, crazy.

*Behold, the devil shall cast some of you into prison, that ye may be tried; and ye shall have tribulation ten days: be thou faithful unto death, and I will give thee a crown of life. Behold, I have set before thee an open door, and no man can shut it.*

You know what they think of my woman here? The cops, I mean? Her name was Ileana. From Guatemala. An Indian woman. Part Indian, *mestiza*. Her girlfriend, who I also killed, was a black Dominican. Cops don't care about these women. They call them dykes, spic dykes, spic cunts, nigger spic dyke cunts. You understand me? Nobody cares that I killed them but me. Jealous rage, manslaughter two, easy plea, do a little time, maybe draw a suspended. Hey, cut a deal, boy. That's what they tried to tell me, the cops, the PD.

But your mother – your mother, white girl – her they cared about.

There's a man out there, a collaborator, a Mr Detective Errol Walker, who told me he was on my side, who wanted me to think he is my brother because he is a brown-skinned man, because he is, like me, descended from Africa and from slaves. But he is not my brother. I am a killer and in all things an enemy of the state, and Detective Errol Walker is a *policeman*. He is on the other side of life from me. He wants to be a righteous man but he is a collaborator and a slave to a system that disrespects him and disrespects me and disrespects Ileana and her girlfriend Virginia, and disrespects you too, Nita. Do you know how they talked about you? What made you into a freak? I'm sorry to say it, girl, but that's what you have become, going off into alleys with strangers at night.

Listen, Nita – the word:

*These are they which came out of great tribulation and have washed their robes and made them white in the blood of the Lamb. They shall hunger no more, neither thirst anymore, neither shall the sun light on them, nor any heat. For the Lamb shall lead them into living fountains of waters, and God shall wipe away all tears from their eyes.*

Let me tell you again about Jimmy Rivers. His mama is a Haitian woman who lived here thirty years. His daddy was a Baptist preacher and he never saw his face. Julian, his little brother – remember him? – he's in the navy now, on the USS *Missouri*, off the coast of Kuwait – Julian's daddy was a smooth-talking jiving man their mama would hardly give the time of day to until he ran off with her employer's little sister, and from that day onward she remembered him with hatred as the one real man and true love of her life. Jimmy Rivers's mama worked every day taking care of other people's children. She still is taking care of other people's children and she threw her own child out for what she thought was good for him and he went on and eight years later killed a woman he loved. Don't worry about him and your mama, which I know you are. He killed a woman he loved. It's the same if he killed your mama or not.

*For God shall wipe away all tears from their eyes; and there shall be no more death, neither sorrow, nor crying, neither shall there be any more pain: for the former things are passed away. And the Spirit and the bride say, Come. And let him that heareth say, Come. And let him that is athirst come. And whosoever will, let him take the water of life freely.*

I'm writing these words to you, Nita. I'm writing these words because I know what is troubling you, in your soul, and I also know the answer. The answer is not in the law, Nita. The answer is not in confession to the law. The answer goes beyond confession. Understand me, girl. Go wherever you have to go beyond confession. Go as I am going. Your mother is dead and it is the same. *I beheld there was a great earthquake, and the sun became black as sackcloth of hair, and the moon became as blood, and the stars of heaven fell unto the earth, even as a fig tree casteth her untimely figs when she is shaken of a mighty wind.*

Don't you worry anymore, I say. I know the truth and I have my reasons.


James Rivers. Jimmy. Part Haitian, part slave. Let me

describe for you, Nita, his interrogations. They went something like this:

– James Rivers?

– James Rivers is a slave name. I don't go by no slave name now.

– What's your name then?

– Don't have a name. You people, you took my name. You took my name when you took my fingerprints. You took my name from my mama and from her mama and from her mama before that. Now you want to take my life. But it started with my name.

– Fingerprints? What fingerprints? Did we take your fingerprints? You got that wrong James. We take your fingerprints you're under arrest. But you're not under arrest yet so nobody took your fingerprints yet.

– I'm not under arrest then maybe I'm leaving.

– Try again James.

– Maybe I should have a lawyer.

– That's only on television James. Bleeding heart fucking television. You know what kind of lawyer you're going to get here? Some incompetent bleeding heart dyke wimp liberal, that's who, glasses an inch thick. Maybe even a Jew. What kind of help you think some dyke shyster's going to give you James?


But maybe it wasn't like that. I remember their voices like out of the twilight zone. I remember talking, telling them about Ileana – I told these leering men about her. They were asking me about your mother.

– Did she humiliate you James? Did she humiliate you the way the dykes humiliated you?

– Someone else was in her bed. I couldn't see who. They were under the sheet, two of them, moaning. They didn't

know I was alive. I went to the kitchen and looked for a knife.
 – Why did you do that James?
 – She was my woman.
 – Why did you go to the kitchen James?
 – A knife. I wanted a knife. I was mad. My heart was thudding. I was a drum, exploding. My woman was in bed with another man. In the bed where we made love. In our bed. Fucking a man. What would you do?

They have no answer. They ask the questions, they say. Why a knife? they say.
 – Why not a knife?
 – You're a big man James. Why not fight? Why not use your fists? I'm asking you why a knife?
 – It came to mind.
 – Why?
 – Did. I don't know.
 – It wasn't because two days before, you killed another woman the same way with a knife from her kitchen?
 – I never killed any other woman. I never killed anybody first. Only my woman that night and the woman in her bed.
 – Were you sober James?
 – I was drinking.
 – What about crack?
 – What about it?
 – Did you do some crack James?
 – I never did any crack.
 – Cocaine James?
 – A little cocaine maybe.
 – What time was it?
 – After four.
 – The bars had closed.
 – Right.

– And you were in the bar.
– Right. I was in the bar.
– Were you drinking in the bar James?
– Sure I was drinking in the bar. I told you I was drinking.
– How long were you in the bar James?

It goes on like this, Nita. For hours it goes on.
– How long were you in the bar?
– Since, I don't know, midnight maybe. I was supposed to be at her place.
– You stood her up.
– She stood me up. She was supposed to meet me there, at the bar. I was late. She wasn't waiting. I kept calling. She didn't answer. Finally I went over . . .
– What were you drinking while you were waiting James?
– She should have been waiting there.
– What were you drinking?
– Vodka. I don't know. Vodka.
– What else did you have at the bar?
– What? I don't know. You tell me. What did I have?
– Cocaine.
– Somebody tell you that?
– You just told us James.
– I never told you that. I never said so.
– You did James. Was it the truth or wasn't it? Did you do cocaine that night or didn't you?
– I think a lawyer should be here before I talk to you.
– You don't want that. Some bleeding heart fucking Jew lawyer who can't get her eyes off your dick. Is that what you want James?

Like that. That's how they talked to me, these representatives of decency and law. Tell us about the dykes, he said,

the collaborating black man, Detective Errol Walker, but I
resisted him, I said it was my business, and he answered
me they were dead, that made it their business, and it was
all far away and unreal until finally I was telling them the
story again, how I went and got the knife and went back to
the bedroom, but in the bedroom it wasn't a man with her,
it was her roommate, another woman. I hear them laughing
under the sheets. I see their hands moving up and down
their bodies and I hear them laughing, both of them, I
hear their voices. I go cold—

But I can't stand talking to these guys anymore. I'm not
talking I tell them, I tell them to get me a lawyer.

– I didn't hear that James. Did you hear that D'Amico?


Hear what? says the other one, the white one, Sam
D'Amico, and they start pushing me, about you, about your
mother, until it turns out they know everything about me,
they get me going again, and I'm shouting at them, it's not
their business, I killed the woman I loved, I was drunk and
angry and crazy and I was in pain because she was fucking
another man who turned out to be a woman and she'd been
fucking her all the time I was in love with her, and I cried
and I killed the bitch. She was the woman I loved and
suddenly she went dead on me, she was a bitch and she
disrespected me, and her friend who I thought was my
friend was a bitch and disrespected me, and they were
fucking each other, and lying and laughing and disre-
specting me, and I could smell how they were fucking, the
smell was all over them, and I loved her. It is not their
business.


But the thing is, Nita, they're paying no attention. They
don't care about Ileana and Virginia. What they care about

is your mother. They kept asking me about you, asking me if I fucked you. When I said no, he said, Detective Errol Walker said, No, hunh? Why is that? You afraid of white girls? Afraid their mamas do you harm? I asked you did you fuck her James.

— We were kids.

— I think you fucked her James. I think you fucked her real good. She's a regular little whore these days. Maybe you taught her how? Didn't her mama think so?


I'm sorry Anita. It's what he said. Then he got to where he was trying to go.

— Your mother says Mrs Palatino drove her out of the building.

— She was behind in the rent. She was always behind.

— She told us she'd been behind in the rent before. She told us Mrs Palatino went to the landlords. Mrs Palatino was the cause of all the trouble. When you moved was when you started drinking and when you got into drugs and when you came home to your mother's house, no more than twelve, wearing a gun. That's what she told us James. All because of Mrs Palatino.

— Why don't you arrest my mama you looking for somebody who hated Mrs Palatino?

— James James James. Why did you use a knife on the dykes James? Talk to us James.

— Because it came into my mind. I told you.

— Not because you used a knife a few days before on Mrs Palatino?

— I told you.

— Were you having trouble with your woman before that night James? A few days before were you having trouble with her? For a few weeks or even months weren't you having trouble? Did you drink behind that James?

— Sure I drank behind it.

— And weren't you drinking behind it for days, even weeks, before the night you found her in bed with her lover? Did you ever black out James in all those days and weeks?

— Sure I blacked out. But I didn't black out the night I killed them.

— And what about the night you killed Mrs Palatino? Did you black out then?

— I didn't kill Mrs Palatino.

— Did you think of Mrs Palatino when you went to the dykes' kitchen to get the knife James?

— . . .

— James?

— I did.


For a minute they almost had me believing them, until I remembered reading about your mother's death in the paper. I even saw you on TV.

— I didn't kill her. I was with *her* that night. I was in her bed listening to her lying, listening to her and knowing she was lying, feeling my blood burn while she lied and lied, and letting her lie, tasting her lies on her lips and on mine. She was a bitch, my woman, she lied, she ate me and she lied, she ate that other woman, she touched her, she let herself be touched, she let that woman . . .

— Your dead girlfriend is the only witness to your whereabouts on the night Mrs Palatino was killed?

— . . .

— James?


After that I stopped talking. They did all the talking from then on. They told me they were going to take a walk and leave me a while, but before they went they wanted me to know what questions they were going to ask me, they wanted me to know what kind of answers they were looking for. They told me they were going to turn the video camera on when they came back and someone was going to come and write everything down for me to sign. They told me what their questions would be. They told me the whole story. They gave me everything in their questions. It was as if I already agreed to something I couldn't remember agreeing to. They seemed to know I would cooperate. They wanted to know why I didn't kill you, Nita, after I killed your mother. They wanted to know if you were in the shower. They wanted to know if I stared at you naked while you stood in the kitchen using the knife I killed your mother with to quarter an orange. Did I go back out the way I came in, through your bedroom and up the fire escape? Or didn't I just go out the door? Were you in bed asleep? Why did I take time to wipe the knife on the sheet and rinse it off and put it away? That was what I did, wasn't it, while you were in the shower? They would need an answer to this question. Were you in your bed or in the shower? I would have to tell them which way it was, one or the other. Did I understand? They told me to sit tight and think about it. They would need answers to all these questions for the statement. They would need to know how I got up on to the roof to come down the fire escape and in the window. They would need to know what bee got into my bonnet, what bug got up my ass. Did I understand? They would want as many details as I could come up with, and anything I got wrong or couldn't remember they would blame on the drunk, maybe drugged, state of my mind.

They explained everything to me. The white man, Sam D'Amico, said he was uptown there in Detective Errol Walker's precinct because he had just two suspects in the murder of your mother. He had you and he had me. You were a young woman, an unhappy woman, who ran around at night with boys you didn't know and lived like a nun in the daytime, never even going to work with bare legs or skin showing at your wrists or your neck, not even in summer. You were the victim's daughter and you were pretty and you were tragic and you were white. Did Detective Sam D'Amico think you killed your mother? Or did he think it was me – a punk with a chip on his black shoulder who had already confessed to knifing and killing two other women, one that I claimed to love? He asked me another question: Did it matter what he thought? What would the press think? was the question that mattered, he said. What would the public think and what would the teachers think – because your mother, of course, was a teacher – and the politicians and the neighbors? What would his own mom and pop think? What would his parish priest think and the people of Bensonhurst and the people of Howard Beach? Did I understand him? According to all your friends and neighbors, Nita, you are gentle and kind – troubled yes – but wouldn't hurt a fly, etc., certainly not your mother, you loved your mother, and so on. So, Detective D'Amico asked me, who does that leave?

Solitude is good for the memory, he said.

Then the two of them went out and I sat in there alone.


But maybe it wasn't quite like that, Nita. Maybe I make it sound like they knew I was innocent of killing your mother, like they knew they were setting me up. They didn't. I don't think they did. I think these guys believed I killed your mother, because sitting in there listening to them, I began to believe it too. I resisted them – while they were in there hammering on me I resisted them, I kept asking for a lawyer and telling them the truth. But then when they were gone and I was sitting there alone, I thought about what they were saying to me. I thought about Ileana, who was dead, and her friend who was also her lover, who was also dead. I thought about killing them, how I killed them, how it was me who did it. I thought about the rage inside me and how these men talked to me like dirt – like dirt themselves, Nita. I thought of the dirt they put on your name and I remembered your mother and how she talked to us when we were children and how she tried so hard to keep you to herself and away from the life of the street and away from me and I thought about what they were saying about your life now and as I thought about all that while I sat in that room that smelled of my sweat and the policemen's sweat and my fear too because they made me afraid but also angry and the room smelled of my anger and their tobacco-soaked bodies and the coffee they were drinking, as I thought about it, Nita, I asked myself what demon lives in me that I could kill them like that, Ileana and Virginia. I wanted the policemen to take me out of that room. I wanted to confess and get it over with and ask them to take me away. But the thing was they wouldn't do it. They knew what I wanted. But they didn't care about Ileana and Virginia. They cared about your mother, Nita, and when they finally left me alone there, I knew what I had to do.

For myself, Nita. I did it for myself, not for you.

As for you coming to see me, I have to say no to that. I don't want to see you, I don't want you to come, not now or anytime later. This is my place. I live in the truth here. The man's law, the white man's law, isn't the law that matters. What matters is the law of your own heart. You find that law, you live there. The rest is bullshit. I rage in here. I'll keep on raging until they kill me. That's my law. You go find yours.

*For in those days shall men seek death, and shall not find it, and shall desire to die, and death shall flee from them.*

I see that. I see that, Nita. I have visions since I've been here. I see New York City burning. Don't worry about me. Don't worry about yourself. It isn't time to worry. The preachers say worry is the devil's meditation, and I know it's true. *For the kings of the earth shall bewail her, and lament for her, when they shall see the smoke of her burning, Standing afar off for fear of her torment saying, Alas, alas, that great city Babylon, that mighty city, for in one hour is thy judgment come. For in one hour so great riches is come to nought. For in one hour is she made desolate, for God hath avenged you on her.* We were children in the city of death, Nita. A stench rises up there, the stench of slaughter and slavery and suffering bodies – only fire can make us clean, the cleansing fire of the one God of man and heaven. What you do doesn't matter. The God of war is loose in the world now, and fire to purify us all. Don't trouble yourself about me or about yourself or about your mother or living or dying. God is making war on man and we live in the belly – we are the belly – of the great Satan, God's victim and God's instrument. *He that leadeth into captivity shall go into captivity; he that killeth with the sword must be killed with the sword. Here is the patience and the faith of the saints.* Hear it, Nita. Hear the words of the God of truth and war, the one God of all the nations, whatever name the nations want to call God by. The days are come when God's mystery is finished. The days are come when God's voice reaches down from heaven saying, It is done. These are the days when the angels pour out the wrath of God upon the earth, *far Babylon is fallen, is fallen, that great city.* Are you watching what's happening in the world? Are you paying attention? Do you see the armies massing? *And he gathered them together unto a place called Armageddon.* The armies are massing, Nita. Are you ready for the Rapture? You want to ask me what you should do now, girl – well here's your answer: pray. *Come out of her, my people, that ye be not partakers of her sins, and that ye receive not her plagues. For Babylon the great is fallen, is fallen, it is become the habitation of devils, and the hold of every foul spirit, and a cage of every unclean and hateful bird. Her sins have reached into heaven and God hath remembered her iniquities.*

The time has come to stop protecting that old Satan, that old white man, Nita.

*For behold, I come as a thief. Blessed is he that watcheth, and keepeth his garments, lest he walk naked, and they see his shame.* For Babylon the great is fallen, Nita. *Reward her even as she rewarded you. How much she hath glorified herself, and lived deliciously, so much torment and sorrow give her: for she saith in her heart, I sit a queen, and am no widow, and shall see no sorrow.*

Forget your mother, Nita. Your mother is dead. Forget whatever big fat white man you're protecting. It's time to leave, Nita. Leave your dead white mother and your bad white father. Leave the life they gave you and the lies they told. Leave the world they made. Pray, Nita. Words. Find the words. There is no freedom without the words. You want to ask me for help, for a sign. I'm giving you signs, Nita. Signs are everywhere. Freedom is in the signs. Time is over.

Word:

*A mighty angel took up a stone like a great millstone and cast it into the sea saying, Thus with violence shall that great city Babylon be thrown down, and shall be found no more at all. And the voice of harpers and musicians and of pipers and trumpeters shall be heard no more at all in thee; and no craftsman shall be found any more in thee; and the sound of a millstone shall be heard no more at all in thee; and the light of a candle shall shine no more at all in thee, and the voice of the bridegroom and of the bride shall be heard no more at all in thee; for thy merchants were the great men of the earth; for by thy sorceries were all nations deceived.*

That is what I'm telling you, Nita: *In her was found the blood of prophets, and of saints, and of all that were slain upon the earth.* You figure out what's at the bottom of your sorrow, Nita, you go all the way down to the bottom of it, you root that fucker out, you tear him out of your soul, you kill that sucker, you stop protecting that old white man, and then you be free – you, your mama, and maybe even me.

That was the end of the letter. He had signed it, *Your old friend, Jimmy Rivers*, and then beneath the signature: *PS – Or did you think I would forgive you? Is that what you wanted? Not from me, girl. You get no forgiveness from me.*

# helen lynch

## *half-mast*

The parents had gone to speak to the neighbours about sewerage arrangements, on which Mrs Corby appeared vague. Gone off down the lane, taking two children. The place was almost derelict, they had said earlier, as they drove the mud-spattered Mini over the flints of the lane. It would need a lot doing.

The child stood among the cypress trees, letting them breathe for her, the cracked path and Japanese anemones in grey-pink motion between her and the failing porch. No one noticed that she had remained, even Mrs Corby lingering oddly before the house as though uncertain which steps to take.

It was late afternoon, a strange November day, the light moth-veined, like moonrise, in a purple sky. The girl gazed beyond the house to the splayed damson trees, the mound where a wave of ivy swept up over a fallen fence, the hedge brambles sprawling in rusty coils on old rockery stones. They would leave the council house in the large town, with its white kitchen cupboards and strip of grass beside concrete strewn with tricycles, to come here.

This was the first time they had all been together to see the house. It was hoped that the sale would be concluded today, as indeed it had been – though the nephew had not turned up as promised – drinking tea with Mrs Corby from cups as cracked and stained as the sky was now, waiting in the stone-flagged kitchen for the kettle to boil.

The lady being out of the room, the father hoped that the poor old dear's expectations of her nephew were well-founded. She'd be in an old folks home by Christmas, *he* reckoned.

'Michael!'

'Well, next Christmas then.' Though *they'd* to be grateful, he said, for he did not believe she'd ever have sold up otherwise.

'It's an ill wind,' the mother agreed, seeking to grow comfortable with this idea by resorting to uncharacteristic proverbial wisdom, and drawing her mouth into a wide droop like a frog's until it should pass. Mrs Corby set great store by her relations, it appeared, and the house, of Victorian brick and faintly eccentric design, occasioned much reference to 'my father the Captain' who built it.

During their tour of the house, the parents had directed their children to the points of interest, with suitable historical explanation: the pump, the former bell-board in the kitchen, fireplaces everywhere 'before people had central heating', the marble-topped washstand in the old lady's bedroom. The wallpaper there was dried forget-me-not blue dusted with small flowers. The eldest girl had stared for a long time – the first thing to claim her among so many strange things. This pattern, this hue, these pallid sprigs, had been arrived at long before she was born. They breathed an older air, spoke of a world unknown to, preceding, her.

'Come here, child,' Mrs Corby said, beckoning where she stood. The girl, startled amid the dark cypress trunks, edged forward, rubbing socks together. Mrs Corby did not wait but turned along one side of the house for the child to follow.

Fish lay entranced on the black waters of the pond, like orange rhododendron leaves, eyes upward among the twigs and dead leaves. Perhaps others glimmered below the oily surface, and the two stooped to peer down.

'Take to it kindly,' the old lady said, not looking at her companion but rubbing the sticky backs of her own hands. 'It is as it is'.

The child had no inkling what to say. It did not seem to matter. Mrs Corby spoke either to no one, or as if the girl *had* replied. Still, the little girl felt as you do when hiding in those moments before the seeker comes looking for you.

Mrs Corby's hat, a species of panama, appeared to have dropped from a great height on to her rose-grey hair, and to be about at any moment to re-ascend. This in contrast to all else about her, which gestured *down*: stockings the colour of weak coffee nagged at her calves above socks, and slippers of bulging corduroy. Her flowered overall was somehow battened over the blue skirt and beige sweater which protruded from it.

'That is where my father used to raise the flag each morning.' She flapped an arm towards the hedge, where nettles rose behind a clump of honesty, dangling paper moons. They might have grown from the old sea charts the Captain had buried there, the child thought, as the toffee tree grew from the wrappers in a story she had read.

They had come to the back of the house, tangling with golden rod gone peppery brown and the charred-looking currant bushes to make a way through.

'My father found many things ugly, and in the end I could not agree. He felt something was being concealed. I was a great disappointment to him.' She spoke as though assenting to something the child had said. 'My father built this place but he did not possess it – he could not understand that. He was not permitted to construct the house as a ship (he wanted more than just the one porthole you know) but he always thought of it as a ship – as something he *steered* in an element somehow opposed to him.

'Will is such a heavy thing in most people,' she observed. 'I saw it in my father. It wore down his teeth – like a horse's, grey and yellow. Transfiguration, on the other hand,' she said confidentially, 'transfiguration is light. It is easy. When you see, things change. It is not difficult, there is simply a shift of some kind.'

The child did not know these words. Like all her family she was inclined to be quick and to talk a lot (when she was allowed). At six she knew that to be intelligent one is required to show understanding, to *say*. Her parents liked to encourage use of the dictionary, so it was seldom fruitful to *ask* for meaning. Yet now she tried.

'What is it, that Transifigation?'

It was not clear that Mrs Corby had even heard.

'When the deer come, stepping into the garden, I wait with them. And there are always the birds. I give them bread. I love bread. Bread, too, is easy.'

The greenhouse had fallen, glass turned inside out, dissolving. You could not imagine it had made a sound, that gently imploded chandelier still with traces of vine.

'The strangest things are most perfect, they happen every day.' The woman held tight to the child's arm, then let it go as though she had forgotten what it was. 'You cannot get away from them, unless you stand quite still and go blind – and why should you want to do that?'

The old lady looked straight at her for the first time. Despite a largely benign appearance, the grip on the wrist, the straggling hair, the too-small eyes, more than one face it seemed, made the child in flickers afraid. Yet the tone was kind. The old woman seemed to mind so much what she was saying. The child sensed that it was after all addressed to her, desired strongly to receive, and yet felt herself suspected now of not being in some way up to the mark.

Pursuing this thought, she was not fully listening.

'... and in any case, all that we have is given,' Mrs Corby was saying.

The girl sought to compensate for her inattention: 'You mean you get what you're given – and not to make a fuss?' She *knew* it was wrong as she said it.

'I do not mean that' – but Mrs Corby was unencumbered by this association of ideas, or the child's immediate self-reproach, and the severity of her voice was imagined. She gestured to a stooping apple tree.

'My father hanged himself from that apple tree. I watched him at it – took him all morning'.

The six-year-old stared at the ashy flakes of bark round the knots of the tree.

'I offered to help him, but he did not want it – from me – it was a final insult to him I'm afraid. He would not take my help.'

'To hang himself?' The child wondered, unwisely aloud, and yet with the old lady this suggestion seemed to reinstate her.

'No, no, to prevent him – but it was an insult all the same. I should have seen that. It caused him pain,' she added, addressing the remark to the trunk of a nearer tree.

'Go on, dig,' the old woman advised, seeing the child's eye upon some bare earth at the foot of a mound.

With a stick the girl turned the webby earth. There were small nuggets of white in the loamy soil, bits of plate and green glass, old dog bones, slivers of burned brick, corners of ink-blue tile.

'Gerald shan't have it, you see,' Mrs Corby broke in. Gerald was the nephew, the girl recalled. 'Father would disapprove of course – the male line and what-have-you. As if Gerald wouldn't sell it to the first... Do you think I don't know what Gerald will do? He may dispose of *me* as he pleases – I am not such a fool as to think otherwise – but *this* . . . No, I go because I choose – so that I may choose. I have done what I can to protect it. It has protected me. You will know, I think, what to do.'

The girl heard these words without listening, as, hearing the last chimes of a clock, you often know how many have gone before. For she was putting her hands deeper and deeper into the soil, trailing nets of old root, placing to one side the most beautiful pieces of tile. She thought at last to look at Mrs Corby, but the old woman had gone rapt and fumbling, the light of her face reaching out to touch the bowed shapes of the garden under the dark that trickled down the sky.

'*There* you are,' the mother said. 'We wondered where on earth you'd got to.'

'She's a sly little madam!' the father exclaimed, but without his usual energy – or its usual consequences.

It took no time for them all to be shut tight in the car, the girl's brother and sister squabbling beside her (for once she was not the cause of the trouble). The father was embarked on the pretence of involving them in a decision that had already been taken: 'What did they think of it etc.?' answering the question himself.

'We'd have to clear out that pond,' the mother at last contributed. 'The fish are all dead, did you see? Maybe we could make a garage there – once we've filled it in. There isn't really anywhere for the car at present.'

So they went on, with the car's engine, putting in the central heating, deciding the location of the oil tank, knocking those two rooms into one. The father was looking forward to getting some sense into that garden. It was a shame, but sooner or later those big windows would have to be replaced – the frames were completely rotten. It would be nice to do it in the same style, from a historical point of view of course, but you couldn't always have what you wanted in life. You couldn't easily get sash windows nowadays – not without having them made and going to a lot of expense.

# jude weeks

## *old and long remorse*

All through the holidays, we spied on her house. Watching at dusk, as the summer day faded from powder blue to navy, and the violet nights folded round us like velvet. We would sit, two for company, on the roof of the chicken coop and wait, until the door swung silently open, framing her inside its golden lozenge. We held our breath. One day it would happen. 'Better watch out,' Lolly hissed. 'They're quick as a flash! One false move and you never know how you'll end up.'

I took a deep breath and crossed my fingers. So, in our fractured and powerless childhood, we acknowledged the essence of a chancy and incongruous world.

The evening was motionless. Not a breath stirred the bushes, never a sigh in the trees. The chickens churked softly and settled their feathers. The thick, warm smell of hay and shit rose up and lay thickly around and on our hands. In all the surrounding houses lights flashed on and off like a gameboard, and car headlamps swept across the gathering dark like the arc of a searchlight. I looked at Lolly, and her eyes were wide, the irises brown wheels. Suddenly, she ducked her head. The door was opening slowly, slowly.

The old woman sat very still as if waiting, caught in a tent of yellow light. Stripped away by time, all we could see was a pair of white eyes like golf balls, a mummy with skin yellow and papery as parchment. Her hands twitched like bundles of old twigs, and her lips moved ceaselessly. A lace shawl lay across her shoulders faint as the foggy breath of the dying. Muttered sounds came to us easily over the still air; surely it was a spell she was casting, and us within sight! We slunk like otters into the long, damp grass, and fled into the shadowed safety of our own doorways.

We linked little fingers and closed our eyes. 'Sisters for life, friends for ever, sisters for life, friends whatever.' We had escaped danger again, and our parting thoughts were for each other. But we were younger then.

Next day we were cowboys riding across Arizona, our horse an old rug slung over Lolly's back fence. We had a couple of old carpet-beaters, and every time we got some speed up, the dust flew out in choking clouds. That was OK though, it *was* dusty old Arizona. When thoroughly choked we would open a bottle of dandelion and burdock and have ourselves a shot of Redeye. Nothing since has tasted so good.

Half the fence belonged to HER . . . so we knew it had to be magic, sort of. We hacked pieces off with my mam's nail file and sold them as good-luck charms at school. We all wished on them. To get on to the netball team, or that Mam wouldn't find out we'd looked at Peter Robson's thingy. Although we never did anything wrong, as Lolly said, we never touched it, just looked. I didn't know what all the fuss was about. Mam saying you'll get yourself in trouble. That small thing could never make trouble, let alone make a baby! It was like a little curled-up snail. I laughed at this grand male thing. 'Put it away before the birds get at it!' I told him.

I personally had wished for a dad, but I *really* meant the

one I had lost, not the one I ended up with. Just shows you should never meddle with wishes and witches . . . it's magic, you see, and very unstable, remember the Sorcerer's Apprentice.

Still, all over Tyneside, there are grown women who treasure those slivers of magic wood. They find them at odd moments, tucked into old handbags, or at the backs of drawers still wrapped in tissue paper, and they take them out with hands swollen from scrubbing and mending and hold them tight and remember . . .


An old cat with jagged ears would sit by us, unmoving, staring out of flat yellow eyes. A voice would call out, 'Tinker, Tinker,' and he would amble off into the house. We weren't fooled.

'Code name,' Lolly declared. 'Lull us into a false sense of security. Probably called Beezlebub or Grimalkin or Old Scratch.' She knew loads about witches and spells and The Occult, from a book her brother Mick got out the library. She lent it me, and I was well stuck in when Mam noticed and started flapping like an oilskin . . .

'Wants throwing on the fire, ungodly rubbish filling children's heads with filth, damned disgrace, I'll have a word with that young man.'

For once I was a corrupted innocent. Mam was very religious, and wouldn't hear tell of the Devil. Weird, isn't it, because if you believe in God, why not the other? She was wrong too, for I asked Father Doyle and he told me the Devil was very active in the world, you only had to look around, and young girls had to be very wary.

I told Lolly, the important thing is to believe in both, but not let them spook you. Simple. We decided that the other important thing was always to wear a crucifix. Lolly couldn't get hold of one because her mam and dad were Anathists or something and didn't believe in them. I was lucky, our house was simply stiff with them. No bother to borrow a couple. In fact, if Mam saw me saying a decade she'd probably Thank God, thinking I'd turned over a new leaf.

It was a droning hot day and the cat was drooping on the fence when I remembered that the book had said that Evil Entities hated the Crucifix. So I held my Rosary in front of its face. The cat blinked and yawned.

'It's bluffing, try again,' Lolly urged. So I tried again, swinging it like a pendulum, you are in my power you will obey you are mine to command, but still it slumbered on, with only its tail flicking.

So Lolly tried. She was more forceful and spoke loudly and the thing pretending to be a cat opened its eyes. She rattled the holy beads under its nose and poked it with the silver cross. It was instantaneous, the thing screeched and scratched, fell off the fence, and hit the ground running . . . Lolly held out her arm. Bright-red drops of blood streaked her skin and the wound was like a mouth snarling. Her mam put iodine on it which wasn't nice, but she was a mother like that.

Still, her arm came up like a pudding covered with a rash like raspberry jam. It got worse every day until she looked like a leper. Mam said she wasn't surprised the bairn had got infected, the house was filthy, the woman couldn't wash properly, should be ashamed to hang out grey towels like that for the world to mock at and the curtains stiff with dirt, well cleanliness is next to Godliness, I'm not surprised at anything that goes on with That Lot, turning their backs on The Lord.

Our Davey said jokingly that Darwin had a lot to answer for and Mam looked pained and said that she believed in evolution as part of God's plan, and He had blessed Mr Darwin with the brains to see the truth of it and I don't hold myself superior to any of God's creatures and anyway, who are we to question science? Our Davey was gobsmacked.

And Lolly's arm got worse and worse, so of course we knew we were right about the Familiar. Lolly looked grim. I think her arm was really sore, for she only got pickle-faced when she was hurt. I looked at her in the gathering dusk. Her skin was greasy, her hair stuck to her brow and her lips were cracked. As her face emerged from the dusk all sad and tired, I suddenly saw her as she would look when she was old, and then I knew with certainty that one day I would be old too, with all these long days of wonder lost for ever. I clutched at her.

'Things are getting desperate,' I cried, to break the silence, to interrupt my terrible thoughts. 'We've got to do something!'

I put my arm round her, and for a moment I felt her still and accepting and I sensed a part of us which merged like flames, springing up magically, hanging between us like a wavering light. Then she pulled away with something which smelled like fear and it was gone. In the future I searched again and again to recapture that feeling, and sometimes I did, but most often I didn't. And when rewarded with that sensation I knew it was only ever meant to be transitory: no one could hold on to that feeling and live in the world as an ordinary human being. Most of us never even get close to it.

The fear gets in the way.


When the Familiar came back the next day, we were ready. I had a hatbox left over from our Lena's wedding and Lolly had a tin of tuna which had been in the larder for centuries. The tin looked a bit brown but it smelled okay. The book had said that Evil had great appetites, so we knew it would fall for the fish. We had the note ready too: 'We know who you are and renounce all your evil ways. We have your Familiar and if Laura Skinner's arm is not cured within two days, he will die. Beware, We Mean It. The Avengers.'

We put the tin in the shed inside the hatbox and waited silent and still up on the roof, holding hands. The world seemed suddenly very cold and dark, the security of home very far away. We gazed pensively at the lighted windows and at each other. Someone had to do it, and we knew we had been chosen. It was okay *reading* about evil, but when it gets close it feels like jumping into a dark, cold sea, feeling afraid, not knowing if you'll ever come up again.

Soon we saw the black shadow stretch and ooze its way over the fence. As it approached, its eyes reflected the orange flare of the street lights and its face seemed to swell and grow knowing and watchful, like the Devil himself. It entered the shed fluidly, silently, and we slid down and stood trembling outside. We held on to our crosses.

'Keep praying, sister,' I breathed, and we went into the shed together.


The next day there was a right stink on. All us kids had to look for Tinker, so we said we had already searched the shed. I felt awful lying, and I wanted to tell Mam, because never before in all my born days had I ever lied to her. When I thought of that I felt worse. I couldn't look her in the face, and I felt in my bones that she was getting suspicious.

There was no answer to our note, and Lolly's arm never got better, so we hung on to the Familiar for a while. He didn't seem to mind the shed at first, only he was always thirsty and wanted milk, which was tricky, as we had to keep smuggling it out without any questions. He didn't like any of the stuff we got him to eat, we couldn't get a tuna every day, and so he got thinner which was a terrible worry.

When he started howling piteously, we panicked, as the whole neighbourhood might hear. So we tied a muzzle round his face with a hanky. It worked.

It shut him up. It shut him up real good.

A couple of days later, Mam showed us the note that Mrs Lee had got, accusing her of being a witch.

'That's where that poor cat's gone, some nutter's taken the poor old lady's pet, probably end up as a pair o' gloves,' our Davey said, throwing the note back on to the table. All the time Mam looked at me, in that way she had, and I felt like crying.

It wasn't a game, we didn't want to hurt Tinker, we never knew he'd die, we thought that evil had taken a physical form and we had to get rid of it. The book never said anything about death and sorrow and guilt. It all just got away from us. Then a whisper arrowed through the air straight at me and grew and grew into a shout, and I understood something about growing up and loving and kindness, and pity... And with my mother's eyes on me for ever in my mind, I never forgot...

Next day, Mrs Lee was humping bags of rubbish outside. We ran to help. On the top of the pile lay a cat dish, a toy mouse and a soft tartan rug. Lolly stroked it sadly. 'Couldn't bear to keep them now,' Mrs Lee answered the unspoken question, looking at me from her sad old tortoise eyes. 'It wouldn't be fair on the animal, I'm too old to fall in love again, too old and too tired.'

I picked up a broad red ribbon with *Cat Show* on it in big letters. It slid through my fingers as fast and quietly as time slipping away. Lolly's arm was bandaged up. Her mam had taken her to the clinic. 'Not before time,' I heard myself say in my mother's voice. It was a shock to both of us, we thought echoes only came from the past, not from the future . . . and so we laughed loudly and too long.

# kathy page

## *the question*

'London,' my caller is saying 'I'm in London, by the road. In a phone box.' She has a worn but once-rich voice, a faint accent I can't at first place.

'So what's the situation?' I adjust my headset, tick some boxes on the form. Opposite me, Paula is making one of her Blu-Tack animals as she listens to her own caller. She makes them every night: elephants, whales, a giraffe with a matchstick neck, even the occasional human being, naked and less than chaste – none of them bigger than the top digit of your thumb.

'I need somewhere,' my caller says.

'Can you tell me how come?'

'I'm forty, I've never had anywhere to damn well go,' she says, 'so how do I know how bloody well come!'

'I'm sorry,' I say, as we're taught, 'but I need to ask these questions in order to help.' There is no reply, just breathing.

'Date of birth: you must have been born in . . . fifty-four?' I say.

'No' she says. 'Fifth of May, nineteen thirty-six. It says so.'

'You would be fifty-eight, then,' I say. There's a long pause. I expect her to argue, brace myself. But when she does eventually reply her voice is small and disappointed, like something shrunk in the wash.

'I might be,' she says. 'I must be, then, mustn't I? I have to get back to Birmingham,' she tells me, her voice still small, but firm.

'This is only a London service. All I could possibly do is get you a hostel place here,' I say. Vacancies: female 3, male 4, the screen in front of me reads. I press Next. 'Westminster,' I say, 'Southwark or—'

'*Birmingham*' she interrupts, with absolute authority, 'Birmingham, not somewhere else. It has Birmingham on my birth certificate, so that's where I should be. What it has on your certificate is where you should be – it's best all round. It's people not being in the right places that makes everything so hard, so very hard as they are, very hard and falling apart all the time, just violence and misery. If it's two thousand miles away or two miles away it's the same difference – no good, no damn good. The right place is the one where things fit you exactly, it moulds round you, it keeps you together, stops you breaking up in bits, you see? People should go to there, wherever it is, because then everything fits: it's got to fit you, everything – that's home, you must know that. If you don't you're in the wrong, fucking, damn place yourself.' I can hear her breathing hard.

'When were you last in Birmingham?' I ask.

'I remember,' she says brightly, 'it had a green door.'

'Can you remember the road name?'

'No.' she says. Then: 'Yes! Gallstone Drive. I think it was thirty-six or sixty-six. Call them. They know me there. Tell them Laura.'

'I'll put you on hold,' I say. 'Gallstone Drive!' I hiss at Paula who is taking a call at the desk opposite me, and watch her try to keep a straight face. I ring the emergency social services in Birmingham. Gallstone Drive! But there is a place she might mean, the woman there says, a number 13 Gavelston Road; it is what used to be called a Home.

'Might be the place,' my caller says, anxious. 'Ask about the green door.'

'Laura? Oh, you mean *Mary Coates*,' says the man at Gavelston Road – Alec, who comes from Glasgow – yes, they certainly do remember her. And perhaps they could take her back, though he will have to ask the relief manager, who is currently sorting out a dispute in the television room. 'I'll be right back to you, mate,' he says.

'I don't want to raise your hopes too much,' I tell Laura, or Mary, 'but hang on there, I've spoken to a bloke called Alec; he does know you. I'm on the case.'

'I've got to pee,' she says, 'can't wait all night.' The line goes dead. Immediately Alec-at-the-Home comes on the other one and says Yes: get her up there and they will take her. Unfortunately, I tell him, I may have lost her. But just in case, I make all the arrangements – overnight here, travel grant in the morning. Then I take several routine calls. Another hour passes; it is nearly ten.

'The Gallstone woman's gone off, would you believe,' I tell Paula, whose turn it is to take the mobile home and run the service through the night. 'Maybe she'll call later', I say. 'I'll give you all the details.'

'I hope she doesn't. I hope it's quiet. I feel like death warmed up,' Paula says, then sees the expression on my face. 'Oh, Joe, you just lose some,' she says, stretching her arms above her head and pushing her chair back. 'Never mind.'

We turn off our computers; we remove our headsets. I watch Paula pluck her Blu-Tack animals one by one from the top of her screen, squeeze them into a blob and put that in the top right desk drawer. She has always refused to explain why she does this.

'Look!' she says, pointing. The red light flashes; it is Mary, Laura, whatever her damn name is:

'Hello?' she says. 'It's *me*.' Relief spreads through me, warm as wine.


I've handed my car over to my daughter Lucy so Paula gives me a lift part of the way home.

'I'm thinking of having streaks and one of those urchin cuts. What do you think?' she says as we get into the car, an old Saab. There's a plastic dinosaur glued to the dashboard, a litter of tissues and sweet papers everywhere else. We pull out into the main road. 'You must be so excited, Joe!' she says 'Most people still live in the same sort of place all their lives, don't they? There's a leaving party next week,' she says. 'I'll say it again then, but I might as well now, too: you'll be missed, Joe. And you're a lovely man, you know – now don't say anything or I'll bloody well cry.'

'It is a bit sudden,' I say, obtusely, and she gasps. It's like some kind of explosion. The car swerves.

'Look, shall we stop a bit?' I say.

'No!' she snaps. I'm still not getting the point.

'I'll miss you too,' I say. 'And the job.' She nods silently, her lips pursed, heaves in another breath, says:

'Well here it is – you might as well know, now that it can do no harm – I've always fancied you.' She speaks in a brittle monotone, staring hard at the tail lights in front of us. Now tears run slowly down her cheeks.

'Paula . . .' I say, 'but you know . . .'

'Oh, sure, sure, sure,' she says. 'That's why only now.' It also is shocking, to think of her feeling like that. To think of all those times I have moaned to her about Christina and she has just sat there and said nothing. But also, it is flattering. She is so much younger than me. I've always liked Paula, her quirkiness, busy fingers, quick smiles and sudden absolute hard-headedness. I've never thought of fancying her, but maybe I could. Her face is plump, her body small and tightly round. But she is right, there is nothing much to be said on that subject, now, because Christina and I are moving, just about as far away from London as you can get.

You could say it has happened very suddenly: that it began on a Tuesday evening six weeks ago, when Christina came up to me as I sat at the kitchen table. It was hot; I was wearing shorts. She came up behind me and put her hands on my shoulders. She bent over and kissed the top of my head. I smelled her perfume, her breath – faintly sour because she skips lunch unless it's put in front of her – and the whiff of other people's smoke that clung to her clothes. Joe, she said, I think you'll like this news. She slipped her hands down, over my chest and belly, left them there, and rested her chin on my shoulder.

Or else you could say it has happened incredibly slowly, that it began twenty-two years ago, when Christina and I decided to marry. We had been together all through her endless college years. I liked to look, she to talk. I was her relief, she my stimulus. We agreed on which people and books we liked, politics, the fact that whatever we were supposed to be she was driven and I was unambitious – but we could not agree on where we should live.

I always wanted to be in the country, and not just ordinary, agricultural, country but a wild, open place, or as close to one as possible. I wanted to go on painting my big dark abstracts, maybe branch into sculpture, between this perhaps do a place up, then hire myself out to do other people's places too, hill-walk, come home, take Christina's clothes off, make love, eat, sleep.

Christina was for the city: she wanted to get her doctorate and gradually make her way. Well, we finally agreed, it was only the hill-walking that a city really ruled out, and we made sure that we had a garden every time we moved: York, Sheffield, Leeds, finally here, London. More of a city each time, you could say. At night, when I still used to smoke, I would sometimes sit for half an hour or so in the garden before I went to Christina in bed. I could feel the night around me then and see stars; that was at least part of what I had meant by living somewhere wild.

Lucy and David came; I wanted them, she had them, I looked after them when they were small: this gave me a certain distinction with the various neighbours, and a definite curiosity value with her academic friends. Somewhere the painting got lost. Well, I would joke – I used to paint Christina, but now she's hardly ever in . . .

Naturally I met lots of other women as I carted the kids around; I had an afternoon sex phase. Then a whisky-drinking phase. Depression, which eventually led to job on the line. For a while in the middle of all this, Christina was ashamed of me. When we first came here, she moved another man into the house, a small, bearded semiotician from Hamburg, called Gustav, but I stayed put and he went. Our lives just went on, changing bit by bit, as I often explain to friends who are divorcing and amazed at us. Then of course it all became briefly fashionable and we were pioneers. Last year Lucy left home. David is about to. We've done the whole thing.

'What news?' I asked Christina, idly, that Tuesday six weeks ago. I wanted her at that moment far more than I wanted to know whatever it was. Christina is one of those fine-boned, stringy women who get sparer with time, and more energetic. She's still like a girl, though her curly hair is just beginning to grey. Again, we're different: I'm a soft man, plump, sprawling, my hair thinning in the middle.

'I have been offered a post as head of the Department of Modern History at the University in Anchorage, Alaska,' she whispered in my ear, 'And listen, this is the point: it's a wild place. There are wolves and bears. Elk. Hardly any people and countless trees. Harsh winters. Northern lights. Come in the other room, I'll show you,' she said.

We sat either side of the fireplace, the usual Victorian one. When we first moved here, I knelt for two days stripping it of paint. We sat there in the half-light, because one of my peculiarities is that I dislike electric light, especially at dusk; I feel I see better without it. Christina drew breath and told me that she sometimes thought I must feel I had had something perfectly decent in life, but not what I set out wanting.

'Joe, I am really grateful to you,' she continued. 'I couldn't have had the kids if you hadn't looked after them. I feel you've made sacrifices. This post is a chance for us both to get what we want, for us both to be satisfied together.' The light faded. It was very quiet; her bright voice grew unusually soft. 'Who knows, out there, you might even begin to paint again ... I still love you, Joe,' she said. Then I felt a tender queasiness in my stomach: to do with being loved by Christina, and told so, to do with the idea of painting again. I could see how that might happen over there.

A chance to start over again, she said. A new life, an adventure. A fairytale. And indeed, among the glossy photographs she had brought to show me, the couple who had preceeded us, wearing inflatable jackets trimmed with fur, sledged across an expanse of untroubled white towards a wooden house backed by snow-laden trees.

'I'm going,' I say to Paula in the car 'To Anchorage, Alaska.' I try to make it sound merely fact, but somehow it becomes a rather tactless exclamation. Shut up, I tell myself. Amazing, I think, that there are so many possibilities, hiding where you hadn't thought of them, that life is so full that anything could happen at any time, in fact there are many lives I could have and this is just one of them. And deep down I think also: yes, all this is my reward, for those years in the cold. Things are going to open up, like some extraordinary rose, from now on it will all be wonderful.

Paula pulls in at my bus stop. We kiss cheeks awkwardly and I slam the car door shut.

'Enjoy your days off,' she says through the open window – she seems quite okay, completely back to normal – 'and make that Christina do some of the packing.' People have always made remarks like this, as if I have to be defended from her. Normally I explain or argue, but given the situation it doesn't seem right.

On the bus I sit opposite someone I encountered once when I was doing some photocopying for Christina at the garage: a small, stocky man, very tanned, with a grizzle of grey-blond hair, and bright blue eyes. As then, he's in combat trousers and a khaki vest, and carrying a faded canvas haversack. It was months ago, long before the elections, that he told me he was just about to buy property in South Africa. Wonderful bungalows with acres of fruit trees and flowers were going for less than a flat would cost around here.

'The whites are afraid of trouble,' he said, 'but it'll blow over in the end, won't it? Everything does and that country has it all. Look around you, mate,' he said. 'It's not bad, but it's not good either. Used to be better. We've got a little flat and a balcony' – I wondered who the 'we' was, felt somehow it was a man, tall and spare, rather refined – 'you can put a deck chair in the communal gardens,' he said, 'but I'd rather have acres in the sun and someone bringing me a cocktail on a frigging tray, now wouldn't you?'

I smile at him now, but he doesn't recognize me.

'All these machines,' I remember he said as I bent down and opened the copier to free a stuck sheet, 'copiers, calculators, computers, cars – they weaken you. In the end you can't do something you used to be able to do. Me, I make sure I know how to fix anything I buy. I practise mental arithmetic. I do a crossword every day. In any situation, I think: how would I cope if things went wrong? How would I get out of here if there was a fire? If there was civil war and a power cut here what would I eat?

'Squirrels. It might not be good but it would keep you alive. Most people don't even know how to cook these days, much less skin something. But I do. I'm a survivor, me.' He jabbed his finger at his own chest, looked briefly murderous, then broke into a boyish smile and offered his hand to shake. But he sits on the bus now, face loose, eyes distant. All that, and you haven't gone yet, I think.

I walk the few hundred yards home, passing a blowsy girl waiting for the shuttle bus, and the hunched grey-haired man who always seems to be at the corner of our street, smoking and watching his terrier defecate in the gutter. I inspect gardens: one where everything is in separate pots, which stand on concrete tiles: its owner, Mrs Tyler, is often out, dressed always in a blue checked housecoat, watering, trimming. Another is paved in stone, a large pot with a eucalyptus tree in it stands to one side of the door, a galvanized watering can at the other. Whoever it belongs

to also has a piano and plays rather well: it's unpredicatable
– sometimes I catch it for several days on end, then not at
all for months. How many thousand times have I seen all
this? I think, this typical semi-suburban London street with
trees and Victorian houses, a place where people come to
bring up kids and not be broke. Why is it still so interesting?


I stop walking and listen to the purr of the traffic on the
main road. A telephone rings somewhere, a light is turned
off, a breath of wind runs through the plane trees. I will
miss the milkman, I think, who used to be a priest, and
who told me once when I met him off-duty of his passion
for Dostoyevsky and his intention to write a movie script
that would knock the world flat. I will really miss Carole,
who lives two streets away in the estate and meets or rings
me once a week or so to tell me what further sense she's
made of her mess of a life. I met her during my drinking
phase; she's still in hers. 'Are you there?' she'll say: 'it's this:
there is no Continuity.' Or: 'I'm pretty sure that there is no
Essential Self. Most people can fool themselves but because
of the life I've lived, I can't.' Or: 'There's only memory,
dear, I'm hanging on to mine by the skin of my teeth.' She
hasn't rung so often lately, because I'm going, I suppose.
In eight days' time.


I walk slowly up the chequered path and let myself into our
house.

Christina is in the kitchen, talking on the phone to her
mother in Scotland. She's wearing just a T-shirt, no underwear. Out of habit I stare at the gap between her legs, at
the top.

'You shouldn't worry' she's saying. 'You can come out to
visit – think of that – and we'll be back for a holiday every

year. We'll come once a year and stay twice as long.' She makes a face at me: Christ-my-mother! it says, but I don't return it as I usually would. The pull of Christina on me seems less than it usually is.

I go into the garden to collect the washing, but, surprisingly, she has already done it. So I sit on the bench instead and I remember the smile breaking on Christina's face when I told her, yes, we would go to Anchorage, Alaska. At the time it melted me. I took her in my arms and we went upstairs to bed. But in memory, now, I find something I don't quite like about that smile, a shiftiness, a split second's barely concealed amazement, as if she had got away with something she shouldn't have. Her voice seeps into the garden.

'Oh, but they're thrilled to have us out of their hair!' she's saying, in the kitchen. 'You know what it's like at that age. Besides they've got you and the Aunts.'

I come in again, pass her without looking, slowly climb the stairs. I sit on our double bed and look out at next door's garden, faintly lit from their living room window. Sometimes you can see foxes there.

If Christina was not still on the phone, I think I would pick up the extension and call Carole; she certainly owes it to me. Carole, I would say, it's this – I can imagine the click of her lighter, her first suck of smoke: Go on then, dear, she says, I'm all ears . . .

Suddenly Christina is standing in the doorway.

'Don't put on the light,' I say.

'Excited?' she runs her fingers through her newly cut hair. 'I can't wait. Hey – you've not done a great deal of packing today. What's up? Still, I dare say we'll get through it on the weekend. David says he'll help. I met him and his flatmate for lunch, a strange boy with a stud in his lip, but they seem to get on.'

'I feel odd: I feel as if I don't want to go,' I say. She laughs. Then she asks: 'Why?'

'I love it here,' I say.

'But you hated it to start with. And of course you'll love it there too. You're just like that, you know you are.' She comes into the room and picks up one of my socks from the floor by the bed, drops it into a drawer. I know she's dying to put the light on. Outside the sky melts into indigo – a wonderful hue – and, in a diffuse but final way that perfectly echoes it, I know that something has been disturbing me ever since Christina first told me about Anchorage, Alaska. A question:

'Supposing I said I'd changed my mind, that I wanted to stay here,' I begin. 'Would you still want to go, for yourself?' The air that rushes gratefully into my lungs is ice-cold. My head clears, as if from years of fog. My body settles firm around my bones. I fix her face in my gaze, looking for clues.

'I've resigned, Joe,' she says.

'They'd have you back.' She doesn't deny it. They'd have me back too, I think. Then she looks at me angrily and says:

'Talk about apalling timing.' She's absolutely right. 'It's what you always wanted': again, she's absolutely right, but my heart pounds and I shout:

'So what – answer – would you still want to go? Sorry,' I say, quietly.

'It is such an incredible chance, Joe,' she says, 'for a new life. You *know*.'

But right now I want the one I have. I want to know what Paula looks like with her new haircut. Whether Douglas the milkman ever writes his screenplay, or Mary Coates got to Birmingham. I feel the place where I live around me, attached to me. It seems to me that if I cling on to it, it will protect me from Christina's endless plans, from my own acquiescence, from anything.

'I'm sick of being whisked about,' I say.

'We've been here nearly ten years!'

'Exactly,' I say. 'If you're doing it for me, I don't want to go, I don't want to go, I don't want to go to bloody Anchorage, Alaska. Are you doing it for me, or for you with me on the side? That's my question – so answer it, will you, goddam you, please?'

She turns on the light. We face each other, now, across the room, just a few secrets each between us. Her hand rests on the wall, her eyes are bright, the skin around them ever so slightly creped. 'I want to stay here. Us to stay here,' I say, sitting on the bed with my thinning hair and my soft belly, my unpainted pictures, the empty boxes all around – desperate for a drink I mustn't allow myself.

'Just when I've made it fair, in the end!' she says. Her voice tears at its edges – at me too – but the fact is she still has not told me – is she doing it for me, or for her with me on the side? – and I have never been so angry with her before.

In the same moment, it comes to me that after all these twenty-three years she and I are still the same as we ever were, only more so. A good thing, a bad one?

Her face is just a blur. Her clothes sigh as she crosses the room. Outside it is almost completely dark.

'Joe?' she asks. 'Joe, why cry *now*?'

# about the authors

**Amy Bloom** is a psychotherapist who lives in Connecticut and divides her time between writing and her practice. *Come to Me* was her first collection of short stories and *Love Invents Us* her first novel.

**Pat Cadigan** has published three novels, *Mindplayers*, *Synners*, and *Fools*. Both *Synners* and *Fools* won the Arthur C. Clarke Award for best science fiction novel of the year in Great Britain. Her short story collections include *Patterns*, *Home by the Sea*, and *Dirty Work*. She lives in London with her husband, son, and cat.

**Claire Calman** decided to become a writer when she discovered that it mainly involved drinking cups of coffee and staring out of the window. After several years in journalism, she now spends her time editing books, writing poetry (she has performed her verse on love, sex and health live on Radio 4's *Woman's Hour*), and – when not gazing out of the window – working on her first novel.

**Joan Diamond** is a widely respected practitioner and teacher of the Alexander Technique with many published writings on the subject. She is about to complete her first novel and is also working on a collection of short stories, many of which have appeared in various anthologies. She lives in Cumbria.

**Rosemary Friedman** is the author of eighteen novels (most recent *Vintage* and *Golden Boy*), many short stories, TV scripts and screenplays. Her work has been widely translated and serialised on radio. Her stage play *Home Truths* successfully toured major UK venues in 1997. *The Writing Game*, a personal memoir and reflection on writing, will be published in Spring 1999.

**Catherine Gammon** is the author of the novel *Isabel Out of the Rain*. Her work has appeared in *Ploughshares*, *The Kenyon Review*,

*Manoa, Central Park, Third Coast, The North American Review, The Iowa Review*, and elsewhere. She teaches writing and contemporary literature in the Master of Fine Arts program at the University of Pittsburgh.

**Alyson Hallett** was a mental health worker in Norwich and Glasgow, but she has now abandoned the real world in favour of fiction. She has done various writing residencies and is currently experimenting with performance art.

**Gill Horitz** left London for Dorset almost thirty years ago. For the last fifteen she has been involved in devising and developing arts work, including writing projects. She is currently working as arts animateur with *Artshare South West*, the regional arts and disability organisation.

**Helen Lynch** was born in 1964 and grew up in Hampshire. She studied English at the University of York before working for several years in Poland. She lives with her partner and their two daughters in Aberdeen, where she teaches music. Her translations of *Beowulf* and French medieval romances, adapted for children, have been published on the Internet by Research Machines.

**Kathy Page** has published four novels and an anthology of short stories, *As in Music*. She has recently completed another collection of stories, *Paradise and Elsewhere*, and is working on a novel, *Likeness*.

**Lorna Thorpe** was born in Brighton where she still lives. A sometime clerk, tour operator, singer and social care worker, she took a degree in sociology in the 1980s at Kingston Polytechnic. She now earns a living as a freelance copywriter and is working on a collection of short stories and her second novel.

**Betsy Tobin** was born and raised in the American midwest and frequently revisits it in her fiction. She decamped to London in 1989, where she writes plays and short fiction. Her credits include a stage play, *Home Front* and a radio play, *Between The Sexes*. Her short story, *Joyride*, won the 1995 London Writer's Competition. She is currently at work on a novel.

**Joanna Torrey** is the author of *Hungry*, a collection of short fiction published in 1998. Her work has appeared in the Serpent's Tail anthology *Back Rubs*, the Crossing Press anthologies *Lovers: Stories by Women* and *Love's Shadow*, and in *Room of One's Own*. She is currently at work on a novel. She lives in Brooklyn, New York.

**Rose Tremain**'s work has been translated into fourteen languages and she is a bestseller in Britain, America and France. She has won the James Tait Black Memorial Prize and the Prix Femina Etranger (for *Sacred Country*), the Sunday Express Book of the Year (for *Restoration*, which was also listed for the Booker Prize), the Dylan Thomas Short Story Award (for *The Colonel's Daughter*), the Giles Cooper Award (for the radio play *Temporary Shelter*), and the Angel Literary Award (twice). *Restoration* was made into a film in 1995. Her most recent novel is *The Way I Found Her*. Rose Tremain lives in Norfolk and London with the biographer Richard Holmes. She has taught on the University of East Anglia's MA in Creative Writing and was listed as one of the Best of Young British Novelists in 1983. She is currently adapting *Sacred Country* in four parts for television.

**Janette Turner Hospital** was born in 1942 in Melbourne, Australia, but grew up in Queensland, which is still home although her adult life has been unintentionally nomadic and she now divides her time between Australia, North America and Europe. In 1966 she was Fellow in Creative Writing and writer in residence at the School of English and American Studies at the University of East Anglia, Norwich. She is the author of six novels and three collections of short stories. In 1982 *The Ivory Swing* won the Canadian Seal First Novel Award. *Borderline* (1985) and *Charades* (1988) were both shortlisted for the Australian National Book Award; the latter was also shortlisted for the Miles Franklin Award.

**Erica Wagner** was born in New York in 1967. Thirty years later she finds herself living in London and working as the Literary Editor of *The Times*; in between she went to school, college and graduate school, and worked as a cook, a thatcher, a researcher and editor. *Gravity*, her first collection of short stories, was published by Granta Books in 1997. Her father invented the magnetic knife rack.

**Jude Weeks** lives in Gateshead with her husband and two sons, and works in Newcastle as a Relate counsellor. She has had several short stories published and broadcast, both locally and nationally, and has recently just completed an MA in Creative Writing at the University of Northumbria. She is at work on a novel.